The Children of Magic

P.D. Parker

ISBN: 979-8-9916577-0-9 (E-Book)
ISBN: 979-8-9916577-1-6 (Paperback)
ISBN: 979-8-9916577-2-3 (Hardback)

Cover art by Jess Hickman.
Edited by Amanda Mili and Nicholas C.

Published by Patrick Parker in the United States of America.

First edition 2024.

Published through Amazon KDP.

Contact me at petrichorthegoblin@gmail.com

Acknowledgments

Writing this story has been one of my greatest achievements. I am so proud of how it came out. But this would never have been half as good if it weren't for all the people in my life who helped me complete this book.

I want to thank my beta readers Lolita, Sandra, Skip, Ryan, Helena, Parker, Tia, and Jesseca. This book would have been much duller without everyone's thoughts and feedback. I would also like to thank my editors Amanda Mili and Nicholas C. I know that my lack of proper comma usage must have been a nightmare to get through. And thank you to my cover artist Jessica Hickman. Your art is incredible and I am so happy to have it be an important part of my book.

Thank you, Mom, for always believing in me and encouraging my love of reading and writing. Thank you also for helping me get that job at the library. I never would have gotten the idea for this book without working there and rekindling my love for reading.

Thank you, Dad, for sharing your love for fantasy and sci-fi with me. The movies and shows I watched with you have shaped so much of who I am. It hurts more than I can say that you will never be able to read my book. But I know you would have loved it.

And to my readers, thank you for giving my story and characters a chance to live. I hope you will fall in love with them just as much as I have. Especially the goblins.

Book of Anu: The Beginning

In the beginning, there was the void and a goddess.
In the darkness, she named herself Anu.
But she was alone.

Anu created light to balance out the darkness.
Then, a world and stars to fill the emptiness.
She created sea and earth and fire and air to fill the world.
But still, she was alone.

Anu created plants and animals of every shape and size.
She created a variety of places for them to call home.
But still, she was alone.

The goddess decided to make life that thought and acted like her.
But she could not do so without great sacrifice.
Life can only come from life.

Anu smiled and expelled all her breath onto the world.
From her breath, souls formed.

In time, the souls became her first children.
They named the world Anu
to honor of the now-dead goddess.
And it was they who first discovered magic.

Chapter 1: A Beginning
Cycle 3, Day 24

A wooden wagon rocked and creaked as its wheels gyred ever forward over the rough dirt road, sending the sounds echoing through the dark and otherwise silent forest. It was being pulled down the path by two horses, reigned and steered by a man, assisted by a young boy who was no older than thirteen. Behind the driver's seat, and making up the major portion of the wagon, was a large wooden cell with thick bars barricading its few windows. The cell was inhabited by a single prisoner.

"He's not even bound!" said the young boy. The boy had coal-black eyes and hair dark as night. His hair was cut short and uneven as if it was cut by a dagger in the dead of night under a new moon. He shifted uncomfortably in the driver's seat of the wagon as he looked intently at the older man who sat beside him.

"He's fine, Samuel," said the man. He was in his thirties and had sea-green eyes and sun-bleached hair. Both he and Samuel wore dark brown leather armor that was layered like the underbelly of a snake. The man's armor was faded, battle-worn, and covered in cracks and nicks, while Samuel's seemed to be a size or two too big on him and was unscathed. Underneath their armor were simple black shirts and black pants, and buckled to their shoulders were hunter-green capes embroidered with a golden shield, the symbol of the Wardens. The man chuckled casually as he looked back into the cell, "Isn't that right, boy?"

"Yes, sir," answered the prisoner. It was barely even a

whisper, more of a choking sound hardly able to pass the quivering lips of the sixteen-year-old boy. He wore a sweat-stained yellow tunic, belted tight against his hips, and coarse brown pants. His hair was the color of molten gold coming to a cool. He sat crumpled, collapsing in on himself—as if imploding very slowly. His arms crossed his chest, fingers digging deep into his arms. Samuel noted every movement. Every twitch of the finger. The slight mumbles and lip movements. Is this how incantations work? Would he be able to feel a spell if one was being produced? Do spells have a sound, or a smell?

"He's not fine," Samuel countered, his eyes darting between the man and their prisoner. His gaze also passed between each of their weapons, just to make sure they were accounted for. His short sword and the man's long sword were underneath their seat, just as they had been the last several times he checked. So, too, were their wooden shields reinforced by metal. "He turned himself in to us! It's got to be a setup. I bet even now he's preparing a spell to escape or to get the attention of someone else."

The man smiled in a way that made his green eyes shine with mirth. "Mr. Mage, are you going to try and escape?"

"No, sir."

"Are you or anyone you know plotting anything against us?"

"No, sir."

The man turned to look at Samuel. "Well?" There was no demeaning in his eyes. The boy had his full attention as a flicker of genuine trust crossed the man's expression.

Samuel paused for several beats of the horses' hooves until he finally said, "He's not lying, Dad." He hung his head in placated defeat. At least that's one less thing to worry about. But still, he didn't like this situation and was ready to get to the kingdom's capital, Previa. The sooner they deliver the mage the better. Samuel had heard of an increase of attacks on Wardens, specifically ones escorting mages. His stomach had been in knots ever since they picked up this strange, sad mage.

"Sir!" His father bellowed with a laugh. "Address me as 'sir' while on the job."

"Yes, sir!" Samuel said. "I still think he could be dangerous. When mages discover their magic at a young age, it can be trouble."

"He's older than you, Sam," his father said, the smile never leaving his face, its residency as permanent as the stars in the sky—always there, even when not visible. Samuel stiffened at the nickname, and his father seemed to notice. For a brief moment Samuel saw a falter in his father's smile. But his demeanor quickly recovered and then he spoke louder, obviously for the prisoner's sake rather than his son's. "Anyway, these Warden Wagons are made from null wood, straight from the capital. The stuff repels magic like ducks repel water." The son sat in uncomfortable silence, trying hard not to physically react to such a blatant lie and a horrible attempt at a joke. There was no way in all the hells they could have afforded enough null wood for the wagon, or even the cell. Yes, their shields were made of the stuff, but even those cost a small fortune. The wood is probably the most regulated substance in the kingdom. The father waited through the silence for some kind of reaction from the imprisoned boy.

"Yes, sir," was all he got.

Lowering his voice, the father said, "He seems a bit intimidated by me. I blame my regular fitness and rugged good looks."

"Oh, yes. So says the man who has never met an animal he didn't want to hug and adopt. I can't help but tremble next to you," Samuel said with a crooked grin.

"You laugh now, but when I win over an army of forest creatures with my endearing personality, the world will bow before me." Then, the man's voice gained an edge of seriousness as it became a whisper that only Samuel could hear. "But maybe you can calm him down. He seems to be going through a lot. No one turns themselves over to the Wardens without a reason."

The boy on the outside of the prison glanced at the boy within with uncertainty. "I think you're right. Something's wrong, but maybe it's something he just needs time to sort through. Who's to say interjecting ourselves into his struggle won't do more harm than good? Anyway, our job is to get him safely to the capital. We can't solve everyone's problems."

"A job is more than what it's made out to be. Kindness should never be omitted or overlooked."

There was a brief silence, until resolve dissipated it.

Samuel turned to face the older teen. He attempted a friendly smile, which was only slightly undermined by his piercing stare, and said, "Prisoner—"

His father nudged him.

"You're a farm boy, correct?"

"I was."

"Okay, then." Samuel took a shaky breath, and then a second, less-shaky breath, and finally a third for good measure. "So, you're *no longer* a farm boy. How would you like me to address you? What's your name?"

"It's Caleb, son of Calin." The grip he had on himself lessened.

This was progress. Not great progress, but one must take what they can get. He could tell that at the very least, Caleb still wasn't lying.

"I'm Samuel, son of…" He looked at his father questioningly, who gave a nod of approval, giving Samuel the reassurance to continue, "Seth."

Caleb looked toward Samuel with an expression that generally indicated advanced mathematical equations. He seemed to formulate several sentences in his head, but managed only some incoherent beginnings and the word, "What?"

"Oh, yeah," Samuel said, "It's a regional thing. We are from a larger city in the north with a bigger population than the southern towns like the one you're from. Children only take the first letter of the parent's name. I've heard of even smaller and isolated villages where children take the first three, though the tradition is starting to fade in cities like Previa. From what I've heard, a new norm is to add your profession to your name. Met a boy there who was just called John Smith."

"Oh…" Caleb began to grow distant again before asking, "Are we going to your city?"

"Probably not," Samuel said, beginning to calculate routes. "I mean, we could go there for supplies, but there is a smaller town closer by. We also no longer have a house there, so we would still need to pay for an inn. Though we would be able to get a small discount on supplies if we go to Lena's shop, the discount wouldn't mitigate the extra cost of going there as opposed to the closest town. However, between three people, our food and water supply should last till we get to Previa. We can resupply there and wait for another escort job, which we have been having a dry spell of, so we are due. We may want to consider…" Samuel started to trail off, and as he started to come out of his extended monologue, he noticed Caleb's head had dug deeper and deeper into his knees.

Just as Samuel was about to say something about Previa, Caleb interjected with a meek and almost manic-filled whisper, "At least I will see the capital before I am imprisoned—or executed." These words passed through Samuel's mind like a cold wind and left him momentarily frozen.

"Executed?" Samuel asked, slightly louder than he had meant to. Seth's smile wavered for a moment as he turned his head toward Caleb.

"Yes," Caleb said, "that's what happens when people like me are taken to the capital."

Samuel and Seth turned toward each other with expressions of exasperation that seemed to be all too common between them.

"Cal—" Seth began.

"Even in the smaller towns," Caleb continued, his voice growing more frantic, "we know. We know what happens to those born with magic. They get taken and are never seen again. They get turned in by friends or family who see them using magic, and the mage hunters take them to the capital, where they are imprisoned. But the dangerous ones get executed immediately. They… I am not safe. I don't want to hurt anyone, not again…" Caleb's voice caught in his throat and cracked as building tears began to overflow.

Anything else Caleb had to say devolved into incoherent sobs. He grabbed hold of his shoulders like a man keeping himself together. But the cracks had widened and were releasing all that had threatened to break him.

A thousand sentences began and died on the tip of Samuel's tongue within the eternity of Caleb's downward gyre. But it was his father who placed a hand on his shoulder. He had to have known the exact right thing to say to calm the boy down, right? Samuel eagerly awaited his words of wisdom when they both vaguely heard something in the distance. It sounded like knocking on wood. No, not knocking. Whacking? Beating?

Chopping!

"Sword now!" said Samuel, grabbing his short sword from beneath his seat and looking for the direction of the sound.

"Caleb, get down and hold tight!" Seth tightened his grip on the reins and commanded the horses to run.

Samuel made a closer inspection of their surroundings. Dense, green forest all around, with only the lumpy dirt road clear enough for the two horses and wagon. There were no animals anywhere in sight. How could he not have noticed the lack of bird calls?

The chopping sound became louder and faster, almost desperate sounding.

They were going way too fast. Caleb was trying to keep himself secure but was bouncing painfully against the wood floor. The right front wheel gave a heart-stopping shatter as a spoke broke.

"It's still stable," Samuel said. "Keep going!"

The broken pieces of wood scattered along the road behind them. The wagon wobbled but stayed upright. Samuel looked in every direction, still unable to see who was chopping and which tree. Had they passed them yet?

No, the chopping was getting louder but remained somewhat distant.

The tree line was in sight. Only a few hundred feet, and they would be out of the woods.

That's when the tree fell.

A tall, thin, and sickly tree fell directly across the road with a loud crashing and splintering of dead wood. It would have made a sound regardless of those present because it was just that kind of tree. Unable not to be heard.

The horses had plenty of time to stop. They weren't even close to the freedom the tree line offered. Forward was impassable for the wagon, and backward would take too much time. They were trapped.

"Son," Seth said with a forced calm as he grasped Samuel by the shoulders, "I need you to listen to me. I will buy us some time and distract our pursuers. But I need you to untie the horses, then release Caleb…"

"But Father, I can—"

"Not a suggestion! Release Caleb, then you two take a horse, and I'll take the other. Then we will escape together."

Samuel looked into his father's resolute stare. He saw the projection of a man who would fight the world to protect the people in his care. He also saw the hint of cracks as his father, yet again, fought the fear of losing his family.

"Now!" shouted Seth.

Both leapt into action. Seth grabbed his sword and shield, drew his blade, and readied his stance. Samuel took his shield, attached it to a leather strap under his cloak, and began freeing the horses from the wagon. His hands were trembling. He didn't even try to steady himself. He knew there wasn't time. And as the enemy came out of the underbrush, he realized what this was.

"oh, hells!" Samuel yelled. "It's a goblin ambush!"

From what Samuel knew, goblins are vile, monstrous

creatures, filled with ill will and malcontent. They are the embodiment of evil, born for the corruption of the beautiful. They seek the destruction of everything considered good and stop at nothing to see their desire for pure chaos fulfilled.

At least, that is how they are described in the stories that parents tell their children.

Out from the crevices of the forest, ten goblins spilled onto the path. They were all short compared to the human man standing before them, the tallest of which was eye-to-belly-button with Seth. They had sickly pale green skin, long pointy ears, and noses that looked like they had been squashed onto their faces. Their countenances varied from one to the next, but each had extended eyebrow ridges, violet-colored irises, and sharp, jagged teeth. They wore various articles of clothing that looked like they had been refurbished several times over with stitchwork that could only be replicated by goblins and thumbless animals. Not a single set of clothes coordinated in color or fashion. Two of the goblins used mostly unaltered potato sacks as clothes, and those were the more fashionable goblins.

Each ran at them, brandishing their weapons. One waved his slightly larger-than-average stick above his head, another gripped a frying pan in one hand and a spatula in the other, a third held a sword sheath nearly as long as himself, and another still swung around a pair of boots tied together at the shoe strings. Samuel was nearly positive he saw a flute somewhere in the mix. The only true weapon wielded among them was the axe used to chop down the tree, but that goblin traded up for the aforementioned larger-than-average stick.

Samuel gave a slight sigh of relief, and he saw his father's tension slightly deflate. He knew they were still in danger, but not mortal danger. Goblins want living prisoners, hence their crude choice of weaponry. In small groups, they are mostly harmless, but even a lion can be taken down by the right number of ants. Samuel also knew that goblins, even though they have their own unique language, like to speak Primish, the most common language spoken by humans. The problem was that goblins rarely interacted with human groups, so their general understanding of the language was rudimentary at best.

"Hey, how you," one said, not remembering to add the questioning tone at the end.

"Nice meet you?" asked the second. This one was proud of his inclusion of the questioning intonation.

"Salutations!" the third shouted.

All at once, they leapt toward Seth.

Samuel tore his eyes away from his father. He had to focus. He had to free the horses so they could all escape. He didn't want to go anywhere the goblins wanted to take them.

The first horse, named Thistle, was freed and instinctively galloped toward Seth to help fend off the strange creatures. Moments later, the second, named Juniper, was freed. Samuel clumsily climbed onto Juniper's saddleless back, took hold of his reins, and led him to the back of the wagon. Once there, he leapt from the horse and fumbled for the keys to the cage, all while trying to ignore the sounds of fighting he knew he couldn't focus on. However, Samuel kept finding himself tearing his eyes from his progress to catch the mayhem. Even Caleb was absorbed in the fight.

Seth was a master of the sword. His fluid movements showed a precision that only time and dedication could instill in a warrior. No movement was wasted. Every step, twist and swing served an exact purpose. The problem was, a person using a conventional weapon adheres to the rules of said weapon with a give-and-take that is like a dance between fighters. A person using unconventional weapons like a fork, or an incredibly stale loaf of bread harder than a mallet, follows a different set of rules, mostly none. The fight should have seen Seth dispatching goblins two at a time. However, Samuel noted with a half-hearted groan that Seth was not striking with the edges of the blade but rather the flat of the blade, effectively just swatting them away. All the while, Seth was being hit in the head with a canteen, stabbed in the belly with a fork, and whacked in the shin with a frying pan. He did, however, catch an hourglass, which he threw back at the thrower, hitting them between the eyes and causing them to fall flat on the ground, twitching. Seth gave an excited shout as the goblin fell. It was as if he was cheering himself on. Samuel, however, knew that this was a sign that Seth was really getting into the flow of the fight. He was absolutely sure that if he were to glance at his father at this moment, Seth would have a broad smile just like in their sparring sessions together. Thistle came in at this time and helped separate the number of goblins surrounding Seth. The horse was also showered in praise and encouragement by Seth.

"Pay attention," Samuel said as he finally got the prison door open, startling Caleb back to himself, "and grab my hand!"

Samuel stood in the doorway with his hand extended. Caleb hesitated for a moment and then took his hand. With some difficulty, both boys were on the back of Juniper, with Samuel in the front holding the reins and Caleb, at least a foot taller, struggling to hold onto either the horse or Samuel.

"Dad! Let's go!"

Seth and his horse seemed to act as one as the man leapt onto Thistle's back just as she dipped and rose. Within a few strides, father and son were riding side by side, leaping over the fallen tree and nearing the forest's edge. That was when the final trap was sprung.

A rope was pulled taut across the path. Juniper saw it just in time and jumped over. Thistle, however, was distracted by an oncoming rolling pin. As she dodged the flying kitchenware, she tripped over the rope and toppled over, landing on Seth's left leg with a sickening crunch. Samuel's blood ran cold as he heard the guttural scream of pain coming from his father.

Samuel pulled back on Juniper's reins, stopping just at the edge of the forest.

"Go!" shouted Seth, and through heavy panting, said, "They can't get Caleb! Take him to Previa. I'll meet you there, no matter the cost." Thistle had gotten up and was trying to help Seth onto his feet, to no avail. The goblins were already closing in, with the two who pulled the rope trick being the closest.

Samuel would have jumped off and fought by his father's side, knowing full well the outcome, but he looked back at Caleb. Caleb, whose eyes were full of terror and uncertainty. A mage who, put in the wrong hands, could do irreparable damage. Who could help turn the tide of battle for or against the kingdom. He could not be given over to the Dark Lord. Samuel looked at the farm boy and made a horrible decision.

"You better not be lying!" Samuel said as he coaxed Juniper to gallop away as fast as he could go.

"Of all people," Seth whispered through gritted teeth, "you should know I'm not."

As the first goblin reached Seth, he lowered his grinning face almost nose-to-nose with Seth and asked, "How was trip?"

***

An immeasurable quantity of time passed for Samuel as Juniper kept following the path at great speed away from his father. For the rest of the world, it had been fifteen minutes, long enough to get out of the goblins' range. Goblins had never learned how to domesticate horses or ponies, dogs, cats, birds, etc. Though, to be fair, humans never actually domesticated cats either. Goblins travel light and on foot, but they have learned how to overtake enemies on horses. They just aren't usually successful.

A thousand thoughts flew through Samuel's mind as they traveled ever onward. He barely took note of the open fields that engulfed the road. The fields were the fresh green of spring with hints of blooming, vibrantly colored wildflowers. The sky was cerulean with wisps of clouds spread throughout its vastness. And the sun had already begun its descent. Samuel had, in his hurricane of thoughts, calculated roughly three hours until sunset. He knew they were not outfitted with the appropriate gear for camping. Most of the supplies had been left in the wagon, with only what he could quickly get his hands on straddled on the horses. Even that would now be divided in half. He would have to take stock of what was with him—as soon as they found shelter—so he could properly assess the situation. If his memory served correctly, there was an abandoned farmhouse about an hour's journey north, though he would have to take a detour off the main road, which is always a bad idea. You never

17

know who prowls the paths off of the King's Road, especially in areas long abandoned. But options were limited, and having no shelter, even in early spring, would be just as foolish.

Another lifetime passed in Samuel's mind as they approached a fork in the road. The path splintered to the northeast and northwest, or more simply put, left and right. The left path was obviously the more traveled path; it was wider, looked worn and showed heavy foot, hoof, and wheel marks. The one to the right was barely visible, with next to no recent travel marks. The horse slowed down and the younger boy hesitated for a long, silent moment, and then angled the reins to the right.

"Is this way really safe?" croaked the dry and crispy voice of Caleb.

Samuel reached into a sack that straddled the horse and pulled out a canteen of water, passing it to his travel companion. "No, but there is shelter closer this way, and we cannot risk the night in the open. Also" —he patted the horse's neck gently— "Juniper is tired and needs to rest soon."

Caleb nodded, and Samuel could almost see the resignation taking a deeper hold on the boy. It was uncanny for Samuel to see this older and much more muscular boy acting so timid. He wanted to say something. If only he knew what his father was about to say earlier. If only his father were with them now. Samuel uttered a silent curse and an even quieter prayer. Neither spoke for a long while.

Soon, they could see the growing shapes of an ancient oak tree and a farmhouse. The oak was slow to regrow its spring leaves, and in the approaching dusk, its skeletal limbs splayed ominous shadows along the ground, like bony arms and fingers reaching toward anyone who approached it. The house was in no better shape. Its front door hung off the hinges. Its stone walls seemed to sag under the weight of itself. Its thatched roof had several holes. It was more akin to a long-decayed corpse than a house. As they got closer Samuel saw the surrounding fields, dry and barren. He guessed that the ground had been overused and could no longer produce anything living.

When they arrived at the front entrance, Samuel hopped off of Juniper with practiced grace and assisted Caleb off. He then fountained some of the water from his canteen to the horse and affixed a feed bag to him. Samuel patted Juniper's mane and whispered gentle praises. Caleb assisted Samuel as they took the supplies from the horse and into the decrepit house. It was much worse on the inside. There were several floorboards that had broken or been pulled out altogether. Spiderwebs coated every possible corner and broken glass glistened in the dimming sunlight in a few areas. All the furnishings had long been removed. But there was a fireplace, and that was all Samuel needed. The boys gathered firewood as best they could in the coming darkness. Once all the wood was in the fireplace, Samuel dug into his bag and pulled out a hanging lantern with glass panels—and inside was a stone that looked to be made from living fire.

"It's an elven magic item," Samuel said when he noticed Caleb staring at it wondrously. "Watch this." Samuel opened one of the panels and faced the bundle of sticks and limbs and said, "Burn." Just as he spoke the word, the stone began to glow like a mini sun, and a small ember of flame was spat onto the wood, which lighted easily. Samuel then closed the lantern and placed it back in his bag.

"Wow, that's incredible!"

"Yeah, it's been very useful. It's nearly impossible for humans to get magic items from elves, but if you have enough gold anyone will part with anything."

There was a long silence between the two of them. They just sat there in front of the growing fire; minds lost in the events of the day. Eventually, Samuel brought out a loaf of bread and a few sticks of salted dried meat and divided it between the two of them.

"So," Caleb said after some time, "now what?"

Samuel thought for a moment, then said, "We have enough food to get us to the next town, which is another day and a half of travel, a little less if we don't take any rest breaks, but I'm not going to put Juniper through that. Then I will restock on supplies, and we will part ways. I need to find someone to take you to Previa so I can go after the goblins and rescue my father. I should be able to catch up with the goblins in a few days, depending on how fast they travel. They don't have horses so…" Samuel trailed off into a wandering tangent, no longer speaking for Caleb's sake but for his own.

"You talk about sending me away to my fate so casually. Do us mages mean that little to you mage hunters?" Caleb said. There was so little emotion behind the words that the tinge of sadness behind it was almost silent.

Samuel immediately snapped out of his unending vocal thought process and produced a glare that physically startled Caleb and made him turn pale. Samuel grabbed Caleb by the collar and in a voice wavering with grief and anger he said, "Are you that stupid? My father is about to be sent to the Dark Lord as a prisoner, and all you can think about is a stupid rumor? How in the hells do people come up with this? Mages like you aren't just killed or imprisoned. What ruler in their right mind just tosses away people who can take out armies with a few years of training and a simple phrase?

20

Mages are sent to a sanctuary in Previa where they are taught to use their magic! And we aren't mage hunters; we are *Wardens*. We do so much more than escorting mages!" Samuel loosened his grip as the anger flowed out of him, leaving little more than the remaining grief and newly forming regret.

"But, we heard that the king saw mages as dangerous and executed them himself."

"First, no." Samuel fully let go of Caleb and made a slightly exaggerated show of counting his answers on his fingers. "What king would bloody his own hands? Second, yes, there are dangerous mages that are executed. However, they are the ones who actively use their magic to kill, steal, and break the most severe laws. They are treated just like any other person who would use weapons to the same extent."

Caleb's face contorted in several expressions as he seemed to grasp what Samuel had said. Then a look of startled curiosity took residency as he asked, "Wait, what's this about a Dark Lord?"

"So small towns get rumors about murderous mage hunters but not the actual threat to mages? That's just typical." Samuel turned forward and released the last of his frustration through a long, drawn out sigh. "Look, those goblins that attacked us, they were after you; more specifically, they are after mages. They go after us *Wardens* as we are escorting mages. Unfortunately, goblins aren't the most clever and just capture anyone from the group because, odds are, one is a mage. They serve this person or creature they refer to as the Dark Lord, who surfaced about a year ago from what we can tell, and united a lot of the goblin tribes under his banner. He started abducting mages a few months back."

21

"Why is he hunting mages?" asked Caleb.

"We don't know yet," Samuel said as he turned back to look directly at his companion. He noticed that Caleb had moved slightly closer, narrowing the gap between them. He wasn't entirely comfortable with this newfound closeness, but he wasn't going to give up ground by backing away. "Or at least, the general public doesn't know. If the king and his people know, they sure as hells haven't let us in on it."

There was a brief lull in the conversation, like the calm low of the ocean between waves.

"I'm going with you," Caleb said resolutely.

"No!" Samuel said. "That would completely go against my orders and my job. I need you to get safely to Previa or else the enemy has another pawn at its advantage."

"Honestly, my capture will give them no advantage at all. I have no clue how to use my powers. My only talent is farming. If I were captured they couldn't really use me for anything useful."

Samuel looked at him with uncertainty.

"Look, I know this is your job," Caleb continued, "but he is your father, and I am just some mage trying to atone for what I've done. I would say losing one random mage to save your father is more than an even risk. Plus, you can't take on a horde of goblins by yourself. We will go and rescue your father, and then the two of you can safely take me to the capital." Then Caleb spoke suddenly as if struck in the backside with an idea. "If you don't see me there personally, how do you know I got there safely and wasn't captured by the goblins anyway?"

This was the straw that broke Samuel's resolve. He knew he had to save his father, and he couldn't do that alone, and he knew he had to safely escort this mage. The choice was obvious, but was it the right choice?

However, before Samuel could fully cave to the mage with the expression of a hurt calf, the sound of approaching footsteps made both of them turn around. In the doorway now stood a tall, looming figure. A dark, hooded cloak blocked most of his features except for a bright yellow, crooked grin.

"What have we here?" he said as more cloaked figures gathered behind him.

Campfire Conversations: Feeding Goblins

Cycle 3, Day 24

S eth was lying on a makeshift bed made of layers of surprisingly comfortable blankets, with a poorly stitched pillow filled with down feathers under his head and another propping up his broken leg. After his fall and subsequent injury, the goblins were quick as lightning to put a splint on his leg. He hadn't tried to fight them off, so Thistle was calm and allowed the goblins to work. The goblins pulled out several metal rods from a pack crudely labeled "MEDECEN" and placed the rods strategically around the injury, wrapping fabric around the leg to keep the rods in place. Seth was fascinated watching them work. They had examined the break, thoroughly looking for punctures. They were incredibly gentle throughout the entire process. All the while, another goblin was crushing several different plants and ingredients in a bowl and fed the resulting goop to Seth. He accepted without question, and in a rather quick amount of time, he noticed the searing pain in his leg had decreased by a significant amount.

When the goblins were content with their work, they pulled out a tarp from another pack—this one labeled "CAMPNG"—and unfolded it beside him.

"You don't have to do that," Seth had said. "Give me a big stick, and I can walk."

"No!" said one of the goblins. This one had been the

one giving orders during the whole process. Seth had assumed that he was the leader. However, he wasn't wearing anything that singled him out as leader. He had on a filthy green tunic that fit him like a dress, extending to the knees. Had the sleeves not been ripped just above the elbow, they would have easily extended past his clawed hands. He also had a piercing on the pointed tip of his left ear, but upon closer inspection, it wasn't an earring but a discarded wedding ring that no longer had its diamond. "You broken. Walking more make break more."

Seth nodded and allowed himself to be lifted onto the tarp. Once he was situated, several of the goblins banded together and lifted gently on the four corners and sides, carrying him until they decided to make camp for the night.

Seth watched the group from his bed and couldn't help but be curious about his captors. They had positioned him near the central fire but only near enough to be comfortably warm. He watched as several goblins attached the tarp they used to carry him onto a couple of trees, creating a hammock. At its full size, he realized it could probably hold the encampment of goblins. He also realized, with a pang of guilt, that he was using all of their blankets. Another goblin was cooking a stew that smelled impossibly good. This goblin was wearing a tattered and badly patched baker's apron and hat. They were several sizes too big for him, but Seth found it oddly cute and endearing.

Soon the stew was finished and all the goblins gathered around the pot, each with their own unique bowls. Most were chipped, some were ornately painted, and one was a flower pot. The leader was the first in line and carried a bowl easily twice as big as the other goblins'. However, to Seth's surprise, the leader started to walk directly to him.

The head goblin sat on the dirt beside Seth, took a

25

spoonful of the stew—which looked to be mostly carrots, potatoes, and other vegetables, and a hint of rabbit—and opened his mouth, saying, "Ahhh."

"I can feed myself," Seth said graciously in an attempt to keep his dignity.

But the goblin paid his objection no mind and just continued saying, "Ahhhhhhhh."

Seth obliged with a slightly embarrassed smile and opened his mouth. The goblin was patient with Seth and careful not to burn his mouth. The stew turned out even better than it smelled. There were some spices and flavors that Seth had never tasted before, and they were expertly blended. After Seth had finished the bowl, the goblin gave a very toothy grin and proceeded to get his own bowl of stew, this time in a bowl the same size as the others, if not smaller. He came back and sat beside Seth again and watched as his crew enjoyed themselves, talking in their foreign language that sounded more like frogs croaking, mixed with the occasional hiss or chirp. He also noticed one of the goblins giving special treatment to Thistle and giving her food and water.

"You seem like a happy group," Seth said, his smile like a star in the night.

"Yes!" the goblin leader said with pride. "We one of best goblin groups. Now make two success."

"I hate to disappoint, but I'm not a mage."

"It no matter. Success is success." The goblin's prideful smile never wavered.

"What's your name?"

"Puppies!" At this, Puppies looked directly at Seth with the most genuine smile, which gave Seth the impression of a gleeful shark.

"I am Seth, son of Silas." Seth was taken aback by Puppies' name and debated how to respectfully ask about its origin when Puppies interjected.

"Oh! You named by father. I named by mother."

"Really? I would like to know more about goblin naming tradition, if you don't mind."

Puppies let out an excited croak. "We goblins love human language. We love way it sound. Few speak it good. I am best in group. Parent name child favorite human word. Mother like puppies best."

"I see," said Seth. "So how is it decided which parent names which child?"

"First child named by parent who speak human language best. This determined by goblin tribe leader. Both parents enter contest. Parent that spell most words correct names first child. Then other parent name second. Each take turn."

"That's rather…" Seth took a moment to find the right word, "unique. I guess every culture has its own naming system." He was coming to terms with the fact that this foreign group of creatures didn't quite match what he had imagined. Granted, this was his first time encountering goblins to any meaningful extent. He was intrigued by their way of life and how a bunch of people like Puppies could work for the entity he knew only as the Dark Lord.

"Is it?" Puppies asked with genuine confusion and curiosity. "How is others named?"

Seth gave his best fatherly smile and began to tell Puppies about human culture. Somewhere along his tellings, he had gathered a crowd of goblins who were all quietly listening in absolute wonder. They listened to every word in the same way a starving man devours his first meal.

The night was long and full of well-fed goblins.

Chapter 2: A Beginning… Again
Cycle 3, Day 10

About a half cycle before Samuel's story would suffer from its inciting incident; there was another story starting to unfold. It began with an older man around the age of 70. The man was from what could be considered the "real" world. He fell asleep one night on his comfortable feather bed and found himself waking up in a completely different bed. It was an elegant and almost regal bed. It had a vibrant crimson quilt laced with gold and a bedframe with a canopy. The curtains around the canopy were also crimson and embroidered with gold floral designs; there were even gold tassels. These curtains were pulled open by another person in the bed beside him—an almost entirely naked man—who the old man would soon discover to be the king. Their eyes met, and many words were exchanged without breaking the silence. Eventually, the king did break the silence with a royal yelp that summoned the crown guard.

Many things happened in rapid succession. The old man found himself grappled, cuffed, threatened, dumbfounded, dragged, located to the dungeon, uncuffed, recuffed, and relocated after thirty minutes to an almost empty room, uncuffed again, and finally given food and water.

The room was just a brick, windowless, square room. It had torches on the wall that gave flickering visibility to the room. The door was made of old wood that looked like it had been part of that entrance since before the man had been born. He sat in a hand-carved chair that was made by less-than-talented hands if its wobbling nature was any indication. In front of him was what looked like a table that had been broken down into splinters and glued back together and an empty chair of similar craftsmanship to his own.

The old man was alone with his thoughts, and something that had been nagging at his brain in the background was coming around to the foreground. Something seemed off. Everything seemed right, which is why something felt off. The world around him was too real, too vivid, too tangible. His thoughts were clear, and his actions did not feel as if underwater. His senses were keen and focused, not that muted sensation of touch and smell that would indicate a dream. In fact, wasn't it odd that he would even think he was in a dream if it were a dream? The more he thought, the more he was starting to convince himself that this was not a dream but reality. But accepting that it wasn't a dream didn't explain how the devil it could be real.

After some time, he made up his mind that he was going to treat this reality as if it were not a dream. If worse came to worse and he died, and it was a dream, no harm, no foul. But if he died due to carelessness and it was real all along, then there would be a lot of harm. Though if he were to die and this was all real, he supposed he would not have to worry about it after the fact.

Just as the man made up his mind about this, the door swung open and someone new entered the room. The man wore a flowing gray robe and an oversized pointy hat with a wide, circular brim. He stood at just over six feet and walked with a knotty cane nearly as tall as himself. But his most noticeable feature was his gray beard, which covered pretty much all of his face, aside from his nose and eyes, and extended past his waist. Everything else was covered by either his long, wiry hair or his hat. There was no doubt in the man's mind that this stranger was a wizard, meaning he was far, far, far from home.

The old man looked at his own attire: A pair of black-and-green plaid pajama bottoms and a loose-fitting white T-shirt that once flaunted the logo of his favorite band when he was younger; now, the logo was just specks of fading color. He was also apprehensive of his lack of headwear. He never left the house without a hat to hide his balding head. All he had left was the thinning and wispy white hair that made the shape of a horseshoe around his head. His feet were also completely bare, and the cold stones were trying dutifully to turn his feet numb.

The most-likely-a-wizard pointed at the chair opposite the man and asked, "May I?"

"Yes, of course," the old man answered. He regarded the wizardly man the same way a child would regard a person in a mascot costume. It was a struggle for him not to blatantly stare.

The obviously-a-wizard's beard moved upward as his hidden smile broadened. He sat down, situated his beard, then his robe, then his beard again. "Confounded thing," he said. "I'd get rid of this idiotic mess of hair, but then no one would recognize or respect me." He gave a jolly chuckle. The old man had never in his life considered anyone jolly, but this man fit the word better than anyone he had ever met. "Now, where was I? Oh yes. I am Malguinne, the Royal Wizard to King Andreaus, first of his name. What is your name?"

"I am Robert Miller, a retired mailman, but my friends just call me Buddy."

"Ahhh, a good strong name," Malguinne said with a twinkle in his eye. "I hope I'm not being presumptuous, but may I call you Buddy?"

"You may," answered Buddy. "I mean, yes, please do."

"I expect you have questions?"

"I do."

"Then I will answer as quickly as I can," Malguinne said as he stroked his beard. "I have a few for you as well. But time is of the essence. I fear every moment is a moment wasted."

"How's that?" Buddy asked. He caught the sudden shift in urgency in the wizard's voice which transferred to his own question.

"Ahhh, a clever man you are to get to the point of things so quickly." Malguinne beamed at Buddy and the movement of his beard suggested the smile underneath. "You are currently residing in Previa, the capital city in the Kingdom of Primaria. Your world and our world are considered sister worlds in the grand web of reality. So, occasionally, objects, both living and otherwise, travel from one to the other. Usually, it's a quick there and back, a blink of the eye, but now and again, one such as you comes along and seems to get stuck. It has happened a handful of times in my lifetime, but every time, I learn new things about your world. This time, I believe your arrival is most fortuitous. There is a great evil that has arisen on the outskirts of the kingdom. A being calling himself the Dark Lord has started raising an army of goblins and other such evil, vile creatures and threatens our kingdom."

"Look, I know where this is going. I've read my share of books back in the day. A chosen hero is called to action and must save the realm and is led by a Merlin type; that's you. But it's the youngins that get to play the hero. I'm old and tired. Find yourself a more suitable hero." Buddy said this with conviction but more to talk himself out of the "one last hurrah" that his retired life has been craving.

"That's precisely it, Buddy; I have found the most suitable hero," Malguinne said as he clasped his hands together in a display of petition. "Destiny is a funny and unknowable thing. It sent you at our darkest moment; there has to be a reason. I don't know how you will be the one to save us, but solutions and heroism are always found on the journey, not before it. I will create the perfect traveling party of the kingdom's greatest warriors, and when the time comes, we will all bear witness to what you can do. What do you say? Will you help me save my world?"

Buddy remembered fondly a book he'd read multiple times throughout his life about a certain 50-year-old who met a meddling wizard who convinced him to go on a journey and, in the end, went up against some of the greatest evils his world could throw at him. Buddy knew he could only reject the offer once, but that's just tradition. You can't say no to the journey of a hero a second time and not regret it. He'd had a long and pleasant—if not dull—life. If he were to go out by stupidly playing the hero, would anyone fault him?

Would anyone miss him?

Buddy recoiled slightly at that thought and proceeded to let his mind flow through safer streams of thought. Maybe he could bring back a souvenir for his grandson. What was he interested in now? Is he still into trucks? Or has he out-grown them? How old is he now? How long had it been since...

He let the stream stop altogether.

"If I join you for this, will I be able to go home?"

"Of course," the wizard said without hesitation. "I will begin preparations for the Return Home spell. However, it will take some time for it to be fully charged and ready. By the time we return it should have had enough time."

"How long do you expect this to take?"

"Hmm, let's see," Malguinne said as his brows knit to-gether while he contemplated. "I would say with a small party, we should be there in about a cycle, possibly less, de-pending on good weather. Then there is the return. Prepare to journey for sixty days, give or take."

Buddy froze and felt a flutter in his chest. Panic was sinking in. He closed his eyes and took several deep breaths. His hand instinctively reached for his chest but hesitated as he remembered where he was and the man in front of him. He opened his eyes and made sure to sit up perfectly straight and normally. He could already feel his heart properly beat-ing in sync. But was it slower to return to a normal heart rate than usual?

"Is...everything okay, Buddy?" the wizard asked with searching eyes.

"Yeah," Buddy said. "Just took me by surprise, is all. I haven't been away from my...err...loved ones longer than a week since my last...work conference." All the words sounded correct to Buddy, and odds were Malguinne wouldn't question anything. Two months is a long time—longer for some than others—and Buddy was a member of that some. Buddy weighed his options, which was easy to do with only one real option and nothing to weigh it against. "When do we set out?"

***

Buddy was led around the castle as Malguinne attempted to find the servants' quarter. He was amazed at how unamazed he was. The castle was just a large, dark building made of stone and wood. There were candles, lamps, and other fire-and-wax-based lighting and a drafty coldness that gave the interior of the castle a cave-like ambiance. But it was too real. It's not really a fantasy the second you smell the sourness of mildew and get a splinter in the heel of your foot.

Their journey eventually took them through a courtyard. Buddy thought it was rather odd to have a spot in the middle of the castle completely open to the elements and with a garden. But then again, Buddy had never been inside a castle before, so who was he to judge? It was a beautiful garden, with freshly budding flowers of reds and yellows and the midday sun making it stand out like an otherworldly garden. He could even see some hummingbirds flying around. However, once he took a closer look, he saw that they weren't birds at all. They were little humans the size of playing cards. The wings on their back were the exact same as hummingbirds, moving at impossible speed but keeping them fairly still. They did not have clothes, but they were covered in tiny, glossy feathers. Buddy attempted to ask Malguinne about them, but the wizard was too busy har-rumphing around, refusing to admit how lost he was. The other oddity in the courtyard was a large pine tree. All the plants and flowers in the garden shared similar traits as ones from his world, but they were wrong, whether in shape or size, but the tree was like an exact copy taken from his world. A slight breeze blew a small, twirling pine seed wing

34

toward Buddy, who caught it reflexively and pocketed it.

The peaceful quiet was immediately disturbed by the sound of metal armor clanking quickly against stone. Buddy turned toward the sound and saw a guard unsheathing a sword and running toward him. Buddy's arm instinctively shot up as he prepared to be handcuffed yet again.

"What do you think you are doing, Unari?" The guard held the old man at sword point as her glare bore holes into Buddy's eyes. Buddy felt cold panic shoot through his veins and a sudden realization that every word he had ever known had vanished from his memory.

"Wa…er…ye see…" Buddy would have continued but was thankfully rescued by Malguinne.

"How about we drop the sword," Malguinne said with a calming voice as he walked past Buddy and toward the guard.

"Sir! I'm sorry, but the Unari just—"

"Now, now," Malguinne interrupted. "First, how about you tell me your name?"

"I am Laura, daughter of Leirna, head of—"

"Oh, I don't think any more will be necessary." Then Malguinne's kindly visage shifted into a stone-like seriousness, and for a split second, Buddy could have sworn there was a fire in the old man's eyes. "Laura, I command you to do exactly as I say. I am the Royal Wizard, after all."

"Yes, sir," the guard said with immediate obedience.

"Good. Now, please direct us to the servants' quarter. My friend would like some more appropriate clothes."

The guard led them quickly to where they needed to go. They also came to the realization that the servants' quarter was, in fact, not inside the castle proper. Once they located the undersized and overcrowded living quarters, Malguinne dismissed the guard and talked a few of the royal servants into giving up some of their old clothing to the man in the plaid pajamas. Buddy was fitted in a loose sand-colored shirt, equally loose mud-colored pants, bright red socks that needed small leather belts to keep them up, and a pair of coal-black, or coal-stained, boots with a slight hole in the left boot heel. The clothes were uncomfortable but made him feel less out of place.

"Shouldn't we tell the king we are leaving?" Buddy asked as they exited the front gate and started toward the business district of the city. From the ground perspective, it was hard to grasp the size of the city, but Buddy felt like an ant as he walked through the streets. Everywhere they turned, the path was crowded with people, and the sound was deafening. It reminded him of a trip he took to New York with his son. After seeing the fairies or pixies or whatever in the garden, he expected to see more strange creatures in the city. But from what he could tell, everyone looked human. Malguinne had informed him the proper term for the people of this world was Anuin. At least it sounded less sci-fi than Earthlings.

"It would be wise not to. The king is busy taking care of the kingdom in these trying times." Buddy looked around. The people did not look like they were experiencing trying times, just times. "Waking up in the king's bed might also play a role in our quick departure too." Malguinne gave a conspiratorial wink.

The castle loomed over them as they came out of the shadow of the brick walls that surrounded and protected it. The castle itself was a mass of brick and towers, rising from the ground like a jagged mountain. Buddy could not identify from the outside any correlating inner rooms. It was like looking at a maze from a side perspective.

Buddy would soon find that the city was in the center of a valley surrounded by mountains on all but one side, and through the city cut a river that had an unfortunate coloration—and odor to match.

"I suppose," he agreed, with a growing heat in his cheeks. "By the way, why did that guard rush me like that, and what does Unari mean?"

"Ah yes," Malguinne said. "I haven't the faintest clue. I suppose she was just trying to intimidate you to alleviate the boredom. And Unari is what we call people from your world. In this world, every living being's soul comes from the breath of the goddess Anu. And Unari is a word from an older language meaning breathless. Your soul was not created here, so you are considered breathless."

"I see," Buddy said. "So then—"

"Here we are," Malguinne announced as they stopped in front of a building with a hanging sign that said *Journey's End Tavern*. "Now, let us see who we can recruit."

Excerpt From the Journal of Tyberion
Cycle 3, Day 10

I, Tyberion, son of Tibus, former Royal Knight and current sellsword, bear witness to the quest against the Dark Lord. I write down the events of this quest to be remembered by future generations and to give truthful recollections of what will become history and legend.

My part in this expedition began with a pint of ale generously donated by the Royal Wizard, Malguinne. It was cheaply bought with a taste to match. The wizard spun silver words as quickly as a spider wraps its prey with its silken net. I would have declined, save for the wizard's companion. An old man, younger than the wizard but old enough to be my father. Truth be told, he looked much like my father, whom I buried ten years prior.

The old man said little, but his eyes absorbed everything around us like a child new to life. I wanted nothing more than to tell the wizard his noble quest was one filled with death and misfortune and where he could relocate his proposition and his staff. But the old man looked me in my one good eye and said, "You look just like a warrior from an old book I loved as a kid. I bet you could tell some devilish stories. If you join us, then you should tell me about your past adventures."

I never could tell my father no, and I could do no less for this man. I joined the two, letting the wizard know in no uncertain language my terms and my pay. I will hold him to his word under the pain of death. Their following recruitment efforts were exceptionally unsuccessful. The old man, whom I have come to call Buddy, made numerous misjudgments of customs. His referral of a short man as a "hoppit" was the greater of his blunders. It was a small miracle I joined and was of the ability to de-escalate the situation with a swift punch to the short man's jaw. I will not be welcome in that particular brothel, but that is no large loss. Their soup was subpar, and their beer was like fornicating on a rowboat, if you catch my meaning.

Malguinne was able to convince a shifty and dirty-looking man to join. He claimed to be a surprisingly cheap mercenary. However, it is to be noted that he needed no such convincing. I recognized him as a man who had made some ill-informed business transactions over the past few nights and was secretly in search of a speedy escape from the city. I spoke to him in private on the matter and he gave his word as to keeping to his current obligation. This was also under pain of death.

The final companion was an elf hunter. I found it strange to see him living in the city among humans, outside the protection of elven communities. He had a curious bow in that it was a purely natural bow. The few elves I have met always used magic-infused weapons. Bows that shoot fire, daggers that return to the wielder, and other such fascinating devices.

Magic weapons are fine and have an elegance and sophistication that forged weapons do not. However, adding over-complications to weapons can only lead to disaster in the heat of the moment, where anything can and will go wrong. Give me a greatsword any day, and I will cleave a man in twain. There is little need for theatrics in combat. Perhaps this elf was of a similar mind to my own. However, he did have an arrow in his quiver that was wrapped in heavy fabric. An enchanted arrow, perhaps?

The first day's travel did not take our band of mismatched companions far. I was the one to set the pace, basing it on the group's lack of experience in such long journeys. The wizard, I am certain, has more experience than I ever will in such matters, but I found Buddy getting winded rather easily. Even riding horseback seemed to wear on him.

We made camp just off the King's Road, where Malguinne revealed Buddy's true origins. The mercenary appraised the old man in a similar way that a merchant silently measures the worth of a foreign coin. The elf gave no noticeable change. I assume it mattered not to him whether this human was of this world or the other. The elf holds himself as superior to the rest of the company of humans.

I, however, was enthralled. The old man wanted to know my stories, but I desired to know his. I have never met an Unari before, and what I know of them is naturally clouded by the untruths that always come with such travelers. He told us of his world and their inventions of "electronics," which is their form of magic. I will replicate the conversation to the best of my remembrance.

"I don't have it with me, but I had a device that would allow me to communicate with anyone I knew and even those I didn't know. It is as small as a... um... I suppose a horseshoe is the first thing that comes to mind. It could also allow me to look up common answers like the weather for the week or who was the presi... err... leader when my father was a child."

"Well," the elf said, "who was the leader when your father was a child?"

"Let's see. If we are talking about when he was first

born, I admit, I don't quite remember, though it might have been–"

"Is that so?" the elf scoffed. "Devices such as that have their uses, but dependence on it for simple memory shows your civilization's lack of personal growth. From what I have learned from your world, I would not be surprised that your people would crumble the second your *electronics* were to be taken away. I can see that you are so reliant on your people's method of transportation that basic exertion leaves you weakened and vulnerable."

He would have continued in his belittlement of a world he would never know, but I took it upon myself to say a few words. I am neither proud nor ashamed of these words, but out of respect and lack of necessity, I will not be adding them to this journal. I will note that seeing the elf flustered and at a loss for words was an enjoyable event to watch. He went to sleep rather early and rather farther away from camp than the rest. I will be sure to speak to him in the morning to make it clear there is no quarrel between us. And so that I may offer him some advice…under pain of death, of course.

Chapter 3: Claw and Order
Cycle 3, Day 24

Caleb took in the sight of the five men who entered the abandoned farmhouse. They were unified in their choice of dark, hooded cloaks and their equally dark chuckles as they got closer to the two teenagers. Caleb could see hints of mismatched leather armor underneath their cloaks—but it was their weaponry that caught his eye. The metal of short swords and daggers, and one particularly large and rusty claymore, reflected the flickering light of the fire.

The man leading the pack removed his hood, revealing a shaggy mess of black curls, a rough, scared face, and golden-brown eyes that had their own sinister fire in them.

"Don't tell me you've gone deaf and mute now," he said with a voice that would sound more natural coming from a hungry wolf rather than a man. "I asked you a question. What are two young pups doing in the middle of our territory all alone?"

Caleb felt Samuel getting closer and grabbing onto his arm with trembling hands. He looked at the younger boy and saw a layer of fear masking the unmistakable fire of rage in his eyes.

"My brother and I are just waiting for our father, who should be back from hunting any moment now," Samuel said with an uneasy voice. "He's a Warden, and we are his apprentices." His act took Caleb by surprise for a moment, but he played along and nodded.

"You hear that, boys? We got ourselves Warden brats!" the bandit leader said. As he began discussing with his crew what they should do with the two, Samuel pulled Caleb down closer to his height and whispered in his ear.

"Use your magic on them. Then we can escape in the chaos."

"I can't," Caleb whispered back. "I don't know—"

"Just repeat whatever you did the first time," Samuel hissed, interrupting the other boy's protests. Caleb resisted the urge to argue as he saw the younger boy's harsh resolution. Well, what did he have to lose? If he couldn't use his magic now, it's not like they would be any less dead. He gulped, hoping to subdue the fear he felt grasping his lungs; the invisible fist only strengthened its grip. He closed his eyes and reimagined the scene he had tried so hard to forget. He remembered his friend standing before him, and his heart sank as the words came back to him. He opened his quivering mouth and repeated what he had said to his friend that day.

"What in the nine hells is wrong with you!" Caleb kept his eyes shut as he shouted at the bandits. The men had gone silent, and he knew all their eyes were on him. Tears were building and falling as he remembered the hurt look on his friend's face. But he had to continue. He quickly spat out the last part as if it were poison, he was trying to expel from his soul, "She's my sister! Of course I won't give you my blessing! Stay away from her, or else I'll—"

Caleb opened his eyes as he reached the end of what he had said and raised his right hand, open and pointed at the bandit leader. He could feel something rising from the pit of his chest and spreading down his arm with a painful prickling sensation. He could see the hairs on his arm rising as blue sparks traveled in the direction of the flow of pain. The last thing he saw before collapsing to the ground in a near faint was a blue light shooting from the tip of his finger and striking the bandit's arm, which he raised in an attempt to cover his horror-stricken face.

Caleb was winded, and his arm hurt, but he was still conscious. With Samuel's help, he was getting back on his feet, wobbling but upright. However, the scream of pain and terror coming from the bandit sent a white-hot bolt down his spine, and he watched in horror as the skin of the man's right arm began to peel off.

From elbow to fingertips, the bandit leader's skin cracked and peeled, falling off like discarded snake skin. Underneath was something rough and red that began to expand and grow larger. His four fingers melded together into a red heap of what was no longer flesh, and his thumb expanded, flesh tearing off as a sharp, red shape emerged from underneath. He shouted and screamed in agony, begging the men to cut off his arm, but they all just stood there, dumbstruck and unable to look away. In moments, the red, bloated thing stopped shifting, and it became clear exactly what replaced the man's arm.

"Boss, your arm."

"It…it's a claw."

"A crab claw!"

The four subordinates helped their leader up, but none touched the new arm for fear it was contagious.

"Caleb?" Samuel said while watching the men recoup.

"Ye-yeah?"

"You okay?"

"Yeah," Caleb answered, unable to look away from the man's new appendage.

"Good, now, follow my lead." Samuel pointed at the group of men and shouted, "Let us leave, or my brother will do to the rest of you what he did to your leader."

The four men all backed away closer to the doorway. The leader, however, made a sound like boiling blood as he began to laugh and slowly walked toward the two. He swayed ruggedly as he adjusted to his newfound, asymmetrical weight. His crooked smile became warped with madness, and his eyes were alight with burning hatred. Caleb saw Samuel reach for his sword, but the bandit leapt forward in a blur of red and grabbed the boy by the throat with his pincer, holding the dangling, gurgling boy several feet off the ground. Then he turned his eyes of amber fire toward Caleb.

"Oh, I really wouldn't do that again if I were you, boy." Every word cut through the air like frozen venom. Caleb nodded as his knees began to buckle, and he collapsed to the floor. Samuel was released, and he fell to the ground, gasping and coughing, but alive. "Get the rope. I think we should take them with us. I'd hate to leave two boys alone out here. Who knows what dangerous men might stumble upon them."

***

The two quickly found themselves tied up at the wrists and leashed to the saddle of one of the bandit's horses. The leader and two others rode in front while two more rode behind the boys. One of the rear bandits held a crossbow at the ready in case either tried any more magic. It had taken the men some time to get the horses to cooperate after seeing the monstrous claw hand, but the leader was able to strike just the right amount of fear into them to make them obey. Then

45

they haphazardly strapped their ill-gained loot onto their similarly-gained horse, which had included Samuel's sword. He was allowed to keep his shield attached to the back of his armor; it was not like he could use it. Juniper was heavily resistant to becoming the bandit's property, but after some time and a lot of effort Samuel had calmed the horse down enough for them to attach Juniper's reins to the saddle of the last bandit's horse.

There was a long, uncomfortable silence. Caleb was uneasy and more than a little shaky. He wondered if it was because he could almost physically feel the stare of the crossbow at the back of his head or because he used his magic again. He reflected on the feel of the power flowing through him and how unnatural it felt. It wasn't just the pain but the wrongness of it. The best way he could imagine it was forcing water to flow uphill but only using your mind. But he was beginning to understand what triggers it, more or less. All he had to do was not have strong emotional re-actions to anything. If he could just do that forever, then he would never harm anyone again, right?

He looked toward the captain with the monstrous arm. The sight made his stomach drop like a stone tossed into the deepest part of the ocean as he tried to come to terms with what he was capable of. The man was turning the claw over and over, looking at it from multiple angles, and experiment-ing with opening and closing the claw.

The bandit leader turned to his men with his signature crooked grin that showed way too many teeth. "Why so se-rious, men?" He let out a dark chuckle. "This is a good thing! This claw, by Her Breath, is incredible. It feels no pain, and it has incredible grip strength. No one will dare step on our territory without a second thought or a death wish."

"You know," said one of the men, "I think it suits you. You always were better at close combat, and now you can defend and attack with the same hand."

"You were already unstoppable," said another. "Now you're…uhhh…more unstoppable-er."

"That's not how words work, you bumbling bag of bear droppings." This voice came from the direction of the crossbow. Caleb didn't even chance a glance.

"There's just one thing." The clawed leader's voice registered a note of ice that silenced the whole group.

"What's that, boss?"

"I'm going to need a new title!" he said as he bellowed with laughter. "I need a name that will strike fear in my enemies."

There was a pause when the group began to visibly think. Caleb could see, and almost hear, the effort of their minds at work.

"How 'bout Killer Crab? It's even got them alliterating Ks."

The leader thought it over. The look on his face was not displeased but not quite sold. Then he looked at the two boys, and with a twist of his smile, he said, "You boys got any good ideas?"

Caleb looked at Samuel for the first time in several minutes and saw that the younger boy's mind was worlds away from the conversation. His eyes were on the ground but were darting from side to side, lost in plans within plans. Caleb drew attention away from him by saying the first thing that came to mind, "King Crab?"

The leader forced his horse to an immediate stop, causing the rest to follow suit, and looked directly into Caleb's eyes. Only heartbeats filled the void of silence before the bandit's smile broadened so wide he could have sent predatory animals fleeing from miles away. "That's it! From now on, you will all address me as King Crab! I like you, boy. You're going to go far in this gang." The crew started back at their slow and easy pace.

"Wait." Samuel snapped back to attention at this. "What? You don't mean—"

"What did you think we were going to do with you two?" the man asked with a round of laughter from the gang. "We aren't going to kill such useful new recruits. It's so hard to come by fresh meat in this field of work. People wanting to become…let's say, freelance toll collectors, are always at the end of their rope and are rarely of the ability to learn the techniques that make up the minutiae of the job. Besides, Lockpick has been wanting apprentices for ages now."

The man on the horse to the right of the newly dubbed King Crab raised his hand and gave a meek smile. "That's right, boss. I've had a knack for locks since I was younger than you two. I would take 'em apart just to see how they worked. I'm probably the best lockpicker you will ever meet, and that's satisfying and all, but now what? I'm at the top of my mountain. Course I could find another big challenge, but what then if I climb that mountain? Look for a new mountain and a new one over and over? Every time, it will be the same. It will be me atop that mountain. Alone. I'm tired of being alone at the mountaintops. I want to give something back for the next generation of lockpickers." Lockpick looked at the two boys with a genuine smile and more than one tear trickling down his face. "I want to give what I know to someone that can climb the mountains I could never. I want to look at the next peak over and see someone I trained blazing a new trail."

"That's amazing," Caleb said as he wiped away his tears. "I never thought about it that way. But wait. Couldn't you just go into the lock-making trade? With everything you know, you could make locks that only the best could pick, and you could challenge yourself to make the most unpickable lock. And I'm fairly sure you would have an easier time finding apprentices."

Lockpick's eyes went wide with a newfound possibility. He stopped his horse and seemed to disappear inside himself. The leader shot Caleb a nasty side-eye before turning to his subordinate and said, "There's no going back, you know that, Picks. Deserters don't get free passes to live the lives they want. You can't just wake up and say, 'I'mma remake myself today and start a new life'. Besides, there's no freedom in simple living."

"You're right, boss," Lockpick said with resignation. "A man can dream, though." He gave a halfhearted smile as they started forward again, and Caleb couldn't help but feel sorry for the guy. He looked over at Samuel and saw that he was looking at something in the distance. Caleb followed his companion's gaze and saw a small light down the path they were traveling. He knew they were getting closer to the fork in the road where this path met the King's Road, so maybe they were traveling merchants. He turned back to Samuel, whose eyes were beginning to dart from one bandit to another. Caleb knew a plan was being made, and he silently waited for how he could play a part in their escape.

"Looks like we will get to show you boys the ropes of high-risk toll collecting," said King Crab, as the fire in the distance began to grow closer. "Just stay quiet and watch. This will be over before you know it. If they have any luck, we might not have to kill anyone."

49

He couldn't see the twisted smile, but Caleb knew it was there, the same way that a cat's claws are always there, just beneath the surface.

As the campsite came into a clear enough view to make out individual people around the fire, Caleb noticed Samuel inch away from him. It was slow at first, but it was unmistakable. Why was he distancing himself? Was this part of his plan? Then Caleb considered that perhaps Samuel was distancing himself away from the crossbow pointed at their backs instead.

One of the figures by the fire stood up and looked in the direction of the bandits, and that's when Samuel acted. He drew in a deep breath and screamed at the top of his lungs, "Bandits! Run away!" Caleb turned to look at the man holding the crossbow. As expected, the man took his eyes off Caleb and looked at Samuel in bewilderment. Slowly, his crossbow began to move in the same direction as his eyes. Caleb was about to charge at the bandit, but before either could react, the bandit leader sprang from his horse. With a fluid movement, he backhanded—or, in this case, back-clawed—Samuel. The boy was knocked to the ground with a painful thud.

"Now, that wasn't very smart. After all the kindness we showed you and your brother." There was a thorny calmness in his voice as he raised his claw in the moonlight, preparing to spear Samuel in the throat. "But don't worry. I'll take good care of your brother!" He lunged downward, but Samuel was ready for it. He rolled over onto his stomach so that the claw would strike the center of his back, where his shield rested beneath his cloak. Just as the claw was about to make contact, it stopped in midair for a split second and was repelled with such force that the bandit leader was lifted off the ground before falling onto his back. His head smashed against the dirt with an audible thud.

Caleb was incredulous at this sight, but from the corner of his eye, he could see the crossbow bandit lifting his weapon and taking aim at his leader's assailant. He didn't hesitate as he sprinted toward the bandit. The rope connecting him to the horse in front had just enough leeway that he could reach the man and plunge his teeth into his unarmored calf. The bandit gave a yelp and a kick to Caleb's face, and somewhere between the two events, the bolt was let loose. Caleb turned to look in the direction of the projectile, his heart jumping out of his throat, and was instantly relieved to see that it was buried in the earth several feet away from Samuel.

Caleb's eyes met with Samuel's for an instant, and the older boy could almost hear the unspoken gratitude that accompanied the younger boy's smile. A smile that was remarkably similar to his father's. Caleb watched as Samuel dashed to the bolt, grabbing it and immediately using the tip to cut at the thick rope binding his hands. At this point, all the bandits had dismounted and had their weapons drawn. Caleb edged backward toward Samuel as the circle of bandits closed in. He could see that even the bandit leader was regaining his senses and getting up, and Samuel had barely made any progress on his binding. In his panic, Caleb reached deep inside himself, trying to find the magic. Maybe if the need was strong enough, he could control it. Or maybe it would just make the enemy stronger. But options were in limited supply at the moment.

As he reached deep inside himself, he could feel his skin prickling. He focused on this feeling. Pinpointing it. But there was something off. It didn't feel like before. It didn't feel like it was coming from within himself. He watched as the hairs on his arm rose, and he could feel the hair on his head almost float away from him. It was a strange, lighter-than-air feeling that was almost like—

"Get down!"

Caleb felt Samuel's hands grabbing and pulling him forcefully to the ground just moments before the world above him lit up with blinding light.

True darkness followed—and so did the screams that were almost instantly drowned out by an explosion that left Caleb's ears ringing long afterward. He felt around in the darkness, terrified that he had gone blind and deaf. But he could still feel Samuel beside him, rhythmically and sound-lessly moving. He could also feel the ground shake with the erratic footfalls of the others, who were also presumably blind. A boot crushed Caleb's foot. He couldn't even tell if he let out a cry of pain or not. Samuel's hands grasped onto Caleb's shoulder and quickly traveled down to his hands, where the rhythmic motion started again; Samuel was saw-ing away at his rope.

Slowly, his eyesight began to return along with the sounds of chaos, but he was given no time to recover. Sam-uel had successfully cut through his binding and lifted him to his feet, practically dragging the taller boy in the direction of his horse. There was an explosion of fire from behind them and more screams, but Samuel would not let Caleb fal-ter.

In the distance, they could see Juniper being led away by the riderless horse he was tied to. The other horses, Caleb saw, were also scattered in every which direction. Whatever had caused the explosions had scared them more than the bandits ever could.

"Juniper!" Samuel shouted. He then placed his thumb and pointer finger to his lips and released an ear-splitting whistle.

Juniper immediately stopped, causing him to be dragged forward in the dirt as the horse leading him staggered. Both tugged in either direction, trying to escape from the other until, with a sharp snap, Juniper's reins broke at a key joint and fell off. Juniper, now free, galloped toward the two boys. Both clumsily climbed on, and Samuel directed the horse to the best of his ability. All of their gear had fallen off during the confusion. All they had were the clothes on their backs and Samuel's armor and shield. But they were going full speed away from the explosions of fire and light that continued behind them.

"Why don't we go to the people from the camp?" Caleb asked. "If we explain the situation once they take care of the bandits, I'm sure they would understand."

"Absolutely not!" Samuel said. "I don't know who those people are, but one of them is an incredible mage. We are safer to travel alone than with more strangers."

"Oh," Caleb said, a tinge of sadness lingering with his words. "It's because he's a mage."

"No. It's because the mage's first thought after being warned about bandits was to obliterate everything in sight, including us. I don't know about you, but I'm not going to trust anyone who pointed any type of weapon at me, which includes lightning. And did you see those fireballs? That was incredible! I've never seen magic like that firsthand. The fact that he chose to attack first probably indicates that they couldn't afford an actual close-up altercation, which could mean multiple things. I'm betting they are smugglers who realized they were on someone else's turf, so…"

Caleb smiled softly and held on tighter as Samuel continued his endless outer-inner monologue.

"Besides," Samuel continued, "one mage is enough for me, and for what it's worth, I trust you."

Caleb started, "What? Why?"

"Well, you risked your life to protect me back there. And so far, you've been way too honest. You haven't told a single lie. Well, not intentionally, at least."

"How are you so sure?"

"It's…" Samuel hesitated. "Okay, don't laugh. But I get this weird feeling when someone lies. It's like the feeling of telling a lie but coming from the wrong direction. I can't really explain it. No clue when it started. Probably since I was born. I honestly thought everyone could tell, which is why I thought it was weird when people would just blatantly lie. Dad knows, and now so do you. No one else knows. Though there isn't anyone else to tell."

"The person," Caleb said, after a few moments of deliberation, "I first used magic on was my best friend. He said something that pissed me off, and I got mad. I couldn't control my magic. I didn't even know I had magic."

"Was it like what happened to Mr. Crab?"

"No," Caleb said with a chuckle, "it got his head. He went completely bald, and the top of his head became red and kinda rough and spiky. I didn't even consider it to be crab-like until I did it to Captain Crawdad."

"Well, looks like Crabby is in hot water now."

"I bet he's steaming mad."

Both boys began to laugh—low at first, then growing louder as their exhaustion and stress leaked into it, leaving them feeling lighter and relieved. More seafood jokes were made as they journeyed through the night in a direction they hoped to be the right one.

It was not. But they would figure that out in the morning.

Campfire Conversations: Old Man, New World

Cycle 3 Day 24

Buddy was lost in thought as he and his traveling companions ate a humble meal of roasted rabbits they had managed to catch while traveling. They sat around the campfire in a freshly fallen silence—a silence abruptly shattered by shouts of, "Bandits! Run away!"

Buddy tore his mind from his distant thoughts and turned toward the sound. Sure enough, he could just barely make out what looked to be a small group of men on horseback coming their way. He also saw what looked like two younger boys who were on foot. Tyberion let out a poetic string of expletives, some of which Buddy was unfamiliar with. Their travels had been going so smoothly that they didn't even think to have someone standing guard.

The old man was frantically looking around for any kind of weapon but noticed that he was the only one in a panic. No one else was moving from their relaxed position, except for Malguinne. The elderly wizard gave a pained grunt as he stood up and stretched his back. He then proceeded to bring his hands to his face as if to shout back, but instead, he whispered something Buddy couldn't hear. Just as the whispering stopped, small bolts of electricity began to dance between his cupped hands.

Buddy watched with fascination as the wizard pointed his sparking hands toward the men and shot lightning from his fingertips like it was nothing. A few smaller arcs hit the men, who promptly yelped in pain and fell to the ground. But they were back up in no time, running around like chickens with their heads cut off.

"You're not going to kill them, right?" asked Buddy, who was concerned more for the two boys in the group rather than the men.

"Oh, dear, no," Malguinne said with a kindly chuckle. "This is more an act of scaring the wickedness out of them" he winked, "and a bit of target practice for me. Don't want to get too rusty."

"But the two boys—"

"Are probably part of their trap," Malguinne said as he interrupted Buddy. "Bandits use anything and anyone to trick travelers. Had we rescued them, they would have cut our throats in the night and robbed our corpses. There are risks to kindness and mercy; don't forget that."

Malguinne again brought his cupped hands to his mouth and spoke a few unheard words. A ball of flame coiled into existence between his palms but didn't seem to burn him. Then the wizard took the flame in his right hand and threw it like a baseball in the direction of the bandits. It hit the ground with the force of a meteorite, leaving behind a deep crater and falling earth. As Malguinne continued to chuck fiery baseballs, the bandits were frantically, and ineffectively, trying to capture their horses and pick up their gear—which was scattering like candy from a piñata.

"Show off," Tyberion said.

Buddy looked at his fireside companion and saw that he was rather uneasy.

"Not a fan of magic?" Buddy asked.

"You could say that," Tyberion replied, with a side glance at the wizard. The heavily armored man was built like a bear. Even without his armor on, he was just under seven feet tall. His hair was as black as tar, and because of the length—and the beard that framed his face—it looked more like a lion's mane. He had one large scar that went over where his right eye used to be. He had told Buddy that even though glass eyes were available, he preferred to have it stay empty. In the hours that Tyberion was awake, he would wear his heavily dented, scratched, and scuffed plate armor. At one time, it was silver, but age and use had given it the coloration of fog.

At the moment, the mercenary, John, was eating his roasted rabbit several feet away. He had been keeping a distance from Buddy for some time now. Buddy had already surmised that his name was a fake and that he was as sketchy as he looked, but there was a strange allure to the rugged, roguish types. *Maybe he will show true courage when everything is at its bleakest.*

The elf, Rythel, was nowhere to be seen—as usual. He would usually disappear shortly after eating—and even that, he would do at a distance. Buddy didn't mind that so much. Rythel was an ass. He took pleasure in undermining everyone and had an air of superiority that got stale instantly. But he was a great shot. He could hit the eye of a rabbit nearly a hundred feet away. The mysterious arrow wrapped in cloth he carried piqued the old man's curiosity. In one of the few conversations that the two had shared, Buddy asked about the arrow. Rythel told him it was made from null wood and was one of the only things effective against magic. The elf remained silent for the rest of that day.

The elf was also a surprisingly good cook. They had caught some fish the previous night, and Rythel had cleaned and cooked them to near perfection. He even added some herbs that no one knew he carried with him.

"I wish we had magic in our world," Buddy said. "I mean, we have stuff people call magic, but it's more smoke and mirrors than legit stuff. We have Voodoo and tarot and people claiming to be espers, but most are just snake oil sellers."

"It is interesting to hear you speak, Buddy," Tyberion said with a wistful smile. "Sometimes it feels like you are speaking a different language."

"I've been meaning to ask," Buddy said with a chuckle and a cough, "how am I even speaking your language? Is it some sort of magic?"

"Oh yes. I expected you to ask that sooner or later," Malguinne remarked as he joined the conversation. It seemed the bandit fun was over. "You see, what you are speaking is both Primish and what you call English. About a few hundred years back, we had another visitor such as yourself get stuck here. Well, she and the king of that time got, let's say, well acquainted. Turns out love is a strong motivator for linguistic understanding. The king and his scholars worked with the woman to translate her language to our former Primish and the other way around. Luckily, the sentence structure of both languages was similar enough that it wasn't very difficult to learn. Within a generation, English became well-known among the royal family and nobles. The language was soon used as coded messages within the military. However, overuse caused a verbal pandemic within the next few generations, and even the commoners were picking it up. So, to keep up with appearances, we adopted English as Primish and true Primish became known as the Old Tongue."

"No shit?" Buddy said. That was the last explanation

he expected to hear, but it made a strange amount of sense; if the worlds were connected, as Malguinne said, there would be a lot of bleedover going both ways. Maybe this world is where his world gets their folk tales and magical creatures. "So, does that mean the current royal line is descended from my people?"

"Oh, goddess, no," the wizard answered with a hearty laugh. "There is no solid known reason why, but an Unari and this world's people cannot reproduce. The current working theory is that whatever created your world used... hmmm...let's say, non-compatible building blocks."

"As reasonable a theory as any other, I suppose." Buddy was a little disheartened by this knowledge. Just another reason why he didn't belong here. He couldn't believe it had been about two weeks since his arrival. And as much as he has been enjoying his journey, he knew he had to get home soon. He hadn't been able to take his daily medication since coming here, which had thrown his sleep schedule and digestive system out of whack. He placed his hand on his chest, feeling the lump of metal underneath his skin. He was becoming increasingly anxious about his pacemaker. The day he woke up here was supposed to be the day he got the battery replaced. It's still got juice, but he could tell even before coming here it was running low. His ticker was on a time clock. Well, if he's going to die in a fantasy world, he might as well enjoy every moment he can.

"Okay, now tell me again, but this time in a way I can understand: How does magic work?"

Chapter 4: Climbing Trees with Fins
Cycle 3, Day 1

"**M**agic is an intrinsic aspect of this world. There is a precise give-and-take one must understand before using it. There is real danger in practicing magic for trivial and imbecilic reasons," a man said as he plucked the last shard of glass out of a deep laceration from one of the legs of a teenage boy. There was a similar wound on the other leg just below the knee, but it had already been bandaged, and once the last of the glass was out of the second leg, the man began to bandage it. "That being said, what in the nine hells were you thinking, Emile?"

The boy was only a few years into teenagedom. He wore a thin, white undershirt and loose pants that ended above the knees, which revealed most of the faded pink scars decorating his body—each telling a unique story. Most were stories of teenage idiocy. He was lying on one of the several beds in the candle-lit, stone-walled room and winced as the man tightened the once-white gauze around the lacerations. They quickly turned a deep crimson as the man rummaged through piles of vials and notebooks and loose stacks of papers on his desk. There were a few bookshelves in similar disarray in the few areas where the beds would allow. "I was just trying to make myself grow a few inches. I almost had it, too."

"No, you didn't," the man said as he returned to Emile's bedside. He wore simple black robes and had a thick fabric cloth wrapped around the lower part of his face, covering his nose and mouth. In his hands were two small pieces of torn paper and an ink quill. "You nearly *lost* two feet and two feet. Thankfully, you're as incompetent at being incompetently dangerous as you are at being magically competent. Now, hold still; this will hurt, but it will hurt quickly."

The man drew quick circles on the two pieces of paper. Inside each circle were multiple overlapping shapes of triangles and circles and tick marks. He placed them on one leg each, right in the center of the bandages. While keeping each hand touching a circle, he spoke a single word: "*quicken.*" A few sparks of green left his fingertips, transferring to the circles, causing the outlines to glow green. The wrapping slowly started to turn from bright crimson to a rusty brown, and the wrappings started to deteriorate slightly around the edges. The pain shot through Emile's legs like a spider web. He sucked in air quickly and held it for several counts, trying as hard as he could not to make a sound. He could feel the skin under the bandages moving and the wounds closing.

Just as quickly as the spell started, it ended. The green light faded, and the man took the bandages off. There was still some dried blood matted in the boy's leg hair, but the deep cuts were gone, with only pink scar tissue left behind.

"Thanks, Professor Lawrence," Emile said as he stood on his feet again, testing the recovery. He wobbled a little from fatigue, but other than that, he seemed fine. The boy put on his brown robes that had been tossed haphazardly on the ground beside the bed. "I feel good as new."

"Firstly," Lawrence said as he removed the face cloth, "stop calling me professor. Call me Mr. Lawrence or Doctor Lawrence or even Hey You for all I care. I am tired of the *actual* professors giving me dirty looks every time they hear you students liken me to them. Secondly, you probably shouldn't thank me. Of all the students, you are the one I end up treating the most, so you now have several body parts that are weeks or even months older than other parts of you. I just passed two-weeks worth of time through your legs. Keep this up and you'll have more arthritic issues than the wizard Malguinne, who is half human and half arthritis by this point."

With the facial covering removed, Emile couldn't help but see his doctor as an old dog. He wasn't much older than thirty, probably. But his face kinda sagged a little in the cheeks, and he always had dark bags under his eyes. He and the other students always thought the doctor looked more like their definition of an overworked professor than their teachers.

"You got it, boss," Emile said, giving a mock salute and a cheeky grin. "Oh, can you show me how to use time magic? That would be really useful for our exams."

"Really?" Lawrence asked with an expression of pure incredulity. "You nearly kill yourself on a daily basis with the most basic of magic, and you want me to show you how to tamper with time?"

"Yes?"

"You're impossible," the doctor said, though he looked like he was more amused than anything else as a reluctant smile started to replace his perpetual sullen look. "How is your studying coming along?"

"Not good," Emile said, his tone losing its lackadaisical edge and becoming more stiff and serious. "I'm struggling to figure any of this out. Classes are interesting, and I'm constantly studying. But I just can't grasp it. I'm worried that if

I don't improve, they will send me to get my magic removed."

"That's just a rumor," Lawrence said. "There have been no cases where that was necessary. Worst-case scenario is that you stay and work for the school. It's not as grandiose as being the Royal Wizard, but it's a good life."

Emile wanted to believe the doctor. But even if the worst was a guaranteed job at the school, that still meant he would never leave. Never see his friends and family again. Sure, they might have been hesitant around him just before he came here. But if he could just get his uncontrollable magic in check, they would accept him with open arms. Right?

The boy could see the doctor's wavering resolution. Emile knew he had a particular charm that would make almost all situations work in his favor. Just because that charm was more accurately defined as his ability to generate a perpetual flow of pity doesn't change anything.

"Come back here just after sunset. If a night guard spots you, just say you have a stomachache and are coming to see me. I won't teach you time magic, but I can help you come to understand *your* magic better."

"You won't regret this," Emile said, jumping up with unabashed joy. "I'll be the best student you've never had. Oh! I have to go. Right now. Lunch is almost over, and I can't miss it again. I'll be back." He ran out the door. Stopped. Then came back to say, "For the lesson, that is. Not 'cause I'll hurt myself. Probably."

He dashed through the labyrinthine hallways of the once-monastery-turned- magic-school. He passed by several empty rooms that may one day be classrooms if the school ever got more than a dozen or two students at any given time.

It turns out mages are incredibly rare. And really talented mages are even rarer. This particular school taught teenagers and young adults. It was presumed there was a different place that taught adults. Students were placed into one of three categories that depict rank or magical ability. Emile was in rank three, which is reserved for those with little skill with magic or mages with abysmally weak magic. Rank threes make up the majority, with eight students out of the total thirteen this year.

After eating enough to barely be satisfied, Emile went to his last class for the day. Unfortunately, this class was in the courtyard. Spring may have been coming, but it was still cold. It didn't help matters that the school was situated on the top of a mountain overlooking the Capital. The mountain was not tall enough to have ice caps through more than the coldest parts of winter, but spring was just warm enough to be considered miserable rather than hellish.

Emile joined the rest of his rank-three classmates, all wearing brown robes, and glanced over his fellow students until he found who he was looking for.

"Meredith," he said, as he sat on the cold and slightly damp grass beside the girl with oak-brown hair tied back in a ponytail. He gave a wide grin to his friend and could feel the familiar warmth of what he hoped was a subtle blush. It was anything but subtle. "I'm glad I didn't miss this lesson. The cold dew should help clean the blood stains."

She rolled her eyes, not even trying to hide the smile that was forming. "And *I'm* glad to see they didn't have to remove your legs this time."

"Oh, but they did. These legs are brand new. Got them straight from a rank-one student who had two spare ones just lying around." Emile gave a playful wink.

"Shut up," she said, the smile never leaving. He couldn't help but think she had one of the most beautiful smiles he had ever seen. He wasn't sure if it was because of the perfect shape of her lips, the cute dimple to the right of her smile, or because the smile was specifically hers.

The professor, who Emile just noticed was standing in front of the eight students, made a coughing sound to get everyone's attention. The professor was a rather short man, about as tall as the average student. The feature that differentiated him from the students was his purple robes that marked him as a professor. He was also rather old, perhaps in his seventies, though he was surprisingly agile and quick for his age. He had thinning white hair that stuck out as if he were struck by lightning every morning and had a receding hairline that was quite possibly alive and moving higher every time Emile saw him.

"Yes, yes," the professor said, "I know it's cold, but hopefully, our lesson today can help alleviate that. We are going to pick up where we left off yesterday. Everyone will use the phrase "*I summon the flame of my heart to heat my body*" while focusing your magical energies toward creating a small ball of fire in your hands. If you can do this, you can learn to withstand anything winter can throw at you." He shifted his gaze toward Emile, "Oh, and Emile, I think it would be best if you were to just focus on the phrase for today. The medical staff has probably seen enough of you for one day." The professor said this in a kindly voice and with a warm smile, but the smile was thin and barely covered the thinning patience underneath. There was some polite but awkward laughter from the other students.

"But I'm the doctor's favorite," Emile said. "I've even helped him reconnect with his faith. I hear him say a prayer every time he sees me." The laughter this time was a little

66

more genuine.

"Right, all the same, the best practice is safe practice."

Emile did not argue; he just said the phrase over and over, wanting to be able to connect with his magic. At this point, it wasn't even about getting warmer; he just wanted to show the others he wasn't useless. However, as he looked around, only one student was having any success, and that success was a flickering blue flame that made even the professor nervous.

"Psst, Meredith," Emile whispered, attempting to get the girl's attention beside him. "Merry," he tried again.

She looked over to the boy, not even a spark in her hand. "What is it? Can't you see I'm freezing? I would like to get my flame started before I die of cold."

"You know good and well you aren't gonna produce anything more than an ice cube. I need you to ask the professor how to work this spell. He'll give you a clearer answer."

Meredith put on the most theatrically overthinking expression. "Well, I guess I could ask him. Not that I need the extra help, but you need all that you can get; just don't blow us up." She gave him a sly wink and a giggle that made Emile's heart melt. "I'm sorry, professor, but I really don't get this. How do I get my magic to create fire? It feels like it's pushing back against me every time I try."

"Hmmm?" the professor mumbled in response, looking as though he was resurfacing from a thought. "Oh, yes, yes. Magic is like a muscle. Imagine summoning fire like lifting a heavy weight. It's too heavy at first, and maybe you can only get it an inch off the ground. But if you keep practicing, keep trying to lift it, you will eventually be strong enough to push back against your magic and control it to suit your needs."

"But, professor, it kinda hurts to go against my magic's natural flow."

"Yes, yes. It does at first. But once you build that muscle, it will hurt less and less."

The white-haired professor lost interest and moved on to the next student. Emile noticed that Meredith stopped trying to produce her fire.

"What's the matter?" Emile asked.

"Sorry, it's just…" she started, a little hesitation in her voice. "It's nothing, just tired, I guess."

"Don't worry; I know you will get it. You're talented with anything ice-related. I'm sure you will get the hang of everything else, too."

She gave a halfhearted smile and a quiet thank you. They sat in comfortable quiet for the rest of the class, which wasn't long, since the blue flame the one kid produced started to smell strongly of sulfur, causing class to end early and two students to be sent to the good doctor.

***

Emile spent the last few hours of daylight reading over his countless notes and assigned books. But his excitement over his upcoming lesson with Lawrence was causing all the words to slip off his mind like water on glass. Eventually, the time came, and Emile prepared himself for his stealthy nighttime traversal. He crept through the torch-lit halls with what he hoped was silent grace. Thankfully, he made it to the medical room without coming across anyone on night patrol duty. Lawrence was sitting at his desk with a book open and his eyes nearly closed. Emile wondered if any of the words were getting past the narrow slits. The slight bob-bing of the doctor's head was enough of an answer.

"I hope I'm not cutting into your beauty sleep," Emile said, with just a hint of genuine concern for the school's only doctor.

"Funny, I was thinking the same of you," Lawrence said with mock seriousness. "How do you manage to have bedhead before even going to bed?"

The doctor folded the top corner of the page he was on and closed the tome. Then he picked up an apple that was blending into the decorative chaos that was his desk and dragged a stool to the center of the room. After placing the apple on the stool, he approached Emile.

"Alright," he said, "we are just going to jump right into it. I've seen the outcome of your magic. There are always cuts or lacerations and shards of glass either in the wound or around the area. Though, you are almost always the only tar-get of your magic, which I presume is a choice on your part. Now, I want you to focus and imagine dozens of shards of glass forming in midair and then being shot into the apple like tiny arrows."

Emile debated the ludicrous and oddly specific nature of the request, but in the end, he wanted to see where this would lead. So, he lifted his right hand and pointed his palm in the direction of the apple. Then, he closed his eyes and imagined the tiny shards of glass. He reached inside his gut, where he felt what he thought of as the flow of magic inside of him. The professors had all taught that a mage uses magic by harnessing this unseen flow and redirecting it to force it to the will of the mage.

"Good, you're focusing on the flow; now comes the important part," the doctor said. "Don't force it."

"What?" Emile's eyes shot open.

"You don't need to change the direction of the flow this time. Instead, add your will to it and fuel the magic. Make the flow stronger. When you are ready to make the glass, say "*form*" and then say "*send*." The important part is to say both with the intention of *form*ing the glass and then *send*ing it toward the apple."

Emile closed his eyes before he could roll them. He didn't want to call out the person that's actually trying to help him, but it felt counterintuitive to use magic by not using it. He cleared his mind and felt for the river of magic inside. He imagined the flow getting stronger and felt his own energy draining as the steady flow became a raging torrent. He whispered "*form*" as he imagined the glass shards forming, and with one push fueled by his will and the river's flow, he whispered "*send*" and shot his imagined shards straight into the apple.

Shleeep.

He could hear the sound of small, sharp objects slicing through the air and striking something soft. He opened his eyes again and saw the apple. There were small chunks sliced clean off the edges, and the center was a pincushion with dozens of small pieces of glass. He was amazed; but not entirely because he was able to do exactly what he intended with his magic. But rather because, for the first time, using his magic didn't hurt. It didn't feel like straining a muscle against a heavy weight. It felt like…letting the magic do what it naturally wanted…but that couldn't be right.

"You did well," Lawrence said with a smile that surprisingly continued to his eyes.

70

"But, what exactly did I do?"

"Well, first off," the doctor said, "you proved me right. You have a natural talent, or more accurately, core magic, that uses two of the four known types. You use elemental and shifting magic. More specifically, you can control wind and air, and you can change objects into glass. What you did was change the dust particles in the air into shards of glass, then once they formed, immediately sent them toward the apple with a strong gust of air."

"So, if I use that exact same method, I can use other elements like fire and water?" Emile couldn't hide the excitement in his voice. Unfortunately, the excitement lasted until he saw the mournful look his tutor was giving him.

"That is doubtful." Lawrence walked toward his desk and took a piece of paper, which he ripped into little slips. "Every mage is unique, as is their magic. Some can control all the elements, some can perform all four types of magic, but most can only do one or two of either. Being able to use shifting magic and elemental magic is incredible, and I can see you becoming a powerful mage. But your elemental magic most likely ends with air, and your shifting is most likely limited to glass."

Lawrence drew a circle with triangles enclosing smaller circles on two slips of paper. He lifted the apple just enough to slide one slip of paper underneath and then placed the other slip in his hand.

"I have mastery over time, which is a part of the conceptual type of magic. That type of magic deals with bending and controlling more abstract concepts—like time, in my case. It is a rare talent that no one knows how to teach. The professors here only tried teaching me the *basics,* such as producing flames, causing explosions, creating water, or other such useful skills. I couldn't do any of that. I still can't do any of that." He placed his free hand on the apple. "*Skip and transport.*" With a flash of green, the acupunctured fruit disappeared for thirty seconds and then reappeared in the doctor's hand with the slip of paper. "I had to teach myself how to use my magic the way it wanted to be used, and in doing so, I learned that my ability is actually time and space. I can send things through time, speed up or slow time in designated areas, and send things from one place to another. I can't shoot fireballs, but I can do so much more because I focused on what I could do rather than try and force myself to learn what I couldn't."

"Hold on," Emile said. "You said 'the way it wanted.' You make it sound like magic is alive and has a will of its own."

"I don't know about it being alive," the doctor admitted, "but it certainly has a path of least resistance in which it naturally wants to flow. Maybe a better descriptor is that it is a force of nature that can't be willed by us tiny mortals, but if we know how it behaves, we can predict how best to utilize it."

"I think I understand," Emile said, not even coming close to understanding.

"Don't worry; you will get it in time," the doctor said. "Let's focus on your control of air for the time being. I'm sure that will be a much safer route than slinging more glass around."

***

For the next three nights, Emile came back to the medical room. Each night, he became more and more proficient in controlling his magical talent. His professors were taking note and were incredulous, but pleased, with his progress. Emile could tell they wished he could still do at least a little more in other areas, but they would take any progress that wasn't actively causing danger. On the fourth night, he had a tag-along. Meredith entered the room behind him.

"Oh, goddess!" Lawrence exclaimed.

"I can explain," Emile said, but was stopped by Meredith.

"No, let me," she said calmly. "I've seen Emile getting better and better over the last week, and I kept pestering him until he finally admitted you had been teaching him."

"Pestering?" Emile said incredulously. "You threatened never to speak to me again."

She shrugged. "I didn't mean it. Please, Doctor Lawrence. I'm tired of being useless. I'm tired of knowing I have something incredible inside me but not having the knowledge or experience to know how to access it. You could see Emile's true talent through his screw-ups; please do the same for me."

Emile looked at the doctor with pleading eyes. It had actually killed him to not be able to talk to Meredith about this. He had tried to teach her the way Lawrence taught him, but he didn't even know where to start, and they both got frustrated before deciding the doctor was her best bet too. He wanted Meredith to be happy no matter what.

The doctor looked at both teenagers and gave a long, exasperated sigh. "Fine, but only you two, and only for a week at the most."

***

Three more days went by, and Lawrence found himself with two more learners. He put up even less of a fight that time.

By this point, Meredith had grown more proficient with her water elemental magic than Emile was with his. Emile didn't have any hard feelings about it; if anything, he had grown more infatuated with her.

"An important thing to remember is that shifting magic requires no effort to maintain," Lawrence said. "Think of everything and everyone being malleable. But once a thing is turned into another thing, nothing will turn it back until you use your magic to return it to its original form or someone with a similar magic changes it back. Going back to the previous metaphor, everything is malleable *and* lockable. Shifting magic acts as a key that locks something into being something else. So only that key or another key of the same shape can unlock it. Another thing to mention: Organic things cannot be shifted into non-organic things. For instance, Emile, you cannot change any part of me or yourself into glass. That being said, there are mages that specialize in animal shifting. They can shift themselves and others into an animal designated by their magic…"

***

The week time limit came and passed, and the doctor had somehow become the secret tutor to the entire rank-three class. Emile could see the extra exhaustion forming under the eyes of the doctor, but he could also see a more and more genuine smile on his face with each session.

"Remember," Lawrence said to the room of eight teen-agers, "the key is communication. You must clearly say what you want your magic to do. Incantations are nice and can give a more detailed description of what you are trying to do. But at the end of the day, an incantation is just a nursery rhyme you are saying more to yourself than any-thing else. Choose a word or two to represent what you in-tend. Anything more is useless excess. Now, Emile and Mer-edith, if you would come up front. I need your assistance demonstrating—"

The sound of the door opening caused mass silence as everyone in the room looked toward the intruder. However, it was not just one intruder. It was all of the school's profes-sors. Emile knew that Lawrence was powerful, but he was just the school's doctor. There was no way he could measure up to even one professor, let alone all six of them.

Leading the charge was the headmaster, who wore the same purple robes as the other professors, but with golden trim and floral designs. He had straight, pitch-black hair that reached just above his shoulders. The hair fell around his owl-like face like elegant curtains. On his beak-like nose sat a pair of handleless spectacles. He narrowed his already half-shut eyes toward the doctor and pointed a finger at him.

"Sleeves turn to lead and burden the wearer."

Emile turned to his tutor and watched as the fabric around the doctor's arms changed color and texture as it be-came metal. Lawrence did not even struggle against the newfound weight. He just lowered to the ground, kneeling. There was no surprise or shock in his eyes. Emile was look-ing at a man who had given up–and it was his fault.

"Don't blame him!" Emile said. "This is my fault. I forced him to teach me."

"No!" said Meredith. "I'm at fault. I blackmailed the doctor into teaching us."

The rest of the group stood to defend the man who had helped them; however...

"Sound, shatter through the air and deafen," the short,

white-haired professor whispered as he snapped his fingers. The sound it emitted was like a high-pitched explosion. Emile collapsed to his knees grasping at his ringing ears. His head was splitting, and his vision went blurry. He could see the smudged shapes of his fellow students in the same state as himself. Lawrence, however, just kneeled there, unwavering.

"Doctor Lawrence," said the headmaster, "you have been found guilty of teaching students without permission. Furthermore, you have been teaching them counter to the school's particular curriculum. This can and will be seen as treason. Poisoning the minds of new mages is comparable to the destruction of royal property. This is your second offense. We thought demoting you to the school's nursemaid would be a suitable punishment to persuade you against such reckless actions. It is a pity that you cannot seem to control yourself. You will be escorted to the elves, where you will have your magic removed. Then, you will be brought to the capital, where the king will decide your fate. I am sure we can find good use of your magic without you."

The professors started to march single file into the already cramped room. The students practically fell out of the way to avoid being stepped on.

"This is a good example, students," the doctor said. His voice cut through the silence, and the congregation of professors froze. "Single and precise words are crucial in the heat of the moment. Incantations sound threatening and more powerful, but they carry no extra weight other than dead weight."

"You still persist?" the headmaster asked. "You are powerless without the use of your hands and precious slips of paper, and yet you still defy me. You are not the one in control here. I am!"

"And another quick and final lesson," Lawrence said, purposefully avoiding looking at the fuming headmaster. "Rules of magic are more like guidelines rather than an exact ruling. Everything in this world is malleable. That includes rules."

Emile saw the white-haired professor look nervous. The man raised his hand and said, "*Silence his voi—*"

The doctor smiled. "*Transport.*" A green light sparked underneath the doctor's right shoe, and then he was gone.

No one in the room moved an inch for several minutes. The headmaster spoke several strings of profanities; most were incoherent, but Emile was sure he heard, "Her Breath is wasted on you, you son of a bastard." After the headmaster finished his profane monologue, he hesitated for just a moment and then shot a glance at the students.

"You are to go to your rooms. A proper punishment will be provided in the morning." Then, the headmaster stormed out of the room, pushing aside any professor in his way.

The rest of the professors led Emile and the other students to their rooms, not saying a word. Emile lay awake through the night, staring at his ceiling. He prayed to the goddess that Lawrence would be safe, wherever he went.

Campfire Conversations: Moments Before Disaster
Cycle 3, Day 28

Samuel and Caleb sat huddled together in the middle of the woods. A small campfire crackled in front of them, alleviating the brunt of the night's bitter cold. The bones of the rabbit they just ate splintered in the blaze with the occasional pop and sizzle. They were leaning against Juniper, who was already sleeping soundly.

"How close are we to the next city, or town, or anything?" Caleb asked, with a weak and scratchy voice.

"I don't know," Samuel replied, as he looked up into the star-filled void. "Maybe tomorrow, maybe the next day, maybe…" But he didn't finish that sentence. It had been four days since they escaped the bandits. They had no supplies. No weapons. No shelter. No map. And to top it all, their mad dash away from the bandits put them off course to the point that Samuel was lost. He had no clue where the road was. All he knew was the direction they were heading, and that was only because of the direction the moon and sun traveled. The Dark Lord's domain was northeast of where they currently were, so if they kept going in that direction they would hopefully catch up with the goblins. But he didn't know how to track them. Had they gotten ahead of the goblins? Or were the goblins still ahead of them? Perhaps they should travel to the Dark Lord's domain and wait for them there. Though if the goblins were ahead of them then perhaps they should just go directly to the Dark Lord...and then what? Would he just demand his father be returned to him?

Too many questions hummed in Samuel's head like a swarm of angry wasps. All of which demanded his attention. In truth, he had no answers to any of them. Only a headache from thinking about them all. He decided to put these concerns to the side for now. They had much more immediate concerns, specifically food and water.

They had managed to catch some small animals for food, thanks to Caleb's skill at making basic traps using sticks, sharp rocks, and peeled bark that acted as string. They also managed to have a fire each night, thanks to Samuel's skill at fire-starting by using two sticks, friction, some dried leaves, and a lot of patience. Samuel learned that Caleb and his father used to go camping often when he was younger, and they still made it a tradition to go on a camping trip once a year. Samuel, in turn, told Caleb about how he and his father had been mostly living on the road, going from town to town on peacekeeping-type jobs for the last few months, so he and his father had to learn to make a fire back before they got the magic lantern.

Samuel knew, though, that the problem was water. They had managed to get some water from berries and a few plants. But if they didn't find a better source of hydration, their journey may come to an abrupt end.

"I meant to ask..." Caleb said. "Usually Wardens stick to a specific area or town. Why have you and your father been traveling so much?"

"I guess we are just trying to find new roots," Samuel said, not looking down from the stars. "No, that's not true. We just can't look back right now. We need to keep busy. We need to get the next job. Help the next town. Settle the next dispute."

Samuel did not look at his companion, but he felt Caleb lean ever so slightly closer. But Samuel did not mind. His warmth was comfortable.

"You mentioned before that you no longer had a house to go to," Caleb said. There was a tentative softness in his voice like he was talking to an injured pet. Samuel felt that he should feel offended, but he couldn't help the upward twitch of his lips.

"My mom…" Samuel said. "Well, she died a little over a year ago. She got really sick all of a sudden. We didn't even have time to get a local wizard or doctor to look at her. It was like she was perfectly healthy one day, then the next she was dying. Dad didn't take it well. Honestly, neither did I. We couldn't stay there anymore. Without mom, it just wasn't a home. It was just the place me and dad stayed when we weren't working. So, we sold the house. Dad and I left for Previa so that he could become a Warden. Then, he took me on as an apprentice, once it was official. And now I'm here."

"I'm so sorry."

"Don't be. At least I knew her well enough to mourn her. That's what dad always says." Samuel felt a sharp hitch in his voice in the last sentence, and his eyes started to water. He figured that the smoke was blowing his way.

Samuel was surprised when Caleb didn't say anything. He was so used to all the unsolicited advice people always give. He was used to people struggling to find the right words but still trying anyway. He wasn't used to a silence that didn't need to be filled but could be from his own choice.

"You know what the worst part was?" Samuel tried to say calmly.

"What?"

"Being with her the last few days and knowing she was lying every time she told me she would be better soon." This time, Samuel didn't even try to deceive himself about the smoke. He broke on the last word. His voice got stuck in his tightening throat, and the tears that had been building for an unknown amount of time flooded out of him. He pulled his legs into himself and buried his face between his knees. He didn't want Caleb to see his grief-distorted face as he began to sob in earnest.

Caleb didn't try to give any comforting words while Samuel cried; he just wrapped an arm around his companion's shoulders and shared his warmth. This was the only comfort Samuel needed. They sat like this until the younger boy had stopped crying and became able to speak again.

After a brief silence, Caleb asked, "Would you like to tell me about her?"

Samuel nodded. He composed himself, and when he was ready, he began to speak. "Her name was Ursa, and she was the kindest person I have ever known. She was never quick to anger, but if she ever did get there, she would stay there until everyone forgot why she was angry to begin with, including herself. One time there was a traveling merchant who tried to convince her she needed a magic pot that never ran out of whatever herb you put in it. Mom was adamant that it was a scam, and after many failed attempts at kindly asking the charlatan to leave, he wore out her reserve of hospitality and left town with ten fewer fake magic pots and at least five more cracked beyond repair. The poor idiot came back to town a year later, I guess thinking that the feud was in the past, and found himself being chased out by a mob. Mom even supplied the pitchforks to the townsfolk who joined. She didn't even remember why she was mad at him;

she just saw him and trusted her instinct that told her he deserved to be mad at."

"Why did she have so many pitchforks?" Caleb asked between soft fits of laughter.

"If I remember correctly," Samuel said slowly as he recounted the exact phrasing, "she said she 'wanted to be prepared in case of a mob, or in case of a need for a mob.'" Samuel laughed, remembering the absurdity, and a new layer of tears burned just below the surface. And then there was a thought that rose up with the emotions that wanted to flow. "I miss hearing her call me Sam. It's such a stupid, small thing. I should miss her cooking, her singing, the sound of her footsteps early in the morning as she tried to not wake me or dad. And I do miss them. But what I miss most is hearing her call me by a nickname I always hated. I don't know what I would give to hear her voice calling out to me again, but it's more than I have or will ever have."

Samuel took several moments as he wiped at his face and waited for his voice to steady. When he was ready, he continued reminiscing, and Caleb continued to listen.

***

After some time, the fire shrank to little more than embers.

"Thanks for listening," Samuel said. "I didn't realize how much I needed that. But I need to get some more firewood before we no longer have a fire."

"I can get the wood. I saw a spot earlier that had some good and dry sticks." Caleb got up before Samuel even had the chance to respond, but the younger boy didn't stop him. He just nodded and watched as the older boy disappeared into the darkness.

Samuel stared into the embers, lost in the ocean of memories of his mother. Several minutes went by and Caleb had still not returned. Perhaps he was taking his time. Or perhaps he got distracted. Samuel hadn't heard anything to indicate something was wrong. But no matter how much he tried to convince himself otherwise, with every passing moment, worse and worse scenarios were taking over his mind. As the embers started to die and the darkness became ever-imposing, so too were Samuel's fears. He could feel a cold panic building inside his chest, threatening to suffocate him.

He knew everything was fine. Everything had to be fine. But all the same, he stood up, gave the sleeping horse a gentle rub on the neck, and went in the direction he saw his companion go. The darkness of the night engulfed everything, with only a sliver of moonlight to brighten his path. Unable to rely on his vision, Samuel strained his ears to see if he could hear anything to lead him to Caleb. But he couldn't. He could not hear anyone. No breathing. No rustling of sticks. No footsteps.

Samuel stopped dead in his tracks. He could hear no footsteps, including his own. He took a step forward.

Nothing.

He knelt on the ground, searching through feeling alone for a stick. He found a thin twig. He snapped it in half.

Nothing.

He wanted to test his voice. But his words caught in his chest. He wished he hadn't left his shield at their camp. He felt incredibly vulnerable in the silent darkness. He got to his feet with a slight tremble that shook through his legs, but he pushed forward. One way or another, he had to find Caleb. He wasn't leaving his companion.

As he took another step forward, he heard the crunch of leaves under his feet. But there was no relief in the returned sound because, at that same moment of pause, he felt something sharp against the back of his neck. Before he could leap forward and escape whatever was behind him, he heard a whisper of a voice.

"*Sleep.*"

Samuel's world rose around him, and his senses fogged over as he collapsed to the ground, unconscious.

Chapter 5: Theft of Magic
Cycle 3, Day 29

In the center of a town, there stood a girl. She wore a white cloak with a hood covering her face from the circle of onlookers watching the ceremony. The cloak had no embroideries or designs. It was as if a blank canvas were turned into cloth. The girl stepped forward toward a large crystal formation that marked the exact center of the town. The crystal branched in every direction, with the highest section of the cluster reaching ten feet. Every imaginable color swam within the structure. One who is unfamiliar with it would assume it was the light that caused these colors. However, the girl, along with the rest of the small town, knew otherwise.

When she was within arms' reach of the structure, she stopped and removed her hood. This revealed a child-like face and long, pointed ears. Even though her features were human in concept, they were also unnatural. Her face was human in the way that a porcelain doll's face is human. Young, yet ageless. Beautiful, but a crafted beauty. She was an elf, as were the rest of the crowd.

She reached out her hands and placed them on the closest crystal. Two more cloaked and hooded elves came to stand beside her. They each wore blue instead of white. One elf held out a wooden box that he opened to expose ten wooden needles that were the size and shape of acupuncture needles. The second elf took the needles and held the first needle at the center of the girl's back. The girl took in a breath and nodded. The man pushed the needle through her cloak and into her skin, just deep enough to stay in place.

The girl grimaced but did not retreat. She stood completely still as the man stuck more needles into her shoulder, down her exposed arms, and finally on the back of her palms. With every needle, there was a strange feeling inside of her being pushed from point to point. It felt like the blood inside her was rushing away from the needles. It hurt in a way the needles couldn't. The needles at least gave physical pain. This other pain was something that reached further into her soul.

Had this just been the girl's memory, the scene would have played out as it had on that day so many years ago. The elf who stuck her with needles would remove them and present her with a green cloak. The crowd would cheer and congratulate her. She would be happy.

However, this wasn't just a memory, and she began to realize this when the elf did not remove the needles. She looked over at him, but to her horror, neither of the elves were there. The crowd had also disappeared. As did the ground, the sky, and the city. Everything had been replaced with an empty void, except for her and the crystal cluster.

She tried to remove her hands. But they were stuck. She tried to yell out for help. But her voice was swallowed by the void. The soul-rendering pain caused by the needles sharpened. Tears welled up in her eyes.

And then she saw the tips of her fingers disappearing. No. They weren't disappearing. They were dissolving. Flakes of herself were leaving her body and changing shape. She watched as the pieces of her began to turn into butterflies and flutter away.

She tried to pull away as the rest of her fingers dissolved into a flurry of butterflies. But she could not.

Bit by bit, more of her was gone. Transformed. Leaving her behind. She was going to be completely gone soon if she didn't do anything. But try as she might, she couldn't do anything. She was helpless.

Just as I was when you abandoned me.

She heard the voice echoing through the void but could not see where it came from. And she could not respond.

✳✳✳

The girl bolted straight up in her cot. Cold sweat drenched her. She took several deep breaths as she attempted to slow her heart rate down. This was not the first time she had this nightmare. She knew that once she separated herself from the dream, with enough time, she would calm down. She had nothing to worry about. All the same, she touched her fingers to make sure they were all still there.

"Morning, Za'rie," came a friendly voice from beside her. "Was your nightmare about the Hunt Offering tonight?"

Za'rie looked at the elf hovering over her. She gave a practiced scowl. "Oh no, this was just my normal nightmare. You know, the one where my annoying cot sister would drink my blood while I sleep."

"I would never," the other elf replied with mock shock. "Your blood would upset my stomach, like that time you ate—"

"And that's enough of that!" Za'rie said, not wanting to relive any more memories at the moment. "I need to go watch over my catch until the ceremony tonight. How long was I asleep for, Aila?"

"About four hours," Aila answered. "Breakfast isn't

even ready yet. I'm sure whoever is on watch duty can wait at least until you eat."

"Not hungry," Za'rie said. "I'll try and join for lunch." Images of the nightmare still lingered, and she was sure that she wouldn't be able to eat until the ceremony was over. She looked around the room. It was a moderately sized room. Large enough to fit the twelve cots for her, her six cot sisters, and five cot brothers. All of them, other than Aila, were still asleep. She quietly slipped out of her bedding and went to the communal clothes rack for the girls. All the clothes were either white or tan dresses or loose-fitting shirts and pants of similar color, although pants did come in the options of brown or black as well. Elvish fashion was generally nondescript and more for practicality rather than individuality.

Za'rie took down a dress and took a quick sniff. She nearly gagged as she said, "Lyra, this one still smells like you." She threw the dress onto the bed where Lyra was attempting to sleep. "Put it in the wash bin when you get up. No one wants to live in your stink for the day."

"Hah, she told you!" said a half-sleeping male elf, who went right back to snoring after saying his piece.

Za'rie rolled her eyes and proceeded to put on a tan shirt and brown pants. They smelled clean enough. She then went back to her cot and grabbed her green cloak hanging from a peg in the wall. An elf's cloak is the one item they don't share with the community. They are responsible for keeping and maintaining it until they complete certain rituals to get a different colored cloak. The upcoming ritual would see her receiving a blue cloak to replace her green one.

She gave Aila a half-hearted smile and left the sleeping chamber. From there, she went past the lavatory, then the kitchen. The smell of breakfast cooking made her feel hungrily nauseated. Finally, she went through the dining room, where two long tables with benches on either side quartered the room, and exited the front doors into the town.

The first light of dawn was just breaking through the morning darkness, and there was a damp chill in the air. No one was walking the main street this early in the morning except for the lamplighter, who was going to each metal lamp post and turning the shining crystal until it went dull. She gave him a quick wave, and he returned it with a smile. He was standing nearly seven feet in mid-air and casually walked to the next lamp post as easily as if he were walking on the ground. The gemstones in the rim of his boots shone with imbued magic.

This was Prymbleton, one of the few elf towns throughout the predominantly human Kingdom of Primaria. Compared to human towns, it was significantly smaller, with a population that seldom exceeded 50. The town was well isolated from the outside world by a vast forest that encased it. It was a sleepy town that thrived on its solitude and was suffocated by it.

She continued down the brick path, passing by unopened smithies and other crafting-based buildings. None of the buildings had signs, but it was a small enough population that everyone knew every building and its occupying craft by heart. After passing the bakery, she rounded the corner and came to her destination, the spyglass room—though everyone would politely call it the security room while talking in groups. It was a small, plain, brick building, with no windows and only one door.

Za'rie knocked on the door, and after several moments of locks and chains being undone, the front door opened just enough for a single green eye to be seen.

"I'm your relief, Nymier," Za'rie said, trying not to sound as impatient as she was with the elf, "unless you want to stay and guard all day."

There was a hesitation as if Nymier didn't dislike the idea of staying shut in all day. But after a moment, the eye, which was at Za'rie's level to begin with, rose several feet, and the door fully opened. Nymier stood as tall as the doorway, and even that was with a hunch so he could fit through it. His eyes were wide and constantly darting around. He grasped the edges of his blue cloak, making sure to cover as much of himself as he could. He had a face that looked perpetually exhausted, but there was still an eerie beauty to it as it contrasted with his golden hair that flowed flawlessly to his chin.

"Thank you," he said, visibly struggling to keep his eyes focused on her. "Let me show you the device before I leave you."

Za'rie nodded and followed him inside. It was a cramped, dark room, with nothing but a hard wooden chair and a table that took up the entire side wall. It was easily ten feet long, and every inch was covered with metal-encased crystals. Each device had a dial, and one in particular had a large red dial. Several of the crystals projected two-dimensional images of areas within the town against the brick wall. But for her, there was only one that she needed to worry about.

"As you can see," Nymier said, pointing at the image of two teenage boys imprisoned in a large, metal, hanging cage, not unlike a birdcage, "the mages you captured can be watched from the central crystal image. It shows what is currently happening in the prison. You don't have to touch any of the dials. I have it set up perfectly to pick up even their whispers. They have been properly fed and watered, so if they call out for either, you can ignore their pleas. If they try to use their magic to escape, twist the red dial to your heart's content. It will send a fun little shock through the bars of their cage." He said this with the type of grin a child wears while they tear off insect wings. Za'rie could feel a chill slowly crawl up her spine and, not for the first time, wondered about her safety around Nymier.

"Have they tried escaping?"

"They have not." Nymier didn't even try hiding his disappointment.

"Thank you, I've got it from here."

Nymier gave a quick nod and exited the building, though not without turning back several times. As soon as he was gone, Za'rie sighed with relief, then closed the door and set one of the locks. She sat down, leaned back, and placed her feet on the table.

She noticed that there were some pieces of paper on the table. She leaned forward and picked them up to examine them. They were poorly scrawled notes on the two prisoners. Nymier either got mind-numbingly bored or enthused with dangerous curiosity during his watch.

Prisoner A

Age:16

Name: Caleb (discovered through conversation with Prisoner B)

Magic Type: Undetermined

Pain Threshold: Untested

Notes: Has a protective nature. Low intelligence. High emotions. Physically stronger than average. I theorize that his magic is most likely shifting or conceptual due *to a lack of escape attempts. Elemental mages immediately test out magic on bars. Either he can not use his magic or it is useless in cage-based situations. No need for ~~subject~~ prisoner to be kept after the ritual.*

Prisoner B
Age: 13
Name: Samuel (discovered through conversation with Prisoner A)
Magic Type: Undetermined
Pain Threshold: Untested
Notes: Has a cautious and curious nature. High intelligence. Low emotions. Physically weaker than Prisoner A. Based on observation I do not think Prisoner B is a mage. He would be the type to experiment with his magic to escape in a way he feels is clever. ~~Petition for Prisoner B to stay in town as my assistant~~ Prisoner shows too much loyalty to Prisoner A to willingly stay. Shows levels of stubbornness I do not find suitable as an assistant.

Za'rie's heart sank ever so slightly as she read through Nymier's notes. Sometimes she wondered if he was in the perfect line of work or if his job only enables his...unique tendencies. She placed the notes back on the table, making sure they were as close to their original position as possible.

She then turned her attention to the two prisoners. It was going to be a long day, and she was hopeful that the two boys would at least be entertaining to listen to. The image was positioned in a way that the two were directly facing her. They sat side by side with their feet dangling out of the cage and their arms resting on the bars.

"Okay, so dumb question," said the younger boy, Samuel, who had messy black hair and an expression on his face that made her think of a puppy trying to look serious. "The crab claw. Do you think it has crab meat or human meat?"

"Oh hells," said the older blond boy, Caleb, who had a more round and relaxed face. "That's a horrible thought. I guess it would be crab meat. But I don't want to find out."

"It's a serious question," Samuel said as he turned toward the other prisoner. "I'm thinking that if you could do the same to a rock, we would have food at any time. Unless the inside would just be rock."

Well, idiocy is a form of entertainment. Za'rie was curious how much of the conversation she missed and if there was a dial she could turn to go to earlier in the imaging. She looked around at the confusion of dials and knobs and switches and decided Nymier did not have the sense of humor required for her to be able to survive any colossal mishaps on her part.

"Look," Caleb said with a tinge of concern or worry in his voice, "I can't control it. I don't want to try and do anything with magic until I learn what I'm doing."

"Well," Samuel said, "it's not like you're going to be able to learn unless you practice."

"I keep telling you I'm not going to practice anywhere near you."

"I know, I know," Samuel said as he motioned his hands in a "please calm down" gesture. "But the worst you can do is give me a claw for a weapon. Sure, it looked painful to begin with, but you should have felt that thing. It was incredibly powerful. I don't know if that shell even could be cracked."

93

"He nearly broke your neck!" Caleb's face was turning red, though Za'rie wasn't sure if it was from anger or embarrassment.

"But he didn't." At this Samuel rubbed his throat and winced a little as he touched a yellowing bruise.

"You should have told me your plan about warning the camp," Caleb said.

"I said I was sorry. I didn't anticipate you trying to help out." Samuel chuckled and nudged Caleb. "You nearly got an arrow in your ass."

"Are you kidding," the older boy said, sharing in the chuckle and giving the other boy a playful shove, "you're the one that nearly ass-kabobbed."

"That's the dumbest thing I've ever heard." Both boys were going through a fit of laughter. Za'rie thought they were being childish, even though she did crack a smile at their stupidity. She had never heard of crab magic before. It must be a rare shifter variant. That could be useful to the cluster. She still wasn't sure what the other boy's magic was or even if he had any. She also hated that Nymier seemed to be right on both of his guesses.

"But getting back to the point," Samuel said, his voice becoming serious. "There was something off about what you said when you used your magic on crab cakes."

"What do you mean?"

"I mean, what you said wasn't technically a lie." There was a hesitation in the boy's voice as if he didn't know how to say the next part. "But it also wasn't fully the truth. It's hard to explain the different feel of the gray area. But basically, it felt like what you said was a partial truth."

"But, that's exactly what I said when I, well, you know…" Caleb brought his arms away from the bars and crossed them over his chest and his face seemed to sink under the weight of his apprehension.

"Right, I have a little bit of a theory." Samuel was talking slowly, as if working out the sentence as he was speaking it. "Based on the information we know, which sadly isn't a lot, your magic is *probably* activated by a strong emotional response to stimuli. Your magic responds to what you're feeling, but if your feelings are jumbled or not properly expressed, maybe the magic comes out as jumbled and uncontrollable."

"Let's say I understand everything you just said," Caleb said after several moments of puzzling together his companions' unrefined thought process. "What are you saying I should do?"

"Okay, so you're not going to like this."

"That wasn't ever in doubt." Caleb chuckled lightly and his grip around himself loosened slightly.

"I want you to think back to the moment between you and your friend. I want you to put yourself back in your own shoes at the time and think about what you felt. And this time, say the first thing that comes to your mind."

"I think you're right."

"Really?" Samuel's brows jolted up slightly in surprise

"Yeah, I really don't like this idea." Caleb uncrossed his arms and his hands rested on his lap. A playful smile started to break past his worried expression.

"Oh, shut up." Samuel punched his companion on the shoulder. "I'm not going to force you to do this. But I think we don't have very many options right now. Sure, the elves gave us food and water. But we were found in their territory, and we will be prisoners until they decide otherwise." He hesitated before saying, "I didn't want to scare you unnecessarily, but there is a widely believed rumor that elves capture humans like this to steal their magic. I don't know if it's true or not, but with the king and the Dark Lord both trying to hoard as many mages as they can, I don't think it's a stretch to say the elves are doing something similar."

"Wait, they can take away my magic?" Caleb asked.

Za'rie was surprised by the amount of hope in his voice.

"That's not a good thing," Samuel said. "From my understanding, the only mage that can undo a magical transformation is the mage that cast it. If you want to help your friend, then you need to learn how to use your magic and change him back yourself. If you lose your magic, you can't do that."

Za'rie was pretty sure she could see the horror growing on Caleb's face, and for a moment, she actually felt pity for him. She considered how he would feel after having this piece of himself stolen. This part of him that he is scared of, but is still part of himself nonetheless. Would he ever feel complete without this fragment? Would she? Za'rie shook her head and readjusted her priorities. Magic is just a material that happened to be mined from people. Magic is a tool. Nothing more, nothing less. If this is the truth, then why couldn't Za'rie fully believe that?

"Oh," Caleb said solemnly. Several moments passed as Caleb looked like he was processing everything at the speed of a dying snail. Za'rie was now sitting properly in the chair, her hand hovering over the big red dial. She didn't want to use it until she was sure she had to, but she also wanted to see the boy's magic in action. She had never seen a mage use magic before. Sure, she has seen magical items, but that's not the same. Magic is so much stronger when it comes from the source. "Okay, I'll give it a try, but you stay behind me."

Za'rie watched as Samuel positioned himself behind his prison mate, and Caleb readied himself into an almost meditative sitting position. She was enthralled and barely breathing, as if her breath was a distraction. She leaned closer to the image, watching for any movement. Caleb sat completely still, his eyes closed, and his face still as stone, his hands subtly trembling in his lap.

Then, she could see waves of emotions and the shadows of his memories as they rippled through his features. Za'rie's heart was racing as she waited impatiently, hoping for an answer to her nightmares.

"I-I don't know what to say," Caleb said without opening his eyes.

"Just say what you would if he were here right now."

Caleb took a deep breath and began to speak, slowly at first, as if his words could start a rockslide. "I'm sorry. I'm so sorry. If I could take it back, I would. Right now, I want nothing more than to undo what I did… This feels ridiculous."

"Keep going," Samuel said encouragingly, as he gestured with his hands. "This is new ground for me too."

Caleb sighed and continued where he stopped. "I just felt so betrayed, and sad, and so mad. I'm still mad. I can't believe you! And you expected me to be okay with it!"

"Why were you mad?" Samuel prodded.

"Because she's my sister. She's my responsibility, and you aren't…you aren't good enough for her!" Caleb's face twitched slightly.

"You're lying!" Samuel said with a sharpness to his words.

"No, I'm not! That's the truth!" Caleb's eyes opened, and he turned toward the other. He was no longer facing forward, so Za'rie couldn't see his expression, but she could hear the malice in his voice.

"You don't believe that," Samuel said with a harsh quietness. "Why are you really mad at him?"

"I don't know!"

"That's a lie!"

"Fine! I'm mad at him for liking her!" Caleb said. Blue sparks started to dance frantically along his exposed skin and leaping off of him in every direction. "A girl he barely spoke to and barely knew. How could he like her and not me!" Caleb sat straight up as if shocked.

At that moment, two things happened: First, Za'rie heard him give an audible and almost hollow "Oh." It was just a single syllable, but it carried the weight of sudden clarity mixed with newfound regret. Second, the blue sparks surrounding him turned into small blue orbs and froze in midair for a moment. Then, they all began to converge on one spot in between the two boys. The orbs swirled around and around in that spot like a whirlpool of lights, and when they were moving so fast it was just a blue blur, there was a bright flash. The image cut out for a moment, becoming nothing but a blank space against the wall. Then the image slowly faded back into focus. There were the two boys, and hovering in the air between them was a blue-hued crab.

Za'rie shot up with so much force that the wooden chair crashed to the ground behind her. Her mind was racing. She was no longer paying attention to the prisoners, and all pretenses of turning the red dial were miles behind her. The only thing she could focus on was the blue crab. It imitated a living creature perfectly. Too perfectly. Her thoughts flashed back to the butterfly of her dream and the accusatory voice. If the boy's magic could take form like that, could her magic have done the same? Before she could make up her mind on the right course of action, she hastily unlocked the door and closed it behind her with more force than she realized, and sprinted down the brick path to the town's prison.

She was thankful that it was still early morning and nearly no one was out. She was even more thankful that no one else was at the prison. The two boys were the only trespassers in over a month, and due to the risk of magical injury, the town had implemented the spying system to keep a healthy and safe observation of prisoners. But in truth, she didn't want anyone to know about this discovery until she had all the answers.

She burst through the prison building's door with explosive force. This had startled the two boys so badly they had become airborne for a fraction of a second. But the younger boy was the first to recover and placed himself in front of his companion, who had not too subtly moved the magic crab behind his back.

"Show that to me now!" she demanded, making sure to close the door behind her to keep anyone else from overhearing.

"I have no clue what you are talking about," Samuel said. "You and your people have removed all of our belongings except for our clothes. Don't tell me you want us to remove those as well?"

"Don't play dumb with me," Za'rie said, trying to play the part of Prison Warden to take control of the situation. "I saw your mage friend create that…thing!"

Samuel looked around the room. Similarly to the security room, this one had no windows as well. The walls were solid stone, and the only other things in the building were three other hanging cages, currently empty, and a wooden crate at the other end of the room where the prisoners' belongings were held. He took a pause, obviously thinking through all the possibilities, then whispered something to the other boy. He then turned back to the girl and said, matter-of-factly, "No."

"You are in no place to argue," Za'rie said, trying as best she could to hide her increasing frustration, but the unsteady tapping of her foot didn't help. "If you don't follow my orders, I will activate the shock magic connected to the cage, then we will see how defiant you are."

"By all means, do it," Samuel dared. He even grasped the bars to show her he knew she was bluffing. Caleb's expression of panic gave away his lack of eagerness toward physical harm. "I'm sure threatening and abusing your prisoners are excellent ways to gain trust. Though I'm also sure if you were going to shock us to show dominance, you would have done it rather than just tell us. You came to us directly because we have something you want."

"You are on dangerous grounds, human," Za'rie said, putting as much venom into her voice as she could. She was staring daggers into the boy, and he was returning the glare with equal measure. She was coming up with plans to have them separated so she could have a one-on-one conversation with the actual mage. But as she was attempting to disregard murder, the voice of the other boy broke the field of ice between her and her prey.

"So, Miss Elf, is there something wrong with my magic?"

She disregarded Samuel and turned her gaze to the other prisoner, who was now holding the blue crab in front of him, as if presenting it to her.

"Don't just go showing her," Samuel scolded. "We don't even know what she wants."

"But you already said she doesn't actually want to hurt us," Caleb said, "and if my magic is broken, maybe they won't have a need for it and will let us go."

"It's not broken," Za'rie said, the icy edge melting, "but its behavior is…impossible."

"How so?" Samuel's voice was also losing its sharpness and was replaced with genuine curiosity.

"Magic is just energy," Za'rie said as she started to approach the cage. "It can do a variety of things based on the needs of the user. It can be used to change one thing into another or control certain things. It is supposed to be an energy inside people that can be taken out and harnessed. But his took shape in a way I've never seen before."

"That's not true, is it?" Samuel asked without any hint of accusation. There was a slight tilt to his head as he spoke. "You have seen something at least a little similar before, haven't you?"

Za'rie was taken aback and couldn't stop the shock from showing on her face, "How did…Never mind, not important. Fine, I think I have once before, but I was sure it was a trick of the light or something." She sighed and took a few more steps closer to the prisoners. "When I was younger, I went through a ritual we call magic letting; it's what we are planning to perform to the both of you tonight. We take needles made out of null wood and insert them into key points of the body to force the source of magic inside someone out into a crystal cluster. We use the pieces of the crystal to make magic items based on the selected magic in the fragment. During my ritual, I was certain I saw my magic leave my body in the shape of a butterfly. It was only for a split second, and I tried to convince myself that it was my imagination."

"So, what does that mean?" Caleb asked as he rubbed the top of the crab as if it were a dog. And like a dog, it seemed to actually enjoy it. It would make a bubbling gurgle every time the boy rubbed its shell, and when he would stop, the crab would gently grab the boy's hand with its pincer and drag it back toward it. Za'rie couldn't make up her mind if she thought it was freaky or adorable.

"It means that I was wrong," she said solemnly. "It means that magic isn't just energy, it's something alive. Something with fears. Something that can feel abandoned. And people have countless living creatures stuck in a rock in the center of the town."

"Hey, it's not like humans knew any differently," Samuel said. His voice was trying to match the other boy's natural sympathy, and it came across as unnatural to Za'rie, which is why she appreciated it all the more. "We thought of it as a weapon. I don't think anyone would have even considered the idea that it was alive."

"So…what's the plan?" Caleb asked, looking between Za'rie and Samuel.

"What plan?" Za'rie asked.

"I mean, we have to tell the rest of the elves. And I'm sure you want your magic back. Also, I kinda don't want to get rid of mine now that I know about Hermy."

"Oh no," Samuel said as he crashed his face against the metal of the cage.

"Hermy?" Za'rie asked with a raised eyebrow.

"Yeah, Hermy, short for Hermit. It's his name," Caleb said as he continued to play with the magic creature.

"You named it?" she asked with exasperation.

"He names every creature he sees," Samuel said, matching her exasperation. "Do you know how hard it is to cook and eat a rabbit with a name? The George incident was an absolute nightmare! And on top of that, that's not even the type of crab it is!"

She sighed and put that thought to the side for the moment. "Okay, I would like to put forward an agreement to a temporary truce. You help me tell the others about magic, and I help the two of you leave safely. Deal?"

Both boys looked at each other. A silent conversation happened between the two. And in unison, they said, "Agreed."

"I think we should introduce ourselves; I am Samuel, son of Seth."

"And I am Caleb, son of Calin."

"I am Za'rie," she said.

There was an awkward silence as the two boys seemed to wait for a continuation of her sentence.

"Of the 20th generation?" she continued.

The boys' confused silence only grew deeper, and the looks on their faces showed no answer to what she was supposed to say.

"What?" she asked.

"Are elves not named after their parents?" Caleb asked bluntly, to which Samuel gave him a smack on the back of his head, causing the crab to wobble and nearly fall off.

"We can talk about differences in cultures later," Samuel said. "Right now, we need a plan."

Za'rie nodded and tried to hide her smile.

***

Za'rie was not too enthused with the plan they settled on. And that wasn't just because she was outvoted by prisoners. She was tasked with speaking to the leader, who in this case was the founding elf of this town, and telling him in no uncertain terms that magic is alive. And if need be, she would lead him to the prisoners to show him firsthand. She couldn't put into words why she felt off about it. Maybe it was because it was too passive of a plan. But an easy resolution was the best solution, and she knew this.

Za'rie gritted her teeth as she pushed through the wooden door that led into the town hall. Though, it was less a great hall and more just a house for a single person. Just past the entryway was the main room. In the center of the room was a desk with a half-dozen neatly stacked piles of paper, enough quills to make up a quell, and an immaculately clean pot of ink. Behind the desk sat a child-sized elf who was humming along as he was writing on the page before him. His face was small and round, and with the addition of his wide eyes and bushy eyebrows, he had the appearance of a kitten.

"Young Za'rie," he said without even looking up, a kindly smile appearing as his eyes kept looking into the distance of the page. "Aren't you supposed to be watching your prey? This is most unwise of you. Nymier would be ever so displeased." He let out a musical chuckle that matched the rhythm of his previous hum. "But we don't have to let him know. What seems to be troubling you?"

"Prymble," Za'rie said, addressing the leader of the town, "as I was watching the two prisoners, I saw something that confirmed my long-held fears."

"Oh my, that doesn't sound pleasant." Prymble placed the quill with the others and gave her his utmost attention.

"One of the boys attempted to use his magic to escape, so naturally, I sent a shock through the cage that knocked them out before anything could happen. But in the split second when the boy started to use his magic, it materialized into a little creature—"

"Ah, what a unique magic," the elf said. "It will make for a great addition—"

"No," Za'rie interjected. "I don't think it's unique at all. It wasn't him performing magic. That creature *was* his magic. It was a living thing. Just like my magic when I saw it go into the crystal."

"We've been over this, my dear," he said with gentle reproach. "Your nightmares are tainting your memory. You are feeling a natural guilt that all elves feel at one point or another. But that guilt goes away as you come to accept that the magic you gave will help the community grow and prosper."

"And what if you're wrong," Za'rie said, her voice growing in desperation. "What if all magic isn't just energy? What if magic is a living part of us, and we have been torturing it by forcing it to be used as everyday tools and weapons?"

Prymble gave a moment's pause to consider this, but Za'rie could see that his decision was made centuries ago. She could see by the distance in his eyes that he never once gave this thought a moment of his time, even now.

"If all that were true," he said slowly, "then I would make the tough decision to continue just as we always have. We need magic to maintain our way of life. Everything we do is for the sake of the community. Would you ask your fellow cot brothers and sisters to live in a world without our magic?"

Za'rie lowered her head, unable to look at her elder.

"No, sir," she said as tears burned the edges of her eyes.

"You are a good and kind girl. I am proud to have you as a member of our community. Now, I think you should go back to your post. I'm sure those two won't stay knocked out for too much longer."

***

"That failed miserably!" Za'rie shouted as she barged into the prison building, a woodcutter's axe in one hand and a rusty key in the other. "Time for plan B!"

"What happened?" Caleb asked.

"We don't have a plan B!" Samuel retorted.

"We do now," said Za'rie, as she unlocked the cage and opened the gate. "We are going to perform the magic letting ritual on the giant crystal, and then we are getting the hells out of this town!"

"There is no way we are just going to go to the center of the town and mess with the town's magic and not get re-captured," Samuel said as Caleb helped him out of the cage.

"That's why I created a diversion," Za'rie said, unable to keep the hurt out of her voice. She then went to a crate in the far corner of the room, pulled out Samuel's shield, and tossed it his way.

Samuel just barely caught the shield in time. The expression on his face looked like he was about to ask about the diversion. But before he could, the world outside the building erupted into pandemonium. There were shouts of panic and heavy footfalls of people in a hurry.

"Fire! The bakery is on fire!"

"Oh goddess, tell me you didn't," Samuel said with widened eyes.

"Calm down," Za'rie said defensively. "No one was in there. They will take care of the fire quickly without anyone getting hurt. But we have to act now!"

She could see Samuel wanting to protest, but Caleb put his hand on his companion's shoulder and just nodded solemnly. It would have looked like a much more serious moment if not for the blue crab sitting on top of Caleb's head like a wobbling helmet.

"Fine," Samuel said with resignation. "Take us to the crystal."

Za'rie timed everything perfectly. They were headed toward the crystal cluster just as the rest of the town had already gathered around the burning bakery. She led them quickly down the path while explaining her plan. She thought it was a rather good plan, considering it took her only a few minutes to come up with it. However, Za'rie was starting to get annoyed with Samuel's constant questioning of said plan. It was going to work. It had to.

After a quick journey through town, they stood in the shadow of the giant crystalline structure. All her life, this was a source of power, a symbol of her family. Now, as she watched the swirling colors, all she could see was a prison. She knew her magic was trapped somewhere in there, and she was going to rescue it.

Za'rie gripped the handle of the axe painfully tight, and without hesitation, she made the first strike. The shock of it traveled like lightning through her hands and arms, and there was the hot friction of wood against flesh. But she had successfully started to chip away at a smaller cluster of crystals along the northernmost edge. Shards flew through the air as she continued to strike. Again and again. All the while, the glowing lights within the areas she struck began to leak out and take to the air like shooting stars in reverse.

Just as planned, Caleb watched the street for anyone who might see them, and Samuel positioned himself at the southernmost edge of the cluster. Za'rie could see Samuel aiming his shield toward the crystal and inching forward. He looked like he was being pushed back by an invisible force, but the strain on his face showed his determination to see this through.

It was working exactly as Za'rie expected. The multicolored lights were fleeing northward away from the null wood and were being funneled out through the damaged areas of the crystal. She went to other sections and kept smashing through the structure like glass. She could feel the flesh on her hands becoming raw and her arms prickling as they started to go numb. She also could feel the painful cuts as shards sliced through the air and made contact with her skin. But she didn't slow down.

That was until Caleb shouted, "We have people coming this way!"

She looked toward the street he was facing, and she could see three elven men in blue cloaks coming their way. She knew them as adults of the previous generation. They were mentors of her childhood who taught her to hunt, cook, and create. And now they were brandishing weapons and running toward her. She didn't want to fight them. She couldn't fight them.

"Step away from our crystal now!" shouted the tallest and leanest of the three. He seemed to be the leader of the group. He was holding an ornate sword hilt that had no blade and pointed it at the two humans.

"You don't understand!" Za'rie shouted back with the full weight of her sorrow and regret. "The magic is alive. We have been enslaving magic all our lives without knowing.

108

We have to free it!"

"The mage is controlling her," said the shortest of the three with ears so long they seemed to droop slightly. He was wielding a stringless bow and stood behind the leader of the trio. "Don't worry, Za'rie, we are here to help!"

"Wait!" Za'rie screamed, but it was too late. The leader tapped on a crystal embedded in the hilt, and fire erupted in the shape of a blade. The one with the bow drew back on an invisible string, creating a shard of ice in the shape of an arrow at his fingertips. The third elf, who was significantly more muscular than the other two and had half of his left ear missing, wore a pair of gauntlets that sparked with electricity after he struck his fists together.

There was a whistle cutting through the air as the shard of ice shot toward Caleb, who dove to the ground, narrowly avoiding the arrow. However, the gauntleted elf took this moment to dash toward Caleb, going for a strike to the boy's face. Before Za'rie could react, she saw Samuel leap forward and intercept the elf's gauntlet with his shield. She waited to hear the clash of metal on wood, but instead, the elf's fist flew backward with enough momentum that he found himself face-up on the ground.

"We can distract them for a few moments," Samuel said. "Hurry and take care of the crystal!"

"Please don't hurt them," Za'rie said, not entirely sure which group she was addressing. She tore her eyes away from the fight and searched through the wreckage for more sparks of light. So many had escaped already. But she still had not found her own. She had a growing fear that it had already escaped, and instead of returning to her, it fled with the others. Or worse, it had already been removed from the source and put into a magic item that could be goddess knows where.

She shut her mind off from her fears and the sounds of fighting behind her and continued smashing her weapon against any undamaged spots. The pain seared into her hands with each strike. Blood was running down the handle, making it harder to grip. And just as she found the last spark of light, she heard another shout from Caleb that cracked with desperation and fear.

"Samuel!"

She turned to see the sword-wielding elf pointing his weapon at the young boy. The bladeless hilt projected a torrent of flame in Samuel's direction and engulfed him.

"No!" she shouted as a shard of terror splintered in her chest. "You're going to kill him!"

The null wood was repelling the magic enough to protect him from the primary fire. But she knew that it wouldn't take long for the heat alone to end him. She began to run to aid her new companion, but then she heard Caleb say something else.

"Hermy, please help!" He ran toward the elf, and the crab on his head turned into a blue orb of light and bounced from one arm to the next. In an instant, Caleb's arms started to enlarge and become red. His fingers were combining and expanding into long, horn-like points. His arms and hands changed shape into that of crab claws. The transformation looked natural, as if his arms could always change in this way.

Caleb seized the hilt of the bladeless sword with both claws and snapped shut. The leader's eyes widened with shock as his weapon broke into multiple pieces, and the fire was extinguished. Before he could recover, he received a punch in the gut with the back of Caleb's claw, sending him coughing violently to the ground.

Samuel, whose clothes were charred and had several burn holes, leapt back to his feet and in front of Caleb just in time to deflect an ice arrow that would have hit the boy in the chest. The arrow shot back toward the short elf, causing him to dive to the ground to avoid it. But just as he got back to his feet and drew back his invisible bowstring, Caleb had already sprinted full-tilt toward him, reaching for the bow. Caleb went to grab the weapon, but was intercepted, as a crackling gauntlet knocked his claw away.

Za'rie broke out of her daze and tore her eyes away from the two boys. She took one final strike against the crystal to free the last of the magic. A large crack spread from the blade of the axe, and the light of magic seeped through. It started as a ball of purple light, and as it flew toward her, it shifted and sprouted butterfly wings. The magic butterfly landed on her trembling index finger and didn't move for several seconds. It slowly started to dissolve back into her hand, and in the back of her head, she heard a sharp whisper. *Your atonement has started.*

Tears swirled and fell as she felt a sense of completion that she never knew she was missing. But she wasn't even given a moment to come to terms with all the thoughts and emotions that raged in her mind when she came crashing back down to the reality surrounding her. Samuel had grabbed her by the arm and pulled her along with him, away from the forming mob of elves behind them. She matched his pace quickly and soon was dragging him along, leading him in the correct direction. She looked at Caleb running along with them, struggling to catch his breath. His arms had already reverted to their regular state, but there was a weariness on his face that made her worry he was going to pass out at any moment.

She led them down the quickest path to the stable. Samuel released his grasp on Za'rie, charged toward the stable, and opened the gate. The boy shared a quick embrace with the horse before helping Caleb onto his newly saddled and provision-equipped back. Za'rie found her own horse, Elentari, and mounted her. She was also saddled and pre-equipped for Za'rie's new journey.

With no time to spare, they rode their horses out of town. There was an attempt by the townsfolk to ready their own horses and catch up, but during the time Za'rie was packing and preparing for the journey, she also sabotaged every other horse's reins and saddles. There were elves falling off their horses, reins snapping, and gates that refused to open. By the time anyone was able to pursue them, it was too late.

Za'rie looked back at her hometown one last time. The familiar shapes of home slowly faded from sight, probably forever. She had her magic back, but was the cost too great? She was exiled from the only family she ever had. Life as she knew it was over and was taken over by the unknown. She turned away just as the tears threatened to undo her. She looked forward and promised herself she would never look back again.

Campfire Conversations: Tears in the Night
Cycle 4, Day 2

Caleb sat in front of the fire with Hermy on his shoulder. Over the past few days, he had learned more and more about how to communicate with his manifested magic. Hermy couldn't talk back, but he seemed to understand everything that Caleb said. However, the crab was more than capable of showing how he felt. Caleb had several red marks on his neck and shoulder from dissatisfied pinches, along with red marks from satisfied pinches. The difference was the intended level of pain. He also bubbled at the mouth when he got excited. And there was one instance so far where the boy was sure Hermy was dancing. Samuel called him crazy when he had suggested this to the group, but neither Samuel nor Za'rie actually gave an alternative.

Caleb had also learned that Hermy didn't need to eat or sleep and could manifest as a physical crab or a flying blue orb. The crab could also disappear into Caleb. Possibly going inside his soul? None of them knew where magic resided inside a person. Za'rie's best guess was somewhere in the heart or chest section.

At the thought of Za'rie, Caleb looked over to her tent. The sun had barely set, but she had already gone to bed. Well, she said she was going to bed, but both boys could hear her crying quietly. This had been her routine for the last three nights. She had talked to them a lot throughout the days but never anything meaningful. She would follow conversations but never add anything. She acted like she was going through the motions but not fully there. Caleb looked over to Samuel, who was seemingly invested in a line of traveling ants.

"We need to do something," Caleb said in a soft and rounded whisper.

"There's nothing we can do," Samuel said. "She just needs time to sort things out."

"It's been three days," Caleb countered. "She isn't sorting things out. She's falling into a mental gyre. She looks like she is getting less sleep by the day. We are her friends; we need to help her."

"*Friends* is a very strong word," Samuel said, with more volume than Caleb expected. "She just met us. There's no way she trusts us enough to open up. And besides, even me and you—"

"Are friends," Caleb interrupted. "Don't belittle our friendship just because it's new."

"Why do you have to make it sound so awkward?" Samuel said with teenage embarrassment.

Caleb gave a soft smile and patted Hermy on the shell. "You are way too serious all the time. Isn't that right, Hermy?" The crab gave Caleb's finger a happy pinch.

"Fine, you win," Samuel said with an exasperated exhale. He turned toward the sound of quieting sobs. "Hey! Za'rie!"

There were a few moments of silence. Then, a quick sniffle.

"What!" came the crackling voice of the elf.

"Just wanted to talk, is all," Samuel said. Caleb could hear the edge of defensiveness in his voice and gave his side a sharp poke. The younger boy sighed and took the hint. "Caleb is horrible at late-night conversations, and I just felt like talking to someone who doesn't fall asleep halfway through one."

Caleb cracked a smile and poked Samuel again. Samuel punched him in the shoulder, which caused Hermy to give an uncrablike gurgling growl.

"I appreciate the gesture," she said with a lot of hesitation, "but I really need to sleep. Elves need more sleep than humans. Something to do with our immortality and all." Caleb could feel the younger boy tense up, as if struggling against calling out her blatant lie.

"Please?" Caleb said with as saccharine of a voice as he could muster.

There was another long pause, but Caleb knew that he'd won. Za'rie emerged from her tent, purposefully not looking directly at either of the boys, as she proceeded to sit on the opposite side of the fire.

"Alright," she said reluctantly. "I'm out here. What did you want to talk about?"

"That is a good question," Samuel said as he turned to Caleb with a mischievous grin. "What did we want to talk about?"

"Well," Caleb choked, "I was curious how old you are. You look like you are about my age, but I don't know how quickly or slowly elves mature."

"I'll have you know," Za'rie said indignantly, "I am at least twice your age."

"Good to know," Samuel said. "Now, this time, can you tell us your *actual* age?"

"What he means is…" Caleb interjected, as he was trying to give a stern glare to his friend without being obvious

115

about it, "It's okay if you don't want to talk about that. It was a bit more personal than I realized."

"Fine, fine," Za'rie said, folding her arms across her chest. "I'm fifteen. Elves mature at roughly the same rate as humans. It's when we hit thirtyish that we stop aging. We are semi-immortal. We can't die of old age, but the things that kill you can kill us too. We are also more susceptible to illnesses. A simple sickness can quickly become life-threatening if not treated quickly. Because of that, most elves don't leave the safety of our hometown." The tone of her voice trailed off into a soft melancholy.

"That makes sense," Samuel said, and Caleb could see the curiosity developing on his face. "So, how do elven towns and cities trade with other cities if there isn't much outward travel?"

"Our communities are very self-reliant," Za'rie said. "We have a surplus of... magic-infused tools and weapons." She took a brief pause where she drank some water, but Caleb was pretty sure it was because she was starting to gyre again and just needed a moment to collect herself. "These items help with all day-to-day survival. We use them for hunting and growing our own food. We use them to make our own clothing, pottery, and so much more. During the summer, we have magical devices that cool our homes, and in winter, we have devices that heat them. There was little need for outside resources except for luxuries, and there were some brave—or dumb—traveling merchants to bring that to us. The smart ones steer clear of elven territory, you know, because of how we steal the magic from stray intruders." She gave a dry chuckle before falling into a deep silence.

"I'm sorry," Samuel said, "I should have asked a different question. I didn't mean to make you dwell—"

116

"No," Za'rie said, "I need to face the facts. But it's hard. Magic was our way of life. To live without it as we currently use it is to take away a core aspect of my people, and it will deprive whole communities of the things they need to survive. However, continuing doing something so horrible just because it's what has always been shouldn't be an option."

"There is another way," Caleb said. "They could learn to live with their magic instead of trying to harness it like a tool."

"I don't know," Za'rie said. "So many of the elves are hundreds of years old and have been abusing magic in this way for so long. Can they really change?"

"You did," Caleb said.

"That's different," Za'rie said. "I'm still young. And I don't even know how to use my magic. Every time I try to connect with it, I feel like it gets further away from me. How did you get yours to work?"

"It's hard to explain," Caleb said as he closed his eyes, trying to recall the feeling he had in the cage. "It was like something inside my chest was tied up in knots, and my magic was sort of trapped inside it. It was only when I was fighting against the knot that my magic struggled back and did things randomly. But when Samuel helped me come to terms with the root of the knot and helped me realize how to untie it, it just appeared."

"Okay," Za'rie said, "now let's try that again, but this time in Primish and with fewer metaphors."

"Fine," Caleb said with a sigh. "I think I have been ignoring how I felt about my friend for a long time, and I just bottled it all up. I didn't even know when it all started. It's not like one day I looked at him and thought, 'I want to kiss him.' I was hiding a piece of me away. You're just going to have to live with that metaphor. And I think Hermy was

117

somehow part of that part of me. I really don't know. It's confusing to think about, and I am still trying to process it."

"So, are you going to tell him when you return home," Samuel said.

"Oh, dear goddess!" Caleb said. "I haven't even thought that far ahead. Maybe? But then again, maybe not? How would he even react? I guess I will lower that bridge when I get to it. But getting back to the point," Caleb said, turning his attention back to Za'rie, who had been quietly listening. "I'm not sure if your magic is the same, but if it is, that means there's something blocking you from it."

At this point, Za'rie had unfolded her arms and was leaning forward. Her expression was pensive and calculating. "But I've dealt with my issue. I destroyed the source of my people's way of living! I got exiled for trying to right the wrongs that I and my community have done! What else can I do?"

The three lapsed into a stillness as they contemplated together. The only sound was the crackling of the fire between them and the bugs and creatures around them. This time, it was Samuel that broke the silence.

"I don't know much about magic. But now that I know where we are, I might know a place where we can learn more about it. Maybe that can help you learn how to communicate and connect with yours, Za'rie."

"What place is that?" she asked apprehensively.

"There is a town called Leabmore that would take us a few days off course, but it has a library that is said to be filled with books about magic."

"Are you sure you're okay taking a detour?" Za'rie asked. "Your father—"

"Was captured alive," Samuel interrupted. "Meaning

118

they won't take him all the way to the Dark Lord just to execute him. And having another member of the group that can use magic will probably be crucial in actually rescuing him."

"Okay, then let's go check out this library."

Book of Anu: Death and Rebirth

The children of Anu should fear not death.
The body may die, but the soul lives on.
The passing of the body allows the soul to be reborn anew.
Rejoice in the cycle of the soul.

A soul cannot be unmade.
But it can become corrupted.
A soul fed on evil acts becomes tainted and malformed.
The body may heal, but the soul bears the shape even after death.

A soul corrupted makes a pilgrimage through the hells.
The hells are realms that clean the soul of sin.
Nine hells shall the corrupted soul travel.
Nine hells to wash away the darkness.

A tenth hell yet remains for a soul tainted beyond redemption.

Chapter 6: Always Meet Your Villains
Cycle 4, Day 7

S eth was impressed by how quickly they had made it to the Dark Lord's territory. After their first night, the goblins came to a cave that had a boulder hiding the entrance to an intricate underground cave system with railways and mining carts. This turned a trip that would have taken a full cycle, if not longer due to Seth's injury, into one that only took thirteen days. This did have the unfortunate consequence of Seth and Thistle being parted for their journey. But a pair of goblin brothers, Honeysuckle and Apple Pie, had volunteered to take her by the overground path and meet them at the Dark Lord's lair. Thistle had grown more comfortable with the goblins by this point and didn't resist too much once Seth said his goodbyes.

Puppies and his goblins may seem clumsy and awkward above ground, but in the underground, they were in their element. Their vision was near perfect in the dark, only lighting torches for Seth's sake. At one point, they had taken a slight detour down an offshoot tunnel because Petrichor, the main doctor and medicine maker of the group, wanted to see what he had called Sparkling Cave. No one had argued; if anything, they all voted in favor of the detour, including Seth, and he was incredibly grateful that they had.

Sparkling Cave, however, was a terrible misnomer. The cave did not 'sparkle'; it shone in a way the night sky never could. It was an underground spring with crystal clear water where blind, colorless fish swam freely. But the cave's namesake came from the plethora of gemstones that encrusted the rock walls and ceiling. Shining a torch caused rays of living color to be cast in every direction. And when the torch was extinguished, the lights continued to shine for several minutes. The colors reflected on the surface of the water like dancing stars.

They lingered in the cave for a few hours, taking their time to eat and collect water from the spring. After boiling the water, Petrichor took a vial from his "MEDECEN" pack and emptied it into the water.

"The water clean now," Petrichor had said with a large toothy grin.

"The water *is* clean now," Seth had replied.

"The water is clean now?" Petrichor asked.

"That's correct," Seth said, returning the too-large smile. "You are learning quickly. I am proud of you."

The goblin turned a deeper shade of green in only the way a bashful goblin could. The water was then divided between all the goblins, and some was used to clean Seth's injured leg. It still hurt like all hells, and he still couldn't walk on it. But the medicine they fed him regularly helped dull the pain.

The underground system finally ended with them emerging near the foot of a long-dormant volcano. Seth had expected to see barren land covered in ash from a volcanic eruption several centuries ago. Instead he was surprised to see beautiful greenery that had grown around and over the petrified ruins of what used to be a human city. Trees were breaching decrepit buildings. Grass was growing through the cracks of stone paths. And from the new growth sprouted a thriving community of goblins. There were clotheslines reaching from building to building, cluttered with what could generously be labeled as clothing. Small goblin children ran through the streets and greenery, laughing and yelling. Mothers and fathers scolding. Older goblins, looking like dried and shriveling onions—white hairs and all—watched in amusement.

He only had a few moments to take in the sights before the community spotted the emerging group. A mob of children of every size circled him, chanting, "Uman! Itsa uman!"

"Back, back," Puppies said, shooing away the giggling children. "The human is injured. We are taking to Dark Lord now."

Seth didn't have the energy to correct Puppies' grammar, but he was happy that he had gotten much better over the journey. The goblins continued to carry him on the tarp as they paraded him through the cheering streets. The group was receiving a hero's welcome, Seth noted. He was curious how many ambushing groups were out in human territory, risking their lives. Seth had to remind himself that he was the prisoner in the situation and was the one at risk. However, he had never once felt like anything less than an equal member of the group. He felt bad for these kind and simple people. They were clearly being taken advantage of by someone who only saw them as pawns.

They came to the end of the road to the largest, but still equally dilapidated, building. Seth braced himself for the worst as Puppies shouted at the front door, announcing his presence.

"I, Puppies, am here with my men to hand over our human prisoner!"

The door opened of its own accord. The edges of the petrified doors crumbled slightly into fine dust. Puppies led the way forward into the great hall, brightly lit by the lack of a ceiling. There were several long tables with benches on either side, all covered with a light layer of dust and sand. At the head of the room was a large black throne, decorated with antlers and horns that could only be from a dragon based on the size. It was not a throne that looked comfortable to sit in. This was probably why it was currently empty.

At the far end of one of the tables sat two figures on either side of each other. The one on the left was human and was wearing black robes, and his expression was that of a sagging, serious perplexity. On the right was some sort of humanoid that was covered head to toe in black plate mail armor. The visor of his helmet was down, so Seth could not see his expression, but he could get the sense that he shared the serious mood of his companion.

Between the two was a board with white and black pieces.

"Ha, I win again," the man in the black robes said as he replaced one of the armored man's white pieces with one of his black ones.

"I demand a rematch," the armored one said, his voice echoing within his helmet.

"Naturally," the other man said. He let out an exaggerated sigh that melted into a chuckle halfway through. "But I think Puppies has a capture to report."

"Right, of course." The armored man looked in their direction and stood up, revealing his massive stature of over seven feet. The more Seth looked at the armor, the more he thought it looked less like actual armor and more like a fancy decorative suit one would see lining a hallway in a nobleman's home or the king's castle. As the man walked closer, Seth realized that his armor wasn't actually black, but rather, it was probably silver underneath the plethora of scorch marks that all blended into one large mark.

"Puppies," he demanded, "report!"

"Yes, sir!" the goblin said as he stood up straight and saluted. "Me and my men ambushed Warden leading mage to human capital thirteen days ago. We lost mage but captured Warden. This is Warden Seth. He was injured in the capture. Petrichor recommends three cycles of bed rest."

"Six cycles at most," Petrichor interjected.

"Puppies!" the armor echoed. "Your Primish has improved incredibly." He bent down and gently patted the goblin on the head as best as one could with gauntlets on. Then he looked over at Seth. "I presume this is your doing?"

"Yes, sir!" Seth said, unsure how to address the person before him.

"You have my gratitude. I have never had good patience at teaching," he said with an awkward head tilt. "Doctor Lawrence, if you would kindly remove yourself from the bench and heal this man's leg."

"Not a doctor," the man said with a grumble. "I was released from that position. If you are going to make me a general, at least address me as one."

The not-doctor crossed the room toward Seth while picking up a piece of paper and a stick of charcoal from the table. He took a quick look over Seth's leg and then began to draw on the slip of paper. Seth could not make sense of the random shapes he was drawing, but either way, he was just along for the ride.

"Before I do this," Lawrence said, "I need you to understand and verbally agree with what I am about to do. I am a mage who uses time magic. I can speed up the healing process of your leg by making time go by faster around that area. This will mean that a few seconds will pass for most of you, but six cycles will pass for your leg. Do you understand?"

"Yes..." Seth answered with growing uncertainty.

"Do you want me to proceed?"

Seth considered for a moment and then said, "Yes. Do what you need to."

"Okay, you're going to feel some uncomfortable sensations along with a lot of pain. I recommend you brace yourself."

Petrichor stuck a biting stick in Seth's mouth just as Lawrence placed the paper on his leg. There were green sparks around the paper as the shapes glowed green. The pain was immeasurable. Had it not been for the stick, Seth would have been screaming obscenities. He could feel the bone moving as it mended back together. It was by far the worst pain he had ever experienced. He could feel himself fading into unconsciousness, but he fought back, needing to stay awake the whole way through. He wasn't going to pass out only to wake up in a prison cell. He knew once his leg was healed, he would have to win their trust somehow and escape.

Then, the pain stopped. Seth removed the stick from his mouth, and with the help of Petrichor, he removed the makeshift splint. It was miraculous. It was as if his leg was never broken. He stood up and tested the leg. There was a tiredness in his joints and bones. But other than that, he was perfectly healthy.

"Thank you," Seth said with genuine gratitude.

Lawrence nodded.

"Who exactly are you?" Seth asked, wanting to ask more, but not in front of the armored man.

"I'm surprised Puppies didn't tell you about me," Lawrence said, giving a greeting smile to the goblin. "I was his first capture. He found me after…Well after I got fired. I decided to go with the flow to see what this was all about. Now, I am one of *The Dark Lord's* most important generals."

He laid on a heavy, sarcastic tone when he mentioned the Dark Lord. Seth really wished he had Samuel with him. He took for granted his son's ability to catch lies.

"Now," the armored man said, "to the important business. You are a Warden, correct?"

"Yes."

"You are not, and never have been, a mage, correct?"

"Correct."

"I see," the Dark Lord said slowly and deliberately, as he gave Seth a once over that seemed to peer straight through his soul. "Okay, you may go."

"Go?" Seth asked. "Go where?"

"To wherever you call home," he said as he began to turn away. "Or to wherever you were originally headed."

"Are you not worried I would reveal information about you to the kingdom?" Seth asked.

"No," the man in the armor said, turning back around to face Seth. "The wizard Malguinne already paid me a visit. He has learned not to face me on his own again. I expect he has gathered a party to try and defeat me by now. My scouts should be reporting at any time to inform me of his movements. However, it matters not. I have no equal in this world, and I will not be stopped."

"I see," said Seth. "I was starting to think I was in the wrong place. But you really are the Dark Lord. The one who threatens this world."

"If that is how you wish to address me and my plans, then so be it." There was no hostility in the tone, only a tiredness.

"He prefers Grand Magus," the time mage interjected. "Though I've just been calling him Magus."

"It is not that I prefer it," Magus said. "It is just a better descriptor. I prefer not to need a name."

"An army can't receive orders from no one," Lawrence said. "That's how you get soldiers saying stuff like 'no one needs help' and another saying 'if no one needs help, then shut up about it.'"

Magus gave the mage what Seth figured was a death glare. Or it was possible he was just having a moment of silent reflection. Eventually, Seth decided it was in his best interest to speak up.

"If I am no longer a prisoner, then I am just going to leave."

"You can not leave," cried Puppies. "Your horse is not here yet. You must stay."

Seth had completely forgotten about having to wait for Thistle. Maybe he could just leave and catch up with Honeysuckle and Apple Pie on their way here.

"I did not realize," said Magus, "that you were waiting on your horse. If that is the case, you may stay here until it arrives, and then you can leave in peace. I will prepare you a room if that is your wish."

"Thank you," Seth said, "but I will have to decline. I cannot stay in the home of a person who wages war on my people."

"Before you leave," Lawrence said, in a tone of voice that made Seth think of a man juggling several razor-sharp blades while blindfolded, "I think you should see what it is the *Dark Lord* is actually doing."

"It is true," Magus said, "I need to check on the Well anyway. You are welcome to join us, Warden Seth."

Seth saw his opportunity to leave anyway and never look back. But there was also a curiosity that he was struggling to deny. Magus was nothing like he expected. He had also grown close to the goblins who took care of him, and he wanted to make sure that they weren't being abused or taken advantage of. Because of this, Seth agreed and followed both Magus and Lawrence back toward the volcano.

As they walked down the path, all the goblins out and about gathered around Magus. A mother showed off her newly born baby, whom she named Tempest. A farmer gave Magus the biggest potato of his crop. Several of the younger goblins begged Magus and Lawrence to play with them. Magus gave each goblin attention and referred to them by name. He accepted the potato and praised its size and healthy look. He told the kids that he would send Lawrence out to play once they finished their business in the volcano. Lawrence was nonplussed about this development. But he did not resist either.

The path eventually led to the foot of the volcano and an entrance to a different cave system. Seth was not entirely enthused about returning underground, but he had made it this far. Once they were deep enough into the cave that Seth could no longer see, Magus lifted his gauntleted hand and produced an orb of bright light that stung Seth's eyes at first. It illuminated the tunnel well enough that he noticed this was not a normal cave. The rocks along the wall had a melted texture to them and the shape of the tunnel looked more like a tube than any of the cavern formations he saw while traveling with the goblins.

"Do not worry," Magus said, "the lava that once flowed through this tunnel is no longer a threat."

"I see," Seth said, not sure what else to say in return. "So what exactly is this Well that you mentioned earlier?"

"It is an old pathway," Magus said in a reminiscing voice. "It once led to the core of this world, where magic originated from. You could call it the Wellspring of Magic. Unfortunately, a volcano seemed to form on top of it. The Well is a constant, so the changing of the world would not alter it. However, lava tends to harden and block pathways. I have a team of miners excavating it, but it is slow going."

"These miners…" Seth started, "are they the mages you have been kidnapping?"

"No," he answered plainly, "it is the goblins who are creating new pathways. The mages are brought here to test a theory."

"You've been experimenting on them?" Seth said, unable to hide the disgust in his voice.

"No," Magus said, no shift in his echoing voice, "I only ask them to use their magic and take note of the shape and behavior of it. I then ask them to leave or send them back with an escort, if they request one."

"Why?"

"His theory," Lawrence interjected, "is that magic is alive."

"That is inaccurate," Magus said, with an edge of annoyance. "As I have told you, magic *is* alive. I am testing to see how much it has evolved. My theory is that magic is gaining sentience, or what you would call free will."

"How is magic alive?" Seth asked.

"Magic is a lifeform," Magus said. "It resides alongside the soul of another being. It is a part of that being while also being its own individual entity."

"Okay, let's pretend I understand what you're talking about," Seth said. "What does this mean, and what does it have to do with you?"

Just as he asked this, they emerged into a large, circular, hollow chamber. There were large stalactites pointing down at them like the jagged teeth of the volcano. And in the center of the cavern was a pit that was at least 40 feet across. When they approached it, the light from the orb projected shadows deep down into it that were as dark as what nightmares are made of. He could also make out stairs carved out of the edges of the pit, leading all the way down in a seemingly never-ending gyre.

Magus released the orb of light so that it would stay in the air beside him and reached up toward a stalactite. Instantly, the tip of one broke and fell directly into his grasp. He took the stalactite in both hands and did something that Seth could not see that made it glow a faint red, and then he snapped it in two. He tossed one end of the rock into the pit and waited. After what might have been a faint thud in the dark, Magus took the half of the rock in his hand and moved it toward his helmet, speaking to it.

"Clover? Can you hear me, Clover?"

There were several heartbeats where nothing happened, and then a voice came out of the rock.

"Yes, boss, I here."

"Good," he said with a soft edge of relief. "How is the progress of today's work?"

"Not good," came the gruff voice from the rock. "Ran into dwarves. Got punched. I punched back."

"I told you not to fight back. That will only stir up the rest of the nest. Close off that tunnel. Start on the next one."

"I sorry boss," the voice said after a moment's silence.

"It is okay, Clover," Magus said.

"Don't forget," Lawrence said, "his wife wants him back early tonight; something about making him a special meal."

"Right," Magus said. "Go ahead and close off that tunnel for now, then you and your workers head back to town. You have done good work today."

"Thanks, boss."

Magus placed the rock on the ground and then turned to Seth, as if just now remembering why he took the man here.

"To answer your question," he said, acting like the previous exchange didn't happen, "I do not like the way your people use magic." At the mention of *your people*, Seth got the sense that he wasn't referring to just humans. "You hurt and abuse it. Trap it in crystals. Force it to act on your will alone. Making it do things against its own nature. And unlike the animals of the land, it cannot bite back. I am going to go to the source of magic and speed up its evolution to give it the free will it needs. The trouble lies in getting there. The path is blocked physically, but it is also blocked chronologically."

"What he means," Lawrence said, "is that the source of magic is located at the bottom of this Well, but at a different time. Supposedly, at the beginning of time, if you can believe a man who doesn't clean his armor."

"That is another reason I am searching for mages," Magus said, ignoring his subordinate's lack of reverence. "I do not possess the ability to open the temporal path. I was hopeful when I found Lawrence, but his magic is that of forward temporal movement. He cannot reverse time. However, I am sure—in time—I will find a way."

There was a lull in the conversation in which they allowed the silence to breathe as Seth digested the conversation and what it meant if Magus were to succeed. "I don't know if I can fully condone your goal. But I would like to stay here until my horse arrives. I want to learn more about you and your mission."

"You are welcome to stay," Magus said. "Just so long as you do not hurt my people."

"You don't have to worry about that," Seth said with a toothy goblin grin. "Those little guys have grown on me." He then grew somber and quieter as he said, "I do have one last question: What exactly are you?"

"I am the first mage," he said, pride resonating with the echo of his voice. "I came from the source of magic and climbed out of the Wellspring of Magic 10,000 years ago."

Scout Field Report

Cycle 2, Day 10

For the Dark Lord's eyes only! All other eyes will be plucked.

Me and my subordinate begin our following of the Royal Wizard Malguinne. He an excellent enemy. After his defeat at your hands, he licked wounds and is retreating to the human capital (he did not actually lick wounds; that is human phrase. It sounds cute as if he were cat. But he is not cute). To think, he capable of surviving your wonderful magics. As you commanded, we will watch only. No attack.

Your humble Captain

Cycle 2, Day 14

The wizard making good progress back to the human capital. It was gracious of you to spare his horse. It a beautiful creature. He crossed the great river that separates your land from theirs. It was calm today, and he used his magic to freeze large section to cross over. We are finding it struggle to keep up on foot. But the wizard seems to need many rest periods to relieve himself of water.

Your willing Captain

Cycle 2, Day 21

My subordinate found a cute rabbit. It made for tasty lunch. The weather been cold but Spring soon coming. We seen some pretty blooming flowers. Would you like us to pick some for you on return?

Your subservient Captain

Cycle 3, Day 2

We nearly to the human capital. There been no conflict except for instance with a stray dog. He vicious, and the battle made for good practice. I sad to report that we lost the fight. But a few days' rations are a fair tradeoff for our lives. Oh, did you know great wizard Malguinne, a sleepwalker? I take back previous statement. He a little cute during his sleepwalking incidents. Me and subordinate had to lead him away from steep hill. It would been bad if he died that way. But we made sure he safe through the night.

Your sleep-deprived Captain

Cycle 3, Day 10

It been a few days since the wizard Malguinne reached the human capital. But as expected of such worthy enemy, he already acquired a group of adventurers to try again at beating you. There an elf archer, a roguish human, another human (I think) heavily armored and with a giant sword that at least three goblins tall, and an old man. The old man not the wizard; he a different old man.

Your well-traveled Captain

Cycle 3, Day 15

Me and subordinate finding it easier to keep up with the group pace. The armored one has been setting a slower pace and has been keeping close to the not-wizard old man. This new old man may actually be stronger than Malguinne if they are keeping pace with him and not Royal Wizard. We will keep a closer eye on new old man.

Your ever-cautious Captain

Cycle 3, Day 24

The wizard Malguinne took out a bandit ambush with powerful magic. It fun to watch. There were great explosions and lightning. The bandits were funny. They scattered and lost many supplies. Me and subordinate searched the area later and filled a bag with the supplies they left. We also found useless lantern. But it had pretty stone in it, so we keep it.

Your excited Captain
Cycle 3, Day 30

The wizard Malguinne sleepwalking again, but the other old man saw him and brought him back to campsite.

The man stayed awake rest of night to watch over wizard. He truly the leader of group.

Your grateful Captain

Cycle 4, Day 10

There has been significant increase in the movement of bandits in area. We have not been spotted. But we noticed the same bandits that the wizard Malguinne had attacked with magic have been stalking the group since the attack.

Your most literate Captain

Cycle 4, Day 12

The weather turning bad. I feel the wind strengthening. The group will be passing over great river in just a few days. We hope they cross before storm comes. Otherwise, there may be trouble.

Your nervous Captain

Chapter 7: The Book Wyrm
Cycle 4, Day 5

In the quiet and peaceful town of Leabmore, there was a quaint and cozy library. It was a simple, two-story wood building. On the first floor, there was a large main area surrounded by three book-covered walls, just in front of the service counter. The furniture in this section consisted of an oval table surrounded by wooden chairs, each with a worn but soft green pillow. There was also a rocking chair that was situated in front of a window that separated two book-shelves along the wall facing the service desk. To the right of the service desk was a staircase that led to a second floor of bookshelves, just past the "Restricted" sign.

Behind the desk sat a middle-aged woman with half-moon spectacles and curly red hair, messily tied up in what could kindly be called a bun. She wore a double layered dress with the frontal section of the dress being a dim gold and the secondary surrounding layer being dark green. She had a sleepy expression and yawned heavily in between sips of hot tea. The library had been open for the last hour, and she was performing her morning routine of sitting and wait-ing for anything to happen. Truthfully, the town of Leabmore was more of a small farming town than a book lovers hot spot. The mayor of the town had this library built and funded in the hopes of bringing in wealthy scholars and mages in order to generate more finances for Leabmore. It was a nice idea in theory; it just failed in execution. Once every few cycles, one of these clientele would stay in the town to utilize the library. But they never stayed long. Instead, the main crowd that visited the library were the townsfolk. There were a few regulars who would borrow a few books at a time and not return for several weeks. Eventually, they would remember that they forgot they had the books and return them unread. And then they would repeat the process. Others would come to the library, find a book, sit in the rocking chair, and read until the sun went down. The librarian would make these patrons some tea and would enjoy their comfortable silence.

The bell chimed as the first patron of the morning came into the library.

"Good morning, Colette," the librarian said with a smile. "I'm glad to see you have recovered."

"Oh, good morning, Ella," Colette said. She was an elderly woman with long and well-maintained white hair, a short, hunched posture, and a face the shape of an aged apple. "Pah, my husband overreacts every time I cough with more spittle than usual. It was nothing a night's rest wouldn't recover."

"I'm glad to hear that," Ella said, choosing not to bring up how she demanded the whole town to visit her one last time as she lay in her self-proclaimed death bed just a few nights previous. "Would you like to borrow anything today?"

Colette ignored this question, as she did every time Ella asked. She had no interest in reading, just spreading and hearing gossip. Ella didn't mind. She found that gossip and hot tea paired perfectly together.

"You know how I feel about you living alone," Colette said, apparently skipping the gossip and going straight to unsolicited advice. "What you need is a man to keep you safe."

"Yes, I know," Ella said. She let out a discrete sigh

from behind a well-trained smile. "But you really don't need to worry. I am doing just fine on my own."

"It's not safe," she insisted. "The men have seen a dragon stalking the town."

"No, they haven't," Ella said with calm exasperation. "They only found a single set of footprints, and they were way too small to be from a dragon. I'm pretty sure it's just the teenagers playing a prank like the one they pulled last year."

"That cockatrice was real! I seen it with my own two eyes," she said with a scoff. "Anyways, you be safe now, okay? No going out after sunfall."

With that, the older lady left before Ella could even respond.

"Yep," Ella said to herself once the lady left. "She is back to her old self." She couldn't help but smile with fond irritation. Ella began to clean the shelves for the tenth time that morning and paused as she found a book about a man cursed to be a dragon. She figured that one sounded interesting enough to distract her on this slow day.

***

The day progressed at a sluggish pace. Ella enjoyed the quiet as she attempted to read. But her mind kept trailing off. She found herself daydreaming about the types of adventures mages go on. Ella had only met a handful of mages, but they were always so secretive about their personal stories. She imagined a group of powerful mages marching to the Dark Lord's domain. Mowing down mobs of goblins with incredible magical force. And when they finally came face to face with evil, they would work together to seal him away after a grueling battle. Maybe one or two would become mortally wounded. Maybe the Dark Lord would come back after a century and begin his evil scheme all over again.

Her gaze was on the pages of her book, but her mind was several miles away when the bell rang again, and the second patron of the day came in.

"Good morn—" Ella began to say, until she saw the person who had entered. "The answer is no!"

"You didn't even hear me out," said a tall, thin man. He looked like he fought against sleep deprivation every night and always lost. His shoulder-length black hair fell from his head, heavy with greasy slickness. Under his bloodshot eyes were large dark bags, and his face was a patchwork of dark, poorly groomed facial hair. "I have the goddess-given right to read whatever I damn well please!"

"And as I have told you over and over, Vincent…" she said, making sure to pronounce every syllable with exact sharpness, "once you get a signed voucher or show proper identification, I will gladly let you read them. But until then, you will just have to make due."

"I just need to borrow one book," Vincent said. "One book isn't going to kill you!"

"It's not about me," she retorted. "It is a law mandated by the king. I can't even read them."

"No one has to know."

"My answer is final. No!"

There were several long moments where Ella was not sure what he was going to do. His gaze kept going from her to the "Restricted" sign leading to the second floor. She knew he had the strength to overpower her, but it would be a short-lived victory. The second a resident of the Leabmore discovered the altercation, he would be dealt with swiftly. Part of her wished he would go ahead and lash out so that she wouldn't have to deal with him anymore. But the rest of her hadn't quite decided what level of dangerous he was.

"You're going to regret this!" Vincent shouted finally and bashed his way through the doors.

She dropped herself into her chair as her hands and legs started to shake slightly. This man had only been in town for a week, and he had managed to get under everyone's skin. She began to write a letter to the mayor to get him to do something about this menace to her library and sanity when the bell chimed again. She was about to yell some colorful profanities toward the man she thought had returned, but she instantly changed her greeting as soon as she realized it wasn't him but three teenagers. An elf girl and two human boys. The girl was the tallest of the bunch and had long, waist-length hair. One of the human boys had blond hair, and the other human, the shortest, had black hair. They had patches of dirt and what she hoped wasn't dried blood on their faces and arms. Their clothing was similarly dirty and torn in places. The shortest boy had burn marks on his clothing. Ella fought against the urge to clean them right there on the spot. She considered at least feeding them or giving them a rag. Maybe a good spot in the conversation could lead up to something along those lines.

"Good evening," she said as she regained her composure. "Welcome to the library. I am Ella, daughter of Ellanor. How may I help you three today?"

"Good evening," said the shortest one. "I am Samuel, son of Seth."

"I am Caleb, Son of Calin," said the other human boy.

"And I am Za'rie, erm, daughter of an elf," said the elf girl with more than just a little awkwardness. "We are looking for some books about magic."

142

"You are in luck," Ella said with a practiced smile. "We have quite a number of fictional stories filled with magic and adventure. Do you have a preference in authors?"

"No," Samuel said while glancing around the shelves. "We are looking for books about how to use magic."

"Oh," said the librarian. "I am so sorry, but our magical non-fiction collection is unavailable to the public. It is restricted for mages or preapproved scholarly use only."

"I am a mage," Caleb said as he produced a blue orb of light in his hands that turned into a blue crab. The crab then proceeded to crawl up Caleb's arm and rested on his shoulder. "So, does that mean I can use the collection?"

"Of course," she said, mystified by his display. "If you have the appropriate documentation and identification provided by the Council of Magi."

"The what now?" Caleb said with a slight head tilt, a tilt that the crab imitated.

"Right," the librarian said with patient annoyance. "If you want to get proper identification, I would recommend going to the mage school near the capital. They can give you the required training as well. But until then, you are welcome to use the rest of our collection here, just not any of the material from the restricted collection. If there is anything else I can help you with—"

"Look!" Za'rie said, her voice sharply picking up in volume. "We need to learn what we can quickly and be on our way. We don't have time to do things the proper way."

Samuel gave Za'rie a sharp look that the elf completely ignored or didn't notice. Caleb's face contorted into a pure panic as his eyes darted between both of his companions as if they were fire and alcohol only inches from collision.

"Unfortunately," Ella said, putting as much authority as

143

possible into each syllable, "that is our policy here at the library. I would gladly have a town guard *properly* escort you off of the premises if you would like to continue down this futile path."

Both Za'rie and Samuel were opening their mouths to say something, though to different people.

"Thank you, Ella," Caleb said before the others could speak. "You have been very helpful. I think we are just going to see if we can find something to eat in town before we move on. I hope you have a great day."

His speaking quickened with every sentence as he held onto both his companions and practically dragged them through the door. Ella was glad to see them gone. Why are there so many people trying to view these books all of a sudden? And why aren't they going about it the right way? She rubbed her temples and tried to relax in her less-than-comfortable wood chair.

The rest of the evening was mostly uneventful. She had a few more people coming in to look for books. One elderly gentleman came in just to talk. He was a sweet old man who lost his wife years ago, and his children had scattered across the kingdom. She had accidentally become his talking buddy. She didn't mind, though. He was pleasant, even if he told the same handful of stories every visit. As her last visitor of the day had left, she began the process of closing down. She put up the books that patrons had returned and cleaned up some newly formed clutter around the reading areas.

After locking up, she went into her private area behind the desk. She lit the hearth and cooked a few potatoes for dinner and then went to bed. She reflected on the events of the day and remembered she never finished the letter to the mayor. She told herself that she would get to that tomorrow.

***

Ella woke to loud banging on the front door. She groggily lifted herself out of bed and into the coldness of night. There were some embers still alive in the hearth, which she used to light a candle. The frantic sounds of fists on wood continued as she made her way to the main area of the library. She was wearing a pale lavender nightgown that had since aged to a dull white, and it was as warm in the spring night as a blanket of snow.

"Not open yet!" she yelled at whoever decided midnight was the time for books. "Come back in the morning!"

But the barrage of explosive knocking on the door continued and was accompanied by panicked shouts.

"Let us in!"

"You're in danger!"

She recognized the voices as two of the teenagers from earlier in the day. She didn't know what this was about, but she didn't get a bad sense from the kids. She approached the door with trepidation, and upon unlocking and opening it, all three burst into the library. Caleb took her by the arm and led her away from the door while Za'rie and Samuel relocked the door and grabbed what furniture they could to barricade it.

"What in the nine hells are you three doing!" she demanded, recoiling her arm out of Caleb's grasp.

"We screwed up!" Za'rie said. Her eyes were bloodshot, and she looked like she had just finished crying.

"We screwed up?" Samuel yelled back at her. "I told you that guy was crazy!"

145

"Fine," Za'rie said, matching his volume and stepping toward him with clenched fists. "I screwed up! Are you happy to hear that? But at least I *did* something. All you did was hesitate and overthink. If it were up to you, we would still be planning with no progress."

"And now we are several steps backward!" Samuel shot back, stepping toward her so that there was nearly no space between them.

"Will the two of you stop bickering for five seconds and explain what happened?" Ella exclaimed. The two were immediately silenced as they turned to look at the librarian and then turned away with embarrassment written all over their red faces.

"We started to ask around town about the magic books," Caleb said once he realized the other two weren't going to speak up. "Everyone said the same thing as you about needing permission. Some seemed annoyed. Others just took it as the norm. But a man named Vincent found us while we were asking around, and he started to rant and rave about the unfair system and how knowledge was being kept away from the people. He told us he had a plan to change things. Samuel turned him down without hesitation or our feedback."

At this, Caleb gave Samuel a scolding look. Samuel said nothing but grew a deeper shade of crimson. "We had a bit of a tiff over the decision afterward, and well—"

"That's when I went to Vincent of my own accord," Za'rie continued with a guilty grimace. "He told me about his plan. Or at least he told me exactly what he wanted to. He asked me to track down a creature that had made a nest nearby. He said he wanted to scare it away from town and win everyone's favor and that would gain us access to the books. So, I helped him track it down only to find out it was some kind of large lizard, or small, wingless dragon. That's when the man turned out to be a mage. I think he can control animals, or at least he thinks he can. Last I saw, he was trying to dominate the creature, but I expect he should be here any minute."

"Oh dear goddess," Ella said. "It's not a dragon. It's probably a drake."

"What's a drake, and how do we fight it?" Caleb asked.

"By Her breath…give me a second," Ella said as she attempted to calm down and recollect what she knew about drakes. "Okay, so even though they look like dragons, they are significantly inferior. They don't breathe fire. Their scales are easier to pierce. And their underbelly is scaleless, so that is where they are most vulnerable. It will try and attack with claws and biting, but if someone can get underneath—"

That's when something large and heavy crashed against the doors. The three teenagers rushed toward it, putting their weight against it. Ella froze, dumbfounded. This library was her life. And now both it and her actual life were on the line because of a madman wanting to read books. How did it come to this?

"Ella!" Samuel called out behind him. "Do you have anything here we can use against it?"

"I'm a librarian!" she said, her voice overflowing with rage. "I have books!"

There was nothing she could do. She had no weapons. No magic. No secret knowledge. She was going to die here, unable to even defend herself.

The thing outside continued to bash through the front

door. The hinges creaked under the strain. There was the sound of splintering wood from the other side. The three teens were struggling. But the lock and the barricade did not break. Then, all at once, it stopped. For several moments, the world was silent as they all held their breath, listening to the fading footfalls on the other side of the door. Ella was about to break into a hysterical fit of relieved laughter when the sound of shattering glass broke the silence first.

She looked over to the window and saw a large, horse-sized creature crawling through effortlessly. It was a lizard-like creature with dull, laurel green scales covering every inch of it, except for the faded silver underbelly starting just below the throat. On the back of the drake was the outsider from the previous day with an expression of pure mania.

"Oh, hello, my dear librarian," Vincent said with a tilt of his head. "I think I'm going to read some books. But first…" He pointed at a bookshelf and said something in-comprehensible, to which the drake responded by slashing at the books with razor-sharp talons.

"Not the books!" Ella yelled.

"Stay back," Caleb told her. "We will buy time until the town guards get here."

"Za'rie, Caleb, flank it. Go for the underbelly," Samuel said. "I will get its attention."

"Got it!" they said in unison.

Samuel pulled a wooden shield out from under his cape and charged forward, raising the shield to protect his face. Za'rie unhooked an axe that hung at her waist and took the left side of the creature. Caleb said something that Ella could not hear, and she saw a flash of blue light that passed through his arms, causing them to grow into large, red crab pincers as he took position on the right side.

"Ah, a fellow mage," Vincent said. "If you stay out of my way, I may let you read one of my books."

"It's not too late to stop this," Caleb said. "We can talk this out!"

Vincent gave a cracked smile and commanded his beast to attack. It raised its right claw and struck at Caleb. But Za'rie took this opening to strike the underbelly with her axe. Ella expected the axe to sink into the creature. But all it did was nick it. There was a small trickle of blood, and the drake hissed as it disregarded its attack on Caleb and continued its momentum to slam Za'rie with a whip of its tail. Samuel rushed forward in front of her and took the tail to his shield. Both he and Za'rie were sent flying backward, crashing to the ground beside each other with loud grunts of pain. Ella ran to them and helped them back onto their feet once she quickly checked them for any broken bones. Caleb was attempting to jump into reach of the unarmored area with his claws, but the drake kept swatting him away.

"Its soft underbelly isn't very soft," Za'rie said as she looked at her axe. "Now what?"

Ella's mind was a whirlwind of thoughts. However, most of these thoughts were panic-induced and held little substance other than imagining how she was going to die. Then she remembered a passage from a book she read.

"He's using mental magic which requires concentration!" she blurted out. "We need to focus on Vincent. Can you knock him out?"

Samuel's eyes darted in every direction, calculating. Then his gaze fell on his shield. "I have an idea. Caleb, fall back with me! Za'rie, keep it distracted."

"Right," they said.

"And be safe," Samuel said to Za'rie. It was not an order

but a plea.

"You too," she said, returning the concern.

"What can I do?" Ella said.

"If you have meat, get it," Samuel ordered.

Ella nodded and dashed for her room. She didn't have anything fresh. But she did have some dried meat in her pantry. She quickly got a handful and ran back to the chaos. She now saw Za'rie being swiped and snapped at by the drake but managing to dodge out of its reach. Unfortunately, the drake's attacks were still landing against the bookshelves. Torn pieces of paper were scattering like leaves in the fall. She ignored that for now and looked at the two boys. Samuel was positioning himself in clear view of the drake and its rider. He was kneeling on one knee and held his shield on his shoulder like a plate, angling it toward the creature. Caleb was behind Samuel, in a position as if ready to spring. She then saw that his boots had been replaced with what looked like sabatons, or armored shoes, made of red crab chitin.

Samuel shouted, and Caleb ran from behind at full speed, jumping just before coming to the boy. He aimed to land on the wooden shield, but just as his feet were about to make contact, he was propelled forward with incredible speed. He flailed awkwardly for a moment before taking control of his fall and reaching out with one claw. Vincent and his beast were so distracted by the elf that the claw to his throat took him completely by surprise. Caleb crashed into the man, sending them both to the ground, with Vincent breaking Caleb's fall.

The drake paused and took stock of his surroundings. It was no longer under Vincent's control. Now, it was a wild animal loose in an unfamiliar environment, surrounded by people with weapons. It began to hiss and bare its fangs, arching its neck, preparing to strike.

"Open the front door!" Ella shouted as she understood what the meat was for.

The librarian didn't hesitate. She waved the food in the air and shouted to get the creature's attention. It focused its reptilian gaze on her hand, its forked tongue flicking through the air, and all of its shock and confusion were replaced by hunger. Cold dread ran through Ella's veins as she made a mad dash for the entrance with the drake scurrying toward her. All she could hear was the horrific sound of claws skittering on wood, getting closer and closer.

Samuel and Za'rie were clearing the doorway as Caleb was restraining a hopefully unconscious Vincent. They swung the door open wide just in time for Ella to pass through and toss the chunks of meat. She dove to the side and watched the drake shoot past her and snap at the meat in midair. It was only at this moment that Ella noticed that a crowd of townsfolk were scattering from the library and reentering their homes.

Once the creature realized it was out in the open air, it looked around and saw the wooded outskirts of town and darted toward its nest like a startled lizard. It would have to be dealt with in a more permanent manner, but Ella would let the mayor deal with that. She had a mess to clean and a heart to calm down.

***

Several hours passed, and several more candles were lit as Ella and the teens started the cleaning process. She tasked the three to sort all the damaged books in one spot. She would take stock of all the books needing to be replaced, calculate the cost, and send the bill to the mayor. He was going to be a busy man in the near future. Vincent had been escorted to the town's jailhouse, gagged and blindfolded to prevent him from using magic. Word would be sent to the closest city, and a Warden would come and escort him to Previa. She looked around at the damaged library. It could have been far worse than broken shelves and destroyed books. The librarian wanted to be furious at the teens for causing all this. But she couldn't really work herself up to that level of anger right now. They were just kids, after all, and were tricked by an absolute psychopath. She glanced at the three and could see that there was a growing distance between Za'rie and Samuel, and they both purposefully avoided looking in the other's direction.

"I hope this has taught you all a valuable lesson," Ella said. "Don't trust everything an adult tells you. I can take care of the rest if—"

"But you are at fault here too," Za'rie said. Her voice was hollow and melancholic and lacked the conviction the words needed.

"Za'rie!" Caleb said.

"Excuse me?" Ella stammered.

"No," Samuel jumped in with the same tone of voice as his companion. "Za'rie's right."

"Samuel!" Caleb said.

"No, I mean it," Samuel continued. "This whole thing started because you keep important information away from people. Telling people that they aren't allowed to know something just because they don't have authorization is stupid. Why have books that can't be read?"

"Look, kid," Ella said with a sigh. "I don't like it either, but it's a royal decree."

"It's a bad law," Za'rie said with growing confidence.

"This is how it has always been," Ella said.

"That's just a lazy excuse," Za'rie said. "If a tradition is bad, stop letting it be a tradition."

"Books on magic are dangerous," Ella said. "You saw what that man did without the books; just imagine what he could do with them."

"If they are so dangerous," Samuel said, "doesn't that mean letting some read them and others not create an imbalance in power?" Samuel paused then added, "How did you know breaking his concentration would work? Shifting magic doesn't work that way."

Ella could feel the heat on her cheeks as she remembered exactly what book she got that information out of, and in which section of the second floor it currently resided. She chose to do the most mature thing she could think of and just ignored Samuel's questions. She was too tired to think of a good justification for any of it, and she just wanted to get through the rest of the night. She looked toward Caleb, who had been silent this whole time, hoping he would talk some sense into his friends. There was no apprehension on his face as she had expected, just a relieved smile as he looked from one friend to the other.

"Stay right there," Ella said with a defeated, deflated tone. She crossed the library on tired, sore legs and went up the stairs past the "Restricted" sign. She quickly searched through the shelf of books on magic and came across a title she had seen a few mages studying: *Magic Theory and Magical Application*. She flipped through the book and noted that it was in excellent condition, minus a little wear and tear of the binding. She rejoined the three downstairs and handed the book to Samuel.

"This book was severely damaged in the drake attack," she said. "I will have to get a replacement anyway, so why don't you take this with you on your journey."

"Thank you," Samuel said.

"Does this mean—" started Za'rie.

"I will consider what you have said," Ella interrupted. "Nothing more. But I recommend that you three leave town before people start to accuse you of assisting Vincent."

They said their farewells and promptly left. Again, Ella was alone. She continued to clean for a time, but the events of the night finally caught up with her. She was drained and at the far end of exhaustion. As she slumped into the chair behind her desk, she started to dwell on the things the two teens had said. The conversation ate at her resolve like a bookworm. Of course, the king was right to put a limit on who could learn about magic. Not just anyone should be able to use magic. Wait, could anyone use magic or just mages? How would you know if you were a mage? Could you be a mage your whole life and never know? If that were the case, not knowing would prevent people from knowing if they should know. She rethought her last mental sentence a few times, questioning if it had even made sense. Ella looked at the restricted section above her, and for the second time that night, she went up the stairs and browsed through the titles. The book titled *How to Tame Your Magic* caught her eye, and she took it down. She went to the privacy of her room and began to read.

Excerpt from the Journal of Tyberion
Cycle 4, Day 13

T he weather has been worsening day by day. Malguinne has managed to divert the worst of the storm from our path. However, one can never truly conquer nature. Today, it is as if all the miserable weather we should have received is compounding on top of us. As much as I enjoy witnessing the wizard struggling, I worry deeply for Buddy's safety. His health is waning to the point that even the elf has taken to watching over the old man, albeit only while Buddy sleeps and when he thinks there are no witnesses to his moments of weakness.

The journey thus far has been easygoing. Our only strife came from the attempted bandit attack. I have had my share of mishaps in past adventures, so it is refreshing for a peaceful one. Buddy, however, seems to be crestfallen by this. It is uncomfortable how fervently he wants to see a dragon. I have seen a dragon but only once in my life, and that was when I had both eyes. If I could go through what is left of my life without even a hint of a dragon again, I would be indebted to the goddess. Explaining to Buddy how powerful, intelligent, and dangerous dragons are in this world yielded the opposite effect as intended. He only became more excited to see one. John is not helping matters by indulging Buddy with the story of how he outwitted a dragon and stole her egg to win the favor of a beautiful princess. This, of course, was a complete fabrication. John has too many limbs for someone who stole a dragon egg.

Buddy's drive to see the most dangerous situations

leads me to believe one of two things in Buddy's world: Either it is mundane and boring to the point that his people actively seek out life-threatening situations for pleasure, or they live in near-constant danger to the point that they have become numb to fear. No matter which way the compass swings, I do not think it is a world I could live in easily.

On a note of the unusual… As we were nearing an elven town, our elf companion became anxious enough that we had to travel off-road to avoid getting too close to it. He was a blubbering mess. Barely able to speak. Always glancing over his shoulder as if looking for eyes in the shadows. I would have found it amusing had the fear in his eyes not been all too real and familiar. I took over the role of cook for the few days when the elf was…unwell. It was unanimously unliked. But my attempts to create something edible allowed for some much-needed mirth among the group. Even Rythel ate with us during those few days. I could swear I saw him crack a smile when Malguinne nearly drowned himself with ale, trying to make his tongue forget the taste of my food that first night.

We are nearing the end of our mission. We will be crossing the Ophidian River tomorrow and entering enemy territory. If the Dark Lord is as powerful as I have heard, then we are in for a battle that I expect will never be forgotten. However, my main concern is Buddy. I do not know why the wizard brought him on such a journey. I am sure he would not answer me correctly if I were to ask, and I doubt Buddy himself knows. If I were to make a bet, I would say the old man is crucial to the wizard's plans. I and the rest of the group were formed with so little thought that I am sure we are just bodyguards to ensure safe travel. Or, perhaps more accurately, living shields. No matter what happens, Buddy's safety is my objective.

Chapter 8: From The Ashes Into The Fire
Cycle 4, Day 14

Buddy struggled to stay on the horse as the wind howled and raged around him. He was drenched, and the cold stabbed into his bones and joints. Visibility was nearly impossible. All Buddy could see through the curtains of rain were the people within arm's reach. Did adventure stories omit bad weather? Or were they usually just another obstacle for adventurers to overcome? Malguinne's magic seemed to only delay the storm, not get rid of it entirely. What is the point of magic if it can't solve all the adventurers problems? He looked at his other companions and felt guilty that he was the only one on horseback.

"I can walk for a little bit if someone needs to rest their legs," Buddy said.

"No, you are not to dismount the horse," Rythel said, not unkindly. "It is the safest location for you at this time."

"R-r-r-right," John said with chattering teeth. "W-w-w-we are j-j-j-j-ust fine."

Tyberion was in front of Buddy, guiding his horse by the reins. He hadn't spoken much today. Though Buddy imagined it was hard to be heard through a closed visor and raging winds. How difficult was it to be fully armored in the pouring rain? Were his metal boot armor things pooling water? Isn't that how you get foot fungus, or is it gang-green or gangrene? Buddy became lost in thought in an attempt to escape the miserable weather. It wasn't working in the slightest.

They had traveled for a few hours in horrible conditions before they finally reached the river. With the rain going on for days, the water had risen higher than the river banks, and the current was wild and forceful. Debris of logs and limbs crashed and splintered against each other violently. There was no way they could cross this river conventionally.

Thankfully, they had a wizard.

Buddy slid ungracefully off of the horse as Malguinne stepped toward the river. He was outside the range of decent visibility, but the group could still see the gray, wizardly shape of Malguinne raising his hands open and skyward. Buddy couldn't help but imagine the wizard spontaneously doing jazz hands and breaking into song and dancing in the rain. He would have stifled a chuckle if the next thing to happen wasn't terrifyingly impressive.

Through the heavy downpour, Buddy could see the river changing direction. Not left or right or even backward, but upward. The water rose and curved as if a tunnel made of glass appeared along their path. The newly unwatered river bottom path was muddy and had several small puddles along with some movement from unknown creatures.

"Hurry through!" Malguinne yelled with a hardness to his voice that did not seem at all like the kindly old man. He continued to hold his hands up.

As Buddy got closer, he could see his arms shaking under what could only be the weight of the water.

"Go one at a time. I will go last. Buddy, you go before me."

No one argued. The roguish man was visibly hesitant, so Rythel went first, taking the horse's reins in hand to lead it across. John went next. Tyberion was on the edge of the water tunnel with Buddy by his side. He hesitated for a moment as he looked at his elderly companion and then took his first step forward.

That was when the curved water collapsed in on itself and splashed onto both Buddy and Tyberion. They quickly turned toward the wizard. Their sounds of shock were engulfed by the storm. Malguinne was lying crumpled on the ground, and standing over him was the dark, looming figure of a man holding a large, blunt-looking hook. Buddy took a closer look and realized that it wasn't something he was holding. If the rain weren't completely obscuring what he thought he was looking at, he would have sworn the man's right hand was a giant crab claw. Dark shadows walked into Buddy's field of vision as more men started to appear.

Tyberion unsheathed his greatsword and charged the leader, who in turn charged forward to meet him. The leader reached forward, grabbing the middle of the blade with his clawed hand, and snapped it shut with a twist. The sword shattered, and Buddy saw the warrior freeze for a fraction of a second longer than he should have. The clawed man took advantage of this moment and struck Tyberion's helmet with enough force to dent it. The knight dropped to his knees, wobbling as he attempted to right himself. A trickle of blood dripped from his chin and mixed with the rain. The clawed villain prepared for another strike, but Buddy could not and would not just stand by and watch his friend be killed in front of him. He ran toward the man, and without a second's thought for his own well-being, he put himself directly in the way of the oncoming claw.

Just as the claw was about to make contact, it stopped

for just a heartbeat and then was propelled backward, causing the man to be knocked back, landing in a mess of mud. Buddy did not hesitate. He instantly grabbed his armored companion, helping him onto his feet, and then the two of them ran.

"How the hells does this keep happening!" shouted the man on the ground. "Kill that iron bastard, but leave gramps to me!"

Buddy didn't know what direction they were running in. He didn't know if they were even able to outrun their pursuers. The rain made it hard to see, but he could just make out the shadowy figures gaining on them. He could feel his heart struggling to keep up. His breath was a stabbing pain in his chest. His every step fighting against the pull of the mud.

When a small green hand grabbed his sleeve, he was sure he was hallucinating.

"This way, human," said the waist-high green creature. Tyberion stumbled as Buddy led him in the new direction. He was sure this was one of the worst decisions he had ever made. But given the choice between following a creature that he could neutralize by sitting on versus letting the people behind catch up, he decided on the former. The creature made them take a sharp turn to the left. One moment, it was just the same empty field as was in the other direction, but the next moment, a patch of ground lifted like a hatch.

"Jump," the green person said, standing before the hole in the ground. It was dark, and its depths were impossible to calculate. Tyberion turned his helmeted head toward Buddy, nodded, and then jumped down the pit. Buddy jumped next, being caught in the dark by metal hands.

The old man was placed on his feet and, for the first

time, was able to catch his breath and slow his beating heart. But it did not slow. It pounded like a rhythmless drum. His breathing worsened as he struggled to get enough air. He fell to his knees. The edges of the world were fading away like the burning edges of a photograph. There was a hollowness in his mind that kept away all clear thought as he lay collapsed on the ground. Then, there was an absolute void that swallowed up the darkness of the underground pit.

***

From the darkness emerged a voice. Cold and bitter. "Get out! I can't even look at you!"

A new pain developed in Buddy's chest as he recognized the voice as his own. Shame flooded through him as he remembered the scene. An image emerged in the darkness. He saw a solitary young man with short brown hair facing away from him and slowly walking deeper into the void of his memory. The man stopped and turned his head to look back one last time. But the face was obscured by swirling emptiness. Buddy couldn't remember his own son's face. He knew his son said something here. But he couldn't remember any of the words. Only his own response.

"I thought I raised you better than this."

The young man froze, and even though his face was a void, there was only pain where his face should have been. Buddy wanted to reach out to his son. But it wasn't him that was there, just the voice of himself from the past, echoing bitterly through the darkness. The young man turned away from his father and disappeared into the nothingness. Leaving Buddy alone with his regret.

***

Buddy opened his eyes. At first he only saw colors. Blobs of green. A streak of silver. Warm, dancing shades of yellow and red. Slowly, the colors grew into shapes. Going from simple to more defined. Buddy blinked over and over. The silver streak became a silver bar, became the tin man, became finally, Tyberion. The blobs of green became two green circles, became finally two creatures that looked like a strange combination of goblin and Neanderthal. Around the three were curved walls of rock and dirt. They were in a large tunnel, presumably where they landed after falling down the hole. The tunnel was lit by a small lantern that had a stone that shone like fire. Tyberion had his helmet off and wore a bandage wrap stained red on his head. And on his face was the heartbreaking expression of a man looking at a filled coffin.

"Don't look at me like that," Buddy said through a coughing fit. "Just lost my breath is all."

Buddy attempted to sit up, but one of the goblins gently pushed him to stay lying.

"Stupid human," the goblin hissed. "You lose more than breath had us no been here."

At first glance, Buddy thought the goblin was wearing a metal helmet shaped like a bowl. At second glance, Buddy realized it was a bowl that was painted to look like a helmet. He, at least the old man assumed both goblins were male, also wore what could pass for a military uniform, as long as the bar for passing was below sea level. A medieval scholar from his world could probably take the hodgepodge patchwork and see the individual pieces from their respective origin. But to Buddy, it was clothing soup.

"You lived at death's door just now," the second goblin said. "You have weak heart. You suffered from Heart Flight

162

and then Heart Fight. My medicine help but not cure."

The second goblin wore a white bonnet and a white trench coat-looking piece of clothing that overflowed from the goblin, extending past his arms and trailing behind him like a wedding dress. He also had a satchel over his shoulder that read "MEDCINE."

"Umm, thank you," Buddy said. "But why did you save me? And where are we?"

"We save you because you needed it," the first goblin said as he puffed up his chest and grinned with all his pointy teeth showing. "You are in our tunnel. We have been given orders to watch over Malguinne. But we cannot watch over Malguinne if his leader dead."

"I'm lost," Buddy said, looking over toward his companion for a better explanation.

"These goblins are servants of the Dark Lord," Tyberion said with an almost convincing monotone voice that covered the melancholic undertones. "It seems he was expecting us and has had spies watching us this whole time. They are a danger to our cause. However, they saved your life. I am not of the ability to lift a weapon against them. That all is momentarily irrelevant. Tell me honestly: How sick are you? They say you have a hard lump over your heart. Is that the cause of your malady?"

"I'm sorry, I should have told y'all," Buddy said with a sigh. "I have…a problem with my heart. It's something I've had for a long time. It's manageable with medicine and a device. The lump over my heart is a thing we call a pacemaker in my world. It keeps my heart beating how it needs to. Problem is, it's out of the stuff that makes it work. It's called electricity, my world's version of magic. I was supposed to get it refilled on the day I woke up in this world. It's not exactly an immediate death sentence without it. But it's not been a walk in the park either. I don't know how limited my time is here, so I need to get home soon."

"I see," Tyberion said, his eyes not quite meeting Buddy's. "I suppose knowing would not have changed the situation, and my resolve to see this mission through remains the same. But I will do everything in my power to see you home. You have my word."

"Thank you," Buddy said. "Though I think our first step is to rescue Malguinne… somehow. And don't think I forgot about that leader nonsense." Buddy looked at the two goblins with cutting eyes.

"If it secret, I apologize for spoiling," the first goblin said. "But it obvious. You set pace for group. They look out for your safety more than their self. You watch over wizard when he sleepwalks. And you throw yourself in front of death blow to save companion. You are leader."

"It would be best not to argue their logic," Tyberion said, with the resignation of one who has already tried.

"Fine, fine," Buddy said. "But I would like to thank both of you for saving my life. I am Buddy, and if my friend hasn't introduced himself yet, he is Tyberion."

"What his name if he did introduce himself?" the second goblin asked. The first goblin promptly removed his bowl helmet and gave his colleague a swift bop on the head.

"I am Captain," the first goblin said as he secured his helmet back on. "This is my subordinate, General."

"I see," Buddy said, figuring the military ranking system must be different here. "I take it you prefer to be addressed by rank rather than name?"

"That are our names," the second goblin said, with a confused lilt to his voice.

Buddy blinked a few times as he let that sink in. A few thoughts started to materialize in his mind, but each was shot down with the fact that there were no words in his dictionary that could even remotely represent these thoughts. Instead, he just nodded and mumbled a polite, "Nice to meet you."

"Once the storm clears," Tyberion started, "we should try and find a way to rescue the wizard."

"No!" cried General. "Your friend not in state to be traveling or rescuing!"

"Thank you for your concern," Buddy said. "But we can't just stay here. I'm feeling better now."

"No," Captain said. "You go, you die."

"Is that a threat?" Tyberion said as his hand went to the hilt of his broken sword, and Buddy saw the hand flinch as if Tyberion remembered the damage just at that moment.

"Not threat, one-eyed monster," General said. "Your friend too weak to travel. He needs treatment."

"Or phoenix magic," Captain said in a thoughtful whisper. "It no work for goblins, but it very effective for human. Phoenix is immortal. It feathers heal and sometime can undo death if fresh enough. We can take you."

"I see," Tyberion said. Buddy could see his companion thinking this through with slow deliberation. "Right then, take us to the phoenix. If this can heal my friend, then I will be in your debt."

"Now, hold on," Buddy said. "What about Malguinne? We can't waste time on side quests. If we rescue him, maybe he can do something about my condition."

"No," Tyberion said. "It would be unwise to conduct a rescue mission in our current state. I am weaponless, and

165

your health is poor. I say we seek out this phoenix; perhaps we can convince it to aid us in more ways than one."

"Fine," Buddy said with a resigned sigh. "Let's get this done and over with quickly. I do hope Malguinne will be okay."

"I'm sure he will be fine," Tyberion said. "Something tells me he has been in worse situations."

The two goblins agreed to lead the way, but only after Buddy had more rest, which he reluctantly did. It was hard to sleep in the cold, damp tunnel, but after General gave him some more medicine, Buddy fell into a deep, dreamless sleep. He woke up hours later feeling significantly better but still felt a heavy tiredness that lingered in his chest.

They traveled down the tunnel for several hours, making sure to take several rests along the way. General kept a close eye on Buddy and checked his pulse almost every half hour. After a few hours, Buddy noticed that the path split into several different tunnels, and the one the goblins took them down started to incline and kept turning to the left. It felt like they were going up in a corkscrew-like fashion.

Finally, the tunnel came to an end, with a large boulder blocking the path. The two goblins pushed it with ease out of the way. It must have been significantly lighter than it looked. The blocked exit led them into a shallow cave, with a large opening letting in a blinding amount of sunlight. After the goblins resealed the tunnel entrance, they led the two humans out of the cave, where Buddy saw that they were near the top of a large hill. The storm had cleared up sometime during their travel in the tunnels, and Buddy could see the great river some ways in the distance; it stretched further than his eye could see. On the opposite side of the river was a dense green forest, and even further were large mountains that were fading due to distance. The new green of spring and the blooming of color made the landscape look like a beautiful oil painting.

"He is just a little farther," Captain said as he led them higher up the hill.

"Hey, so, I'm new to all this," Buddy said. "I'm a little confused about, well, nearly everything. But why exactly are you helping your enemy?"

"You not our enemy," Captain said. "We your enemy."

"I don't see how the order makes it any different," Buddy said.

"You journey to our land to fight," Captain explained. "We don't go to your land to fight."

"Your people have been kidnapping mages in our land," Tyberion countered.

"We don't kidnap," General said with an edge of defensiveness. "Only borrow. We send them back unharmed and well-fed."

"Okay, so why do you *borrow* mages?" Buddy asked.

"Don't know," Captain said. "Dark Lord asks, and we do."

"Well, what is his deal?" Buddy asked.

"He don't make deal, he just do," General said, and Buddy could swear the goblin was resisting a smile.

"No, I mean, what does he want?" Buddy asked. "What is he after? World domination? The enslavement of the kingdom?"

"He want to make world better for magic and for goblin," Captain said.

"Make it better how?" Tyberion asked, his voice edging close to disbelief.

"He explain better," Captain said. "But magic is sad

and hurting. He want to heal magic. Make it like it should be. And for goblins, we want to be part of human society. We tired of living in ruins and alone."

"That doesn't sound evil," Buddy said, trying to hide his disappointment.

"That because he not evil," Captain said.

"Then why do you call him the Dark Lord?"

"Because he wear dark armor and is our lord," General said.

"Please tell me you're joking," Buddy said, no longer able to hide his disappointment.

"Little bit," General said with a dimpled smile that showed too many teeth. "In truth, humans and elves fear him cause he want to change the world and change the way they use magic. He labeled Dark Lord by them. We goblins like name, so we use it too. Us using or not using name don't change other's perspective. Dwarves are indifferent. Merfolk and other sea races no can fight on land. All other races won't fight. They think fighting us waste of resources."

"But—" Buddy began.

"Talk more later," Captain interrupted. "We here now."

Here turned out to be a nearly barren hilltop. The earth was scorched and smelled of a bonfire past its expiration date. What few trees were scattered around the edges looked like burnt twigs sticking out of the ground. As he walked through the dirt and ash, Buddy saw small dots of green. Hints of new life peaking through the aftermath of a fire. Ahead of them, at the center of the hilltop, was a crimson bird the size of a house. To Buddy, it looked like a giant version of a peacock with tail feathers that extended far behind it. As it saw the strange group approaching, its tail feathers lifted and expanded, looking like living flames. The sun hit the feathers of yellow, red, and orange, making them glisten and shimmer. Its plumage of similar coloring on its head also began to rise.

"If you wish to make a request," came a regal voice from inside Buddy's head, "you must first show me your offering."

"Offering?" Buddy asked the two goblins.

"We servants of the Dark Lord," Captain said. "Fulfill our request and be indebted to him."

"I do not foresee your master succeeding in his endeavor, so any debt will never be paid," the phoenix said inside Buddy's mind. It extended its long neck like a crane toward the goblin so that both their faces were eye to eye. "Offer me something now, or be burned to a crisp where you stand."

"Give us moment," Captain said, visibly shaken.

Captain and General ushered Buddy and Tyberion a few steps away and huddled together in a square-shaped circle.

"What's this about?" Buddy asked.

"We miscalculate," Captain said apologetically. "Rok, the phoenix, uses healing feathers on travelers. But not free. Rok demand something she don't have, and then she heal. We thought favor from Dark Lord would do."

"It don't do," General said and was promptly ignored by Captain.

"Well…" Tyberion started. "Do you two possess anything she desires?"

The two frantically searched through their packs. They hardly had anything of note. Captain had common supplies for a long journey, such as a compass, a spyglass, some rations, and parchment, quills, and ink he used for reports. General had roughly the same supplies, plus the healing herbs and medicine-making supplies, along with some premade medicinal concoctions—none of which were useful to an immortal phoenix. Then they remembered the lantern. They sauntered toward the phoenix with a victorious stride and showed the giant bird their offering.

"What is this?" Rok's voice echoed in their minds.

"Magic lantern," Captain said proudly. "It make light without fire and set fire when told to. Found out by accident." Captain rubbed his backside and gave a pained grimace.

"To be clear," Rok said with forced patience. "You are giving a phoenix—with the ability to control fire—an item that sets things on fire?"

"Yes?" General replied.

"I should incinerate you where you stand," the phoenix said. "However, I am feeling rather lethargic today. You have one more chance. Surprise me." At this last statement, her eyes glowed a dangerous crimson, and her voice became deep and sinister.

"Do you have anything?" Captain said as both goblins turned toward the humans with pure panic on their faces.

Tyberion had only his armor and half a sword.

Buddy searched through his pockets frantically, looking for anything, when suddenly he felt something small. He pulled out the winged pine seed he caught while in the king's castle. General saw it, and his eyes became like saucer plates.

"Let me see," he said. Buddy handed him the seed, curious about the sudden interest. "This a seed of null wood tree!"

Tyberion and Captain perked up and stared at it. Even Rok lifted her neck to get a good look.

"How in the goddess's name did you find that?"

170

Tyberion asked.

"It no matter," General said. "I have idea."

General started to dig in his "MEDCINE" bag and pulled out a mortar and pestle, a handful of strange-looking herbs, and a purple and violet flower. He put the pine seed and the other ingredients into the mortar and started to crush it all together in the pestle. After it was all blended, he added a metallic liquid to the bowl and combined it all until it became a goopy mess. Once he was finished, he took a vial and carefully put the new liquid into it. This time, he approached the phoenix with trepidation.

"This a poison," he said nervously. "It made using null wood seed. Seed will counter your magic healing. This can kill you."

Buddy held his breath as the phoenix slowly lowered her head in front of the vial. She took a glance at Captain, whose eyes were filled with a mix of shock and fury.

"You are giving an immortal being an immortality antidote," Rok said slowly. "Are you asking me to kill myself?"

"Forever long time," General said with more than a little bit of difficulty. "If I no could die, I would like to have option. And I thought it something you no have."

Rok's neck slowly extended like a snake preparing to strike. As gently as she could, the phoenix grasped the vial with her beak and brought it toward herself. She lifted herself slightly off the ground, revealing a crater filled with an assortment of what she probably considered to be treasure. She carefully placed the vial in the pile and returned to her normal sitting position.

"I do not anticipate ever resorting to such a method," Rok said. "However, it is perhaps a rare concoction and, therefore, should be treasured. You have my thanks and a favor owed."

General grabbed Buddy by the hand and dragged him forward in front of the phoenix.

"Right," Buddy started. "I have a heart condition that is threatening to kill me. Can you heal that?"

"As easily as I breathe," Rok said. She curled her snake-like neck around to her wing and plucked a long-flight feather. She then brought the feather up to Buddy and placed it against his chest. Nothing happened. Rok tapped it against the man. Nothing happened. Rok tapped it against the man again and released the feather. This time, the feather was repelled a few inches away from Buddy and slowly fell to the ground.

"I'm guessing it isn't supposed to do that?" Buddy asked.

"I am afraid not," Rok said. "Unfortunately, I know why my feather will not heal you. You are not from this world, correct?"

"Right," Buddy said.

"Magic does not work on you for the same reason the null wood seed negates my healing," Rok said. "You and it are from the same world where there is no magic. For some unknown reason, anything organic or living from your world repels magic. No spell can harm you, but no spell can help you either. You have my deepest apologies."

Tyberion walked forward and picked up the feather, then placed a hand on Buddy's shoulder.

"Are you okay, my friend?" he asked.

"I can't go home," Buddy said with a barely audible whisper. "That wizard can't send me home, and he damn well knows he can't! Oh, if I see that bastard again, I'm going to punch him square in the jaw!"

At this point, both Captain and General were on either

side of Buddy. Their faces were a mess of emotions. There were several soggy sniffles as they buried their faces in the old man's pant legs.

"I say we abandon our rescue of the wizard," Tyberion said. "He seems to have received the punishment he deserves. We should meet this Dark Lord and request his aid."

"That sounds like a horrible idea," Buddy said with a mischievous grin. "I'm in."

"I still owe you a favor," Rok said. "I can fly you to where he resides. It is the least I can do in your situation."

"Thank you," Buddy said, and then looked at the tear-stained faces of the goblins. "Let's go meet your boss."

Excerpt From the Journal of The Dark Lord

Cycle 4, Day 15

Wellspring of Magic Progress: Progress has been minimal. The excavation team is running into dwarf tunnels at an increased rate. Tensions between the dwarf nest and the goblins are growing. I will make another offering to the queen before the end of the cycle. I expect that will buy us more time. However, I have yet to locate a mage with the appropriate magika to truly open the way to the center. At this rate, I do not foresee an end to my mission within the year.

Village Update: The people are relatively happy and at peace. Seth has been a great help. The children of the village find him entertaining and he has become a wonderful distraction for them. With the children properly distracted, I have been able to send out an additional Mage Retrieval party. It has also been helpful for Lawrence to have a fellow human companion to prevent loneliness and homesickness that is prevalent in his people.

Reconnaissance Party Update: Captain and General have returned. The phoenix transport was a surprise, but only a small surprise compared to the Unari that they brought with them. Upon arrival, Captain gave me his report and I have since read over it multiple times and congratulated him on his successful reconnaissance. He and General will receive appropriate rest time before I send them out to search for Honeysuckle and Apple Pie. They should have returned with Seth's horse by now, and I worry about their safety.

Assessment of Tyberion: As a member of Malguinne's party, I find it difficult to trust him as I do Lawrence and Seth. However, I have gathered that his loyalty is to the Unari called Buddy rather than Malguinne. He also has no true loyalty to the kingdom due to his fall from grace after relinquishing the title of Royal Knight. I have great respect for people who value their own decisions and morality over that of a ruling party.

Threat Level: Minimal

Assessment of the Unari Buddy: Conversing with Buddy has shown me a side of Malguinne that I anticipated, but I am still saddened to see its outcome. I explained to Buddy that Malguinne had indeed lied to him to use him as a pawn in the wizard's plan to defeat me. I am not ashamed to say I felt the pain of guilt that the Royal Wizard should have felt when he deceived this kindly old man. I have informed Buddy that he is welcome to stay here as long as he wishes. The goblins will be able to provide medication that will temporarily sustain him. And against my better judgment, I swore that I would assist Buddy in returning home as best as I could, once my mission was completed.

Threat Level: Life-threatening. High risk to the mission.

Theory on Buddy's Return Home: There is a land far to the east to which I have never been able to travel due to its danger to my physiology. However, it is the origin of the goblin race and may prove to hold some answers that even I do not know. If I do not survive my mission, I will pass on the task of returning him home to one of my subordinates. Perhaps Petrichor. He has shown great interest in the health of Buddy.

Campfire Conversations: The Elf and the Rogue
Cycle 4, Day 14

Rythel and John sat in the relative silence of the night. They were huddled together in a small, dank cave with the smallest excuse for a fire they could manage to get and stay lit. They were cold, wet, and hopelessly alone together. They were also almost completely naked. Both had removed all but their undergarments so they could keep warm. Rythel had laid out his green cloak, simple white shirt, and black pants on a rock near the fire. John had placed his black cowl, shirt, and pants, along with his leather armor, on the rock beside Rythel's. Rythel avoided looking in the other man's direction, not wanting to see his nakedness, and he expected the other man would do the same. He could just feel the discomfort radiating off of the rogue. Or perhaps that was just his own.

"So," John said, "what are we supposed to do?"

"We wait," Rythel said. He restrained a shiver by clutching his knees tight against his chest. They were cold against his skin.

"Right, I get that. But how long do we wait for?"

From his peripheral vision, Rythel could see that John had spread himself out to catch as much heat as he could. It was a futile attempt.

"Until the others cross and find us," Rythel said, turning his head further away from his companion.

"Okay, but what if they don't? What if they got swept away by the current and are dead?" John had said this nonchalantly, which is his standard of communication, but Rythel didn't miss the hitch in the man's voice as he said the word "dead."

"Impossible. Malguinne is too smart to die. Muscle-for-brains is too stupid and stubborn to die." There was a slight hesitation and a dip in mood before Rythel continued. "And Buddy, he can't die, not before going home."

"That's surprisingly nice, coming from you," John said.

Rythel could just hear the man's smug smile in his words.

"That's because I am nice," Rythel said, turning to glare at the man for insinuating otherwise. Then he remembered their shared nudeness and looked away.

"Well, you sure do have a funny way of showing it," John said with a chuckle.

Rythel thought over his dealings with the group so far and cringed inwardly.

"I know," he said so quietly that it was almost a whisper. "I am nice, but I am not kind."

"Well, that's stupid," John said with a laugh. "They are the same thing."

"No, they are not!" Rythel said indignantly. "They clearly have two different meanings."

"Only if you overthink it," John paused and made an exaggerated expression of a person deep in thought, "or just want to sound more clever than you actually are."

"It is a wonder that someone with your *intelligence* managed to piss off so many people in the capital." Rythel turned toward John, ignoring his nakedness and seeing only the man.

"No, really, think about it," John said as he turned toward the elf with a surprising amount of seriousness building around his usual demeanor. "Sure, they are two different words with two different meanings, but they also go hand in hand. Regardless of whether you want to be nice or kind, just be good and treat people well. It's that simple."

"Says the person running from his debt collectors," Rythel said, unsure how to process this side of the human.

"I never said I was nice or kind," John countered, with a distant sound to his voice. "I will never amount to anything, just like my old man, just like his. If you're born in the slums, you do what you have to to survive. I never had the luxury of looking down on people."

"I—" Rythel stopped himself from refuting the unsaid claim. "I suppose that is a bad habit of my people. I am five hundred and fifteen years old. I have lived so many of your human lifetimes that it's hard to take you seriously."

"So, why did you choose to live among humans?"

"I did not choose," Rythel said with a sigh. "I was banished around five hundred years ago. I have not spoken to another of my people since then."

John whistled in disbelief. "That does make things difficult. Why the banishment?"

"I did not agree with my people's way of using magic." There was a distant pain in his expression as he lost himself in remembrance. "I tried to argue that over-reliance on magical tools and weapons was making us weak, and we would lose centuries of progress if we were to lose access to magic."

"Yep," John said. "Telling people their way of life is stupid tends to do that to a person. Do you miss your old life?"

"Most of my memory is of my banishment," Rythel said, looking out of the cave, into the pouring rain, into the past. "But yes, I miss what I can barely even remember. But that life is far behind me."

Rythel was hoping this was the end of this line of questions. It was an uncomfortable topic to think about and even more uncomfortable to speak about. He wished the rain would stop so that he could find a nice, quiet spot to be alone in.

"You know," John said, breaking the freshly formed silence, "we could just ditch the quest and strike out on our own."

"I can think of a myriad of reasons why that would be a bad idea," Rythel said with indifference. "Firstly, the metal foot-soldier would find us and make good on his threat. Secondly, I can think of no good reasons to journey with you of all humans. Thirdly, taking out the Dark Lord is something that needs to be done sooner rather than later. Need I continue?"

"You need not," John said, with thickly layered sarcasm. "Because I'm pretty sure the main reason is that you want Buddy to return home."

Rythel allowed his mind to travel down this line of thought. He did not disagree that it ranked highly in his unsaid reasoning. However, he did not like that this man could read his motives so easily.

"Why haven't you left already?" Rythel said, trying to steer the conversation away from himself. "We are adequately far away from the capital. You can go anywhere, free from your debtors."

"Not gonna lie," John said. "The metal man scares the living breath out of me. But I think my curiosity has gotten the worst of me. I just want to see how this all ends."

"Then, when the rain subsides, I say we start to search for the others."

"I am of a similar mind, my friend." John hesitated for a moment, then said, "Before I let you go back to your awkward silence, there is just one thing I'd like to say."

"Yes?" Rythel said, mildly curious.

"I feel a little unbalanced with you being the only one divulging your secret past," John said with a mischievous undertone. "So, I would like to formally introduce myself to you. I am Jacob, son of Jonathan."

The elf considered this for a few moments and said, "I am glad to truly know you, Jacob. Thank you."

Chapter 9: Tooth and Claw
Cycle 4, Day 17

T o say Buddy was overwhelmed would have been a massive understatement, as the Dark Lord's main hall was flooded by a sea of goblins. The mass of goblins was creating a cacophony of anguish using both the goblin variation of English and the croaking, growling Goblic, the common goblin tongue. Through the chaos, Buddy could see the time mage Lawrence and the Warden Seth struggling to get a proper answer from the goblins clinging to their arms and legs. Tyberion was not suffering the same fate, mostly because the goblins were a little scared of his bear-like appearance. This was not helped by the fact that his contribution to solving the chaos was to pick up an adult goblin by the head, hold the poor creature to his eye level, and ask him to calmly explain the situation. Needless to say, the goblin instantly fainted. Tyberion was kind enough to lay the goblin on the table, away from the threat of being trampled.

Buddy was in a similar situation as Tyberion in that the goblins were avoiding getting too close to him. However, this was out of fear of harming Buddy and not the other way around. The primary medical goblin, Petrichor, made it abundantly clear to the community that Buddy was not to be mistreated or overstressed due to his condition. Anyone caught in violation of the doctor's orders would be subject to a stern talking to by the Dark Lord, which seemed to be the highest form of capital punishment here.

Buddy turned his attention toward Magus, who was standing stock still in the middle of the green sea. There wasn't a hint of movement from his suit of armor. He seemed as stoic as Buddy expected from the man labeled the Dark Lord. But Buddy had learned by now that this wasn't stoicism that he was seeing. This was a leader, listening to every single word being spoken. Absorbing everything and then processing all the data before making the best decision for the community. To Buddy, Magus was a fascinating scenario of "what if King Arthur was king of the evil, antagonistic kingdom." He made everything feel noble and dignified, even if it was just a room full of scared goblins unable to articulate their problem. As if to prove Buddy's thought, Magus lifted his hand, and the room went still and silent. Every goblin and human turned their attention to the Dark Lord.

"Two of our goblin children are missing," Magus said, his voice echoing through the silence. "They have been missing since last night, so this is not just a case of children playing a harmless game. This area is relatively safe, and all access points to the underground are secure enough to eliminate it from our search parameters. I will break everyone into small search parties, with as many groups having a medical goblin just in case. We will find them, and we will bring them home safely. Of this, you have my word."

There was a roar of celebration, which reminded Buddy of the sound of bullfrog-filled summer camping trips. The crowd quieted as soon as Magus started to form the search parties. Seth and Lawrence each had their groups and were in charge of the more dangerous areas of the search. One by one, groups were made and left the building, leaving only Magus, Tyberion, Petrichor, and Buddy. Magus turned to the three, and Buddy could see the concern written over the

183

expressionless helmet. He could hear the unspoken request for the others to keep him safe. And this boiled his blood and sent his heart racing dangerously.

"Like hell I'd just stay here!" Buddy said, puffing out his chest and facing down the Dark Lord.

"This is not the time—" Magus started.

"You are absolutely right!" Buddy continued. "There are kids possibly in danger. We don't have time to argue. I am going with you, and that's that."

Magus turned toward Tyberion as if requesting assistance. All that was returned to him was a hearty chuckle from his would-be backup.

"Well, if he's going with you," Tyberion said, "then so am I."

"Me as well!" Petrichor said, slightly louder than was necessary. "Old human is under my watch."

"Very well," Magus said, the echo of his voice sounding more like a sigh than words. "Do not overexert yourself. And do not put yourself in harm's way."

Buddy gave an affirmation that seemed to please the Dark Lord, and the four of them joined the search effort.

Magus led them north of the goblin village into a thick, wooded area overgrown with unique plants and flowers. Buddy was constantly surprised to see the differences in nature in this world compared to his own, and yet most animals he had come across were almost identical— aside from pixies, which Buddy had seen in the capital's castle. According to Magus, they were one of the primary pollinators. They still had butterflies and bees and other insects, but pixies were much better at it. They were highly intelligent and knew exactly when various flora needed pollinating, and would even purposefully crossbreed plants to get specific and unique results.

They spent most of the initial search calling out to the two children, Trepidation and Weary, and taking brief breaks, as ordered by Petrichor, for Buddy's sake. During these breaks, they would discuss every topic Buddy could think to ask about.

"Why do the people of this world fear goblins?" Buddy asked the group on one of their breaks. Petrichor's ears perked up at this, and he turned toward the old man with a patient but melancholic look. Buddy continued, "I mean, they only just recently started working with you, but they have been living separately from everyone else for so much longer. Why is that?"

"It not just fear," Petrichor said as he sat uncomfortably on the ground. "It hate. It disgust. It mistrust. We not what they like or want." The goblin turned his eyes away from Buddy and became like a closed book.

"I do not know what your world is like," Magus said, choosing to stay standing, "but here, there are expectations built on centuries of tradition. Goblins are not like the rest of the Anuins. They can not use magic, and they are incredibly resistant to it. That alone makes them outcasts. But it goes deeper."

"When I was a child," Tyberion started, while he leaned against a slightly slanted tree, "I was told countless stories of how cruel and monstrous goblins were. I am ashamed to say that I had believed those stories until just recently."

"People expect to see the monsters from the stories they are told," Magus said, "and are blind to what is right in front of them. They fail to see the person just as equally full of endless potential."

"People can be so cruel," Buddy said, a lump of condensed guilt dropped in his chest. "But I am no better."

185

It was barely a whisper, but Petrichor jolted upright and turned toward Buddy with a leaky face. "That not true! You are good! You are kind! You not see us as monsters!"

"I suppose you could say I saw my son as a monster," Buddy said with a hollow husk of a voice, unable to look any of the others in the eyes. "He opened up to me and showed me a side of him I didn't know, and all I could see was the monsters from the stories I was told. I said horrible things. I abandoned him. Forced him to fend for himself."

Petrichor's eyes grew wide in shock, and even Tyberion had a disbelieving expression on his face. Only Magus seemed unperturbed. Though if one could look perturbed with a helmet on, Buddy was not sure.

"I regretted what I did almost instantly," Buddy continued, "but it was years before I could truly reflect and look beyond my closed-minded upbringing. I tried to reconnect with him years later and correct my mistake. But some wounds never heal."

"I suppose your world is not all that dissimilar to our own," Magus said. "However, the man before me is not cruel. He is but a human, capable of great cruelty and also great kindness. A cruel man would lack the empathy required to see your shortcomings."

"What good is that?" Buddy asked, as he gave a melancholic laugh. "I have already made the biggest mistake of my life. How can I possibly make up for that?"

"I do not know," Magus said, "but that is why you must return home. So that you can find out for yourself. You owe it to your son to try. You are not beyond redemption, my friend."

"And I will personally see to it that you make your return home," Tyberion said as he grasped Buddy's shoulder with the bear paw the man called a hand.

"I too!" Petrichor spoke up from his knee.

"Do not worry, Buddy, you will return home. You have my word," Magus said, his voice echoing with an unseen smile. "Now, let us find these missing children. I am sure they are hungry."

***

They continued their trek into the dense forest for several hours in somber silence. Only the sounds of birds, insects, and the occasional footsteps of small creatures could be heard. The path was becoming more challenging to travel as limbs and overgrowth started to populate the trail. Tyberion had to use his newly acquired claymore, courtesy of the Dark Lord's meager reserve of weaponry, to clear the way. As the day progressed, Buddy started to notice it was getting warmer the longer they walked, even though it had been a cool spring day. He was starting to sweat profusely, and his face was starting to feel like he had just opened an oven door. Then he realized that all the sounds of the forest he was used to hearing had vanished and were replaced by deep, raspy gusts of wind. The weird thing was, the wind would blow in one direction and then back the opposite way. Almost as if something very large was breathing. Every time the wind blew in their direction, a torrent of heat filled the air, nearly suffocating the party.

"The three of you return to the town," Magus said with a dark, knowing voice. "You are not safe here. I will join you after dealing with an old friend."

Before Buddy could protest, a large, scaly, serpentine creature slid into his peripheral vision. Its head was a narrow point with no mouth or eyes, like a worm. It stretched far

187

into the depths of the darkness with no end in sight. The circumference of its body seemed to double over and over with each new foot of its body. His skin went ice cold, and his stomach plummeted as this strange new creature made a wide circle behind them, blocking the path. But it was the deep, growling voice that bellowed from above, as the forest was cloaked in a thick darkness, that nearly made Buddy lose all his senses. Petrichor clung to Buddy's leg with a trembling grip, and Tyberion was as white as a sheet, his hand nowhere near his blade. The only one standing his ground was Magus, who faced the void like a man taking on the abyss, and with the knowledge that victory was the only option.

"Hello, my old *Friend*..." The voice sounded like the growl of a lion as it lingered on every syllable and was accompanied by glowing yellow eyes piercing through the darkness above them. If Buddy were to put a size to them at that moment, he would have said they were the size of a car. And he would have been wrong.

They were much, much bigger.

"What business do you have in my domain?" the Dark Lord asked.

"All is my domain," came the voice in the dark. "Your presence here is by my will."

"There is nothing for you here. Leave now while you still can."

"You dare threaten me?"

There was a horrible inhaling sound followed by a brief silence and a single, sudden click. Buddy found himself and Petrichor face down on the ground underneath Tyberion's weight just as flames engulfed the world. Buddy watched in fascinated horror as the fire circled them in a funnel of wind.

188

Magus was moving his hands in the direction of the wind, controlling it, and pushing it upwards, creating a pillar of fire of biblical proportions. It should have been hot as hell in the funnel, but Buddy could feel a cool breeze coming from above. He was sure that, too, was Magus' doing.

Slowly, the roaring flames started to die down, and Magus resolved his tornado. Several acres of the forest were completely leveled, with nothing but ash to show that there had even been life there. But no one was looking at the destruction around them. Their eyes could only see the mountainous, red dragon. Buddy slowly turned his head to look behind them and saw that the creature that had surrounded them wasn't a creature but the massive tail of the dragon. His gaze followed the length of the dull, rust-red tail until it met the body of the colossal creature that towered over them. The sheer size of it took Buddy's breath away. It was easily as tall as the Pyramid of Giza and could effortlessly dangle a bullet train in its talons like an eagle carrying a snake.

Its body was shaped like how Buddy pictured a traditional dragon: It had four legs, two bat-like wings on its back, and a lizard-like structure with a face that looked like a cross between an eagle and a Komodo dragon. But there is a world of difference between seeing one in a book and seeing it from ground level. Buddy had been to large cities in his world. He had seen skyscrapers; he had gone to the Eiffel Tower and the Grand Canyon. But never in his life had he felt as tiny and insignificant as he did at that moment, as the dragon's head hovered over the group like a wrecking ball with teeth.

The dragon lowered its horned face toward them. Ponds of drool dripped past serrated, crocodile-like teeth. The stench of decay flooded Buddy's senses and watered his eyes. The dragon's head was nearly at ground level as he and

189

the Dark Lord stood their ground, waiting for the other to make the next move. Buddy's heart was pounding uncomfortably in his chest, losing any semblance of rhythm. Darkness was beginning to edge into his vision as he felt himself falling into a faint. That was until he felt a small hand shove something bitter past his lips.

"Buddy, swallow," Petrichor said. "Chew and swallow quickly!"

He did both to the best of his ability, and the effect was almost instantaneous. His vision cleared, and his heart calmed. Goblin medicine was nothing short of miraculous. The plants, herbs, and ingredients they use aren't magic, but they seem to have a near-magic nature that still works on him. It still didn't cure his condition, which would be too miraculous, but it gave him more time to work with. He was about to quietly thank Petrichor, but before he could even try, the tiny goblin was wriggling free of Tyberion's weight. Tyberion tried to stop him, but he popped out from under them and charged in between Magus and the dragon's head, taking both by surprise.

"You will leave!" Petrichor shouted through quivering vocal cords. He stretched out his arms as if to block any attack the dragon would launch at him. "We done you no harm. You had your way. Burn our forest. Scare my patient near death. Threaten leader. Now find your pleasure some elsewhere!"

Magus took a step forward, stood beside his goblin companion, and crossed his arms before saying, "You heard my champion. He speaks with the backing of all my goblins and me. Leave our land peacefully, or you will have a war you cannot even imagine winning."

There was a pause where the dragon looked from one to the other. It was impossible to read his scaly face for any emotion, if he even had any. And then he began to laugh. It was a low, hollow, mirthless laugh that had an edge of murder behind it. It was loud and painful, causing Buddy to cover his ears. But what was worse was that his lips weren't moving with the bellowing laughter. It was a sound that came from his throat as if he were imitating the sound rather than making it instinctively. And when he next spoke, it followed the same pattern.

"You command an army of fools," the dragon said, with unmoving lips and tongue. "One does not fight such an army and expect a pleasurable victory. However, my departure now would be a victory in itself."

"Explain yourself," Magus said.

Instead of speaking further, the dragon brought forward a cupped front claw that seemed miles away and dropped two small goblin children in a calculated, careless fashion. The two quickly jumped to their feet and started to run toward Petrichor and Magus. Their forward retreat was instantly stopped as the dragon surrounded them in a prison of his enormous claw.

"They are children, you bully of a lizard!" The words escaped Buddy's mouth quicker than the sane side of his brain could stop them. The result was the inferno-like glare of the dragon turning to him. He should have been scared shitless. But he wasn't. He was mad. No, he was beyond mad. His soul was ablaze with righteous fury. Like his goblin doctor before him, he wormed free of Tyberion's cover and stood in the line with Magus and Petrichor, and was quickly joined by the knight. "What kind of coward kidnaps children?"

"Brave tongues burn as easily as all others," the dragon said with a throaty growl. "I do not steal children out of some sick game. This is
justice. Your precious goblins have stolen two of my horns, so I will take two objects of equal value from you. I deem two goblin whelps to be equal to my sheddings."

"Horns just lying on ground," Petrichor said quietly to Magus. "We use for throne decoration. We no thought they had owner."

"This is not your fault," Magus said in a reassuring tone. "This particular dragon works on his own logic." He then directed his attention back to the dragon and said, "We will return the horns to you so long as you return the children."

"No," the dragon said, "for they have already been claimed. They are yours now. But a price of equal value must be made. That is the only way."

"Now, hold on," Buddy said, his anger getting the best of him. "That's just plain stupid. How can you say living, breathing people are worth as much as bits of you that have fallen off or been scrapped off."

"Silence, outsider!" the dragon commanded. "You are not of this world and hold no weight in this transaction. Those horns were part of me, and I decide their worth."

Buddy could almost feel Tyberion and Magus tensing up, preparing to attack this mountain of a creature. If it came to that, he knew he would be worse than useless. He would just end up being a bargaining chip. But then he saw Petrichor make a quick jolt, and his eyes widened as if physically struck by an idea. The goblin dropped his MEDECEN bag on the ground and quickly started digging in it head first. All eyes were on him in an almost sympathetic curiosity.

Even the dragon seemed to lose a small fraction of his menace as he observed Petrichor's unexpected action.

"Found it!" Petrichor said, in an almost celebratory tone. He emerged from his large sack with a pair of pliers and turned toward Magus, extending the device to him. "Two teeth. My body, my worth. Equal to two horns."

The Dark Lord kneeled, gently taking the pliers and putting a gauntlet on the goblin's small shoulder. There was a hesitation, and Buddy was sure Magus would try and talk Petrichor out of this idea or question his sanity. But he didn't. He only nodded and proceeded to do as his subordinate asked.

After two quick yanks and some muffled Goblic that even Buddy understood to be swear words, two of Petrichor's teeth had been removed. The goblin's mouth flowed with twin rivers of blood, but he quickly snatched the teeth from Magus and ran toward the dragon.

"Equal value!" Petrichor tried to yell. It was muffled, and there was a gurgling in the words, but he was fully understood.

The dragon lifted his claws away from the children, and they instantly ran toward Petrichor, taking cover behind him. He then extended a talon toward Petrichor, who, in turn, placed his teeth on its surface. Like tiny pebbles at the foot of the Himalayas. Buddy could almost see the dragon's lips curve into a slight smile as he accepted the payment. It did not make him look any less frightening. If anything, it only added to his sinister nature.

"This is acceptable," the dragon said with a satisfied hiss. "I look forward to our next transaction." The dragon paused, then turned his burning gaze toward Magus. "Goodbye, my old friend. I do not see victory in your foolish endeavor. I only see a world with one less to see its ending."

At this, he extended his leathery wings to their fullest extent, blotting out the sun, and after several forceful flaps, he launched into the air. Tyberion had to hold onto Buddy to keep him from falling over, but it was a sight Buddy would never forget. It was like watching a shuttle launch itself into space. A mixture of raw power and majestic machinery, working together to defy all laws of gravity. They all watched the sky as the massive creature shrank into the distance. Soon Buddy would dig into Petrichor's bag and use some gauze to stop the bleeding, Tyberion would end up carrying the two children as they trekked back to the town, and Magus would tell them of how the nameless dragon and he first met 10,000 years ago. But right then, they could only take in the wonder of the moment.

"I never want to see another dragon as long as I live," Buddy said. His fear and rage subsided into a drained emptiness.

"And I hope you live long enough for me never to get tired of telling you so," Tyberion said, equally as devoid of all energy.

Chapter 10: No Good Deed
Cycle 4, Day 16

T he river cascaded down its path with a swollen fe-
rocity. Crossing the river was not an option. However, for the three figures that stood on the wrong
side of the watery path, it was the only answer to the question they each asked themselves. What do we do now?

Samuel paced back and forth. A long string of thoughts
slowly cycled through his mind as he systematically discred-
ited every possible solution. Could they swim across? No,
not without drowning. Could they use magic? Not likely.
Caleb, so far, could only change parts of his body, but it exhausted him to near uselessness after barely using it. Za'rie
still couldn't use hers. No matter how much she studied her
new book, she was still at step zero of her journey of a thousand steps. Going around? No, the river cuts through the
land and divides the land into two specific sections. The side
they need to get to and the side they are currently on. Look
for a bridge? Maybe. But do they go left or right? If they
travel too far one way and there's no bridge then they go the
other way and still no bridge, how much time would they
have wasted?

"Hey!" Za'rie's shout broke through the wall of
thoughts separating Samuel from his friends. "Did you hear
a single word I said?"

"Probably not," Samuel said with hollow honesty.

"I said…the horses might be able to cross if it isn't too
deep," she said, the spike of her anger drilling into Samuel's

already splitting head.

"I thought of that," he replied, ignoring her vexation and turning to face her. However, he was only looking in her general direction. All he could focus on were his own thoughts. "It's too dangerous. It's impossible to see how deep it is, and the rain has probably made it even deeper. If it suddenly gets too—"

"You're overthinking like usual," she interrupted. "If it gets too deep, we just turn around."

"And like usual," Samuel countered, with his temper flaring, "you want to rush head first into a situation you don't know anything about!"

"Well, at least I am talking things out!" she shouted and stomped toward him. "Whereas you just stay silent while we wait to be ordered around by—"

"That's enough, both of you," Caleb said, getting between the two and placing a hand on their shoulders.

Samuel was uncomfortable with the amount of force the other boy was hinting at with his firm grip. He took a step back, and Za'rie turned away with a huff.

"Look, we are all tired, cranky, and more than a little hungry," Caleb continued. "Now that the storm is behind us and the ground is starting to dry, let's make a fire, find some food, and eat something that hasn't been heavily salted and dried."

"I'll start the fire," Samuel said, his voice little more than a whisper.

"Good, and I think I can catch some fish," Caleb said. "Za'rie, could you get some kindling for Samuel? We haven't replaced our stock since last night."

"Fine…" She did not look at either of the boys as she mumbled and started looking for anything that could burn.

Samuel went to Juniper and started to untie a bundle of sticks and limbs from one of the packs. They decided it would be a good idea to have a small collection of firewood to keep on them for whenever they had to make camp in open fields like the one they were currently in. It was Za'rie's idea. Samuel laughed at the thought of her having a good idea.

"This was so much easier when it was just you and me," Samuel said.

"No, it wasn't," Caleb said, with such a cutting edge to his words that Samuel spun around to look at the older boy. "We were lost and on the verge of dehydration. If Za'rie hadn't found us and, well, kidnapped us, we would have died. And the whole time, you never even asked me what we should do. I'm not angry about that. I didn't have a clue what to do. I was more lost than you were. But even with the bandits, *you* made a plan for yourself. Even now, with a river blocking our path, *you* were the one trying to think of a way forward by yourself."

"But her idea—"

"Was absolute horse shite," Caleb said with a hint of a smile. "I know, but that doesn't mean all of our ideas are. You're not alone, and you don't have to do this alone, okay?"

Caleb walked away before Samuel could think of a good response. He continued to think it over as he found a dry enough spot on the ground and set up the firewood. He retrieved the flint stone and chunk of metal that Za'rie had packed for fire starting and began to strike the metal against the stone, creating sparks over the firewood. He was so deep in thought that he didn't realize there was nothing for the sparks to latch on to.

"You are wasting the stone," Za'rie said, as she dumped

a handful of mostly dry leaves and grass onto the wood pile. She sat down on the far side of Samuel and fell into silence as she stared into the distance, pointedly away from the boy.

"Thanks," Samuel said quietly. He restarted his efforts, and after some false starts, he finally got a small fire going. His mind was ablaze with all the things he knew he should say. He could find the words but not the order. Just as he was about to attempt it, there was movement in his peripheral vision. Za'rie noticed it too, and they both turned to get a good look. Baffled gasps were shared between the two as they saw a red crab scuttling toward them. Then, a second and third crab joined to make a small congregation of crabs.

"It's okay," Caleb said, panting as he rushed toward them. "They are with me. Sorry, just gotta catch my breath. Za'rie, can you get the pan, please?"

"Umm, sure," she said and proceeded to do as the mage asked.

When she returned, Caleb took the frying pan and asked the crabs to get in. To Samuel's surprise, the crabs did what they were told, as if they were trained pets.

"Okay, you can change them back, please," Caleb said, and at that moment, the blue orb of Hermy shot through the air and tapped against each crab. After his job was completed he returned to crab form on top of Caleb's head. In seconds, the three creatures that were crabs started to shift shape. The shells turned from red to silver and became smooth and scaly. The legs merged, turning into thin, flat appendages. The faces elongated, and a round, flapping opening replaced the crab mouths. Where the crabs once were, now flopped three gasping, silvery fish.

Words failed Samuel as he tried to grasp what he had just seen. He knew that he should be getting used to seeing

Caleb's strange magic. But when he compared the fireballs and lightning the other mage had used with this crab-based magic, it just left his mind baffled.

"Turns out I can change other creatures into crabs, and with Hermy's help, I can order them around," Caleb said with the enthusiasm of a dog begging for praise.

Samuel was tempted to give the older boy the validation he wanted when a quiet sob caused him to stop and turn toward Za'rie. She had her knees raised and her arms wrapped around her legs. Sounds of muffled sniffles were coming from where her face was buried in her knees.

"Za'rie—" Caleb started.

"I'm fine!" she said with a cracking voice. "Stop staring at me! Please…"

"We can't help you if you don't talk to us," Caleb said in a gentle voice.

"I don't want to talk about it!" she said.

"That's a lie," Samuel said. This was supposed to just be a thought, but it was so loud he ended up saying it. But he was not sorry he did. It was the truth, after all.

Za'rie started to say something, and Samuel was pretty sure she was going to deny his claim, but then she stopped. He was sure she had realized there was no point arguing.

"I have nothing," Za'rie said weakly. "I can't come up with good ideas and plans. I can't use my magic no matter how much of that stupid book I read. I couldn't even do anything against the drake. I am useless to you two. And when this journey is over, I have nowhere to go." She lifted her tear-stained face, and Samuel could see the fear, anger, and self-pity in her puffy red eyes. "And now I'm crying about all this like a child!"

"You're not useless," Samuel said with a sigh. "I am

just not good at any of this. I've only ever worked alongside my father. I'm sorry I made you feel this way. You have provided a lot of important supplies for the journey, and if it weren't for you, we would never have made it this far. I haven't given much thought to what would happen after rescuing my father, but I just assumed you two would join me and my father. Knowing him, Dad would adopt you without giving you an option."

"He sounds like a brash thinker," Za'rie said with a choked laugh.

"You don't know the half of it," Samuel said. "He's stubborn, jumps into the heat of things without a second thought, and always does what he thinks is right, and he is the person I respect most in this world, no matter how pissed his brashness makes me."

"I look forward to meeting and rescuing him," Za'rie said, a shaky smile starting to form. "And Samuel...thank you."

"Yeah," he said. "Now, while Caleb is cooking, let me take a look at that book."

"Hey, who said I was cooking?" Caleb said with mock shock.

"I did," Samuel said, circling the fire to sit next to Za'rie. "You're the best cook between the three of us, and it isn't even a close contest."

"He's right," Za'rie said, wiping away the last of the tears. "He burns things to a crisp, and I can never get meat past the raw stage."

"I guess it is best if I cook Finn, Aqua, and Gillroy," Caleb said as he started to prepare the fish.

Za'rie groaned, and Samuel threw a rock in his general direction. They then proceeded to ignore anything Caleb said as they became engrossed in *Magic Theory and Magical Application*.

"You see?" Za'rie said, "It's impossible to understand. The researcher who wrote it uses big fancy words to make it sound like he knows anything, but it's just circular logic."

"You're right about that," Samuel said, and pointed at a specific passage. "Though this is interesting: 'The apparition of the magika results from internal and external stimuli dependent entirely on an unknown variable as seen in subject A.' It's overly worded, but what is he referring to when he says magika?"

"His major theory is that the stronger one's magic, the greater the possibility of it becoming pseudo-sentient," Za'rie said. "He refers to the pseudo-sentient creature as magika, a being of pure magic. I'm pretty sure Hermy is an example of a magika."

***

After they ate their fill of fish, they discussed their course of action. They ended up agreeing to walk upstream to look for a way to cross or a spot where the river wasn't as wide. They continued going upstream until late in the evening when the light started to dim. As they were preparing to look for a place to camp for the night, Samuel saw smoke in the distance. He informed the others, and they hid behind a large boulder by the river. Za'rie went to the packs and brought out a spyglass.

"Okay," she said, "it looks like it's a small camp of five men about half a mile away. They are wearing dark cloaks with no insignia, so I don't think they are soldiers."

"Do they have a wagon or just horses?" Samuel asked.

"Just horses," Za'rie said.

"So they are probably not merchants," Samuel said. "They could be travelers, but they aren't on the main road, and they are close to the Dark Lord's domain, so that's not likely. I would say highwaymen or bandits, but who do they expect to rob near the border?"

"We should probably head downstream and get away from them just in case," Caleb said, with a look on his face that Samuel recognized as a remembrance of past bandit-based trauma.

"I agree," Samuel said.

"I was wrong," Za'rie said. "It's six men, but the sixth doesn't seem to be one of them. He looks like a really, really old man who is tied up, gagged, and blindfolded."

"Samuel," Caleb said, eyes full of concern.

"No," Samuel said with instant anxiety. "There is no way we can take on five bandits. Maybe we can find—"

"This can't be right," Za'rie interjected, pulling the spyglass away with a puzzled expression. "One of them looks like he has a giant claw for a hand."

"No," Samuel said again. "Why are they out here?"

"Who are they?" Za'rie asked.

"They kind of captured us shortly before you captured us," Caleb said. "I accidentally turned their leader's hand into a crab claw, and that just made things worse. But that's exactly why we need to do something." Caleb now turned to Samuel again with a pleading expression. "I can undo the claw now, I'm sure. If things stay as they are, the old man may die, and they will just hurt more people."

"I'm going to have to agree with Caleb," Za'rie said, as she put away the spyglass. "I can't just turn away when someone's life is in danger. Also, I think it would be good for the two of you to get some nice, cathartic payback."

Samuel was about to go on a whole rant listing off all the reasons this was a bad idea. He was about to put his foot down and tell them that fighting bandits was not their job. He was about to say a lot of things that would go against his conscience. But he didn't because he knew they were right. He also knew this was insanely stupid and dangerous. But it's the exact thing his father would do and what his father would expect of him. He took in a deep breath to calm his nerves and exhaled all the pent-up fear and anxiety.

"Fine," he said, "but we are going to come up with a plan first."

***

They waited until midnight, when the night was at its darkest, and hopefully, when most of the bandits would be asleep. They left the horses behind, out of sight. If this was going to be done, it was going to be done as stealthily as possible. Unfortunately, Za'rie no longer had the magic items she used to sneak up on him and Caleb and put them to sleep. Though knowing now how magic items were made, he had no intention of using them ever again.

They snuck up on the camp slowly. Za'rie kept the spyglass in hand and kept checking to make sure the bandit on watch hadn't spotted them. This area, being an open field, kept Samuel on edge the whole time. He expected to hear shouts at any second. The bandit camp was rather meager; just one large tent into which they had seen the old man get dragged just before sundown. The rest of the bandits, from what they could tell, were spread throughout the camp and sleeping in personal sleeping packs. They had accounted for two bandits that were sleeping and one keeping watch. Samuel kept on guard for the fourth and the leader, hoping they were just sleeping out of sight.

Finally, they made it to the back side of the tent. It had already been decided between the three that Samuel would be the one to infiltrate the tent, seeing as he was the one with the shield and could better defend himself if King Crab was inside. It was not an easily made decision, and each had a reason why it should have been them. But Samuel's reasoning ended up taking precedence. Za'rie handed Samuel an elven dagger as they approached the tent. He unsheathed the dagger and slowly began to slice a slit into the fabric of the tent. The dagger was one of the sharpest Samuel had ever seen, and it cut through the fabric soundlessly as if it were butter. The thought of what it would feel like to cut flesh invaded his mind, and he quickly avoided that thought as he poked his head into the tent.

It was quiet and nearly pitch black. The only light came through the front flaps of the tent from the campfire on the other side. The trail of light led up to the center where the bound-up old man lay. Samuel tried to look around the rest of the tent but saw nothing in the darkness. He continued to inch his way into the darkness, dagger in hand, expecting anything and everything. Each step he took was calculated like the footsteps of a man on thin ice, hearing the cracks but needing to proceed anyway.

When he knelt beside the old man, he placed his hand on the man's chest. There was a steady heartbeat and the rhythmic breathing of deep sleep. He debated on whether he should wake the old man first or free him from his bindings. It was while Samuel was hesitating that he heard the sound of movement. The sound of someone standing up. He turned toward his left, and his heart leaped through his chest as he began to recognize the familiar silhouette of a man with a large clawed hand. Samuel wanted to scream out for his friends. But his voice caught in his throat, as if the memory of the claw was holding back his voice.

"Well, well, well," came the frozen, venomous voice of the bandit leader. "What do we have here?"

Samuel reached for his shield but before his hand could even come close, he was several feet in the air. He struggled to breathe as the claw tightened around his throat. He raised his right hand and thrust the dagger down onto the claw. But it bounced off with a loud *clang*.

"Well, if it isn't the pup returning to us," King Crab said as he got a good look at Samuel's face in the sliver of light. "Where's your brother, little pup? I'd hate for him to miss this."

"Take away his claw now!" Caleb shouted as he dove through the tent, the blue orb of Hermy shooting from his hand and striking the man's right arm.

King Crab's grip instantly loosened, and Samuel dropped to the ground, gasping for air. Out of the corner of his eye, he saw Caleb also on the ground. He looked so frail as Za'rie jumped in beside him, trying to help him up. In front of Samuel, the bandit leader was watching in horror as the shell of his right hand began to peel away, layer by layer until all that remained was a normal human hand.

The man let out a guttural sound that landed somewhere between violent cursing and screams of fury. He devolved into a primal rage as he kicked Samuel square in the chest, knocking out what little air he had just gained. Samuel dropped the dagger as he fell on his back. King Crab fumbled for the dagger before Samuel could catch his breath again, and then he ran full-speed toward Caleb. His voice was no more than a string of incoherent curses. Caleb was still struggling to stand and could not avoid the bandit's attack, which is why Za'rie moved between the attacker and the target. She held her axe, ready to try and intercept. Samuel could just barely make out the expression on her face. It was the look of one who knew the end was coming, but not without a bloody struggle. The man thrust his dagger toward Za'rie's chest, and she swung the axe to strike the man's side. But his arms were longer, and her heart would be pierced before he was in range of the axe.

Just as the blade was about to make contact, there was a flash of purple sparks, and the clawless King Crab was launched skyward by a powerful gust of wind. He collided with the top of the tent. The force of the wind and the man caused the stakes holding the tent in place to pop out of the ground and the support rods to become undone. The wind stopped, and the man fell back to the ground with enough force to leave him gasping for air, and the tent began to collapse.

By this point, the old man was awake and squirming around. Samuel could not see the others, but he still had a job to do. He dragged the old man toward the nearest side of the tent as the fabric fell on him. The newly added element made escape difficult, but with enough frustrated effort, he finally managed to get him and the man out and into the open. Samuel heard the uneven footsteps of men just coming out of sleep, and he hurried to untie the blindfold and then the gag.

"Thank you, my child," the old man said with what was probably a smile under his long and thick white beard. "However, I think I can manage from here."

Samuel was about to protest when the old man started to speak in a whisper, and the ropes that remained around him started to dissolve and melt away. A mage? How in the world could these bandits capture a mage? And why would they? Especially if they were just going to tie him up. Before Samuel's thoughts could make out exactly what was going on, the mage reached out a bony and age-marked arm. The boy took the man's arm and helped him up. At this point, Samuel could see Za'rie dragging Caleb out from under the tent, and the four remaining bandits were digging through the fabric, trying to excavate their leader.

"Oh my," the mage said. "I seem to no longer be bound. What a shame."

The old man held his right hand in front of him and pointed his index finger upward. He began to whisper something that sounded like a chant or maybe a song, and a small flame popped into existence just above his fingertip. He then pointed his finger at the collapsed tent. In an instant, the small flame became a torrent of fire, which he directed toward the unsurprisingly flammable tent fabric. He pointed in several different directions until most of the bandit camp was burning. Three of the men fled as soon as the tent caught fire, running to their panicked horses and galloping away without their leader. The last remaining bandit was Lockpick, who had managed to pull out his boss, but not before a good portion of his clothes got burned and the smell of burning hair filled the air.

Lockpick practically dragged the man, who was no longer King Crab, to the last two horses. It seemed the mage was not satisfied with his magic show quite yet; he held an open palm to the sky, saying more words and phrases Samuel couldn't hear. A bolt of lightning struck close to where the bandit and his leader were just a few moments prior. It did not strike them, but it did send their horses into a wild, uncontrollable run. There was no doubt in Samuel's mind: This mage was the one that had attacked the bandits what felt like a lifetime ago. Mages of this strength were rare, and it would only make sense that the bandits would go after him out of revenge. The only question on Samuel's mind was whether he was dangerous?

"You have my gratitude, young one," the mage said, as he turned toward Samuel. Za'rie was hobbling just a few feet away with an exhausted Caleb leaning on her for support. Samuel ignored the mage and ran to meet up with Za'rie and Caleb.

"Are you okay?" Samuel asked with a breaking, shaking voice. "What happened?"

"Yeah, I'm fine," Caleb said, barely able to speak. "Took a lot out of me. It was about the same as the first time I used magic on him. But so much worse."

"Ah, yes," the mage said with a voice that exuded wisdom. "I would say you had to fight against his will to keep the appendage. It takes a lot of magical energy to shift an unwilling subject."

"Thank you," Samuel said, as he positioned himself between his friends and the mage that had nearly killed him and Caleb not too long ago, "for getting rid of them. But now that you are safe, I think it's best if we part ways. I don't know what your business is out here, but we don't want trouble."

"You are right to be cautious," the mage said, a kind smile forming beneath his beard. "You never know who you will meet this close to the enemy territory. But I mean you no harm. I am Malguinne, the Royal Wizard. I am on a quest to put an end to the Dark Lord, but these fine gentlemen have separated me from my companions."

None of what he said was a lie. But there was something off. Even if the content was correct, it was almost like the packaging was all wrong.

"We had a run-in with them too," Caleb said.

"And we managed to escape after you tried to electrocute and incinerate them," Samuel said. "And us with them."

"Oh, dear," Malguinne said. "I am terribly sorry. Had I known you were their captives, I would have been more careful and attempted to rescue you."

Not a single truth resided in what the wizard said, and Samuel knew it. The lies seeped into his bones like a slow-acting venom.

"All the same," Samuel said with a nervous edge in his voice. "I think we should part ways—"

"If he's going the same way we are," Za'rie said, "maybe we should join him. We do need a way across the river."

"I think that is a marvelous idea," Malguinne lied, with an unflinching smile.

Cold panic started to roll down Samuel's spine. He didn't trust this man, and he needed to tell the other two about the lies. But he couldn't just call for a group meeting without looking suspicious. This man was clearly powerful and possibly uncaring of other people's well-being when he used his power. However, they did need to cross the river, and if they were going to confront the Dark Lord, they would need more than just the three of them.

"Okay," Samuel said, with only slight hesitation. "Let's go back to our horses and find the rest of your companions."

He would just have to bide his time and tell the others what he knew later. For now, he was going to keep an eye on the wizard. Samuel hoped he didn't just make the worst decision of his life.

Campfire Conversations: Declawed Leader
Cycle 4, Day 17

T he man formerly known as King Crab just sat there, in the middle of the woods with his four companions, completely silent as the golden rays of morning light started to illuminate the world. He and his men sat on the cold, wet, slightly muddy ground, with no fire and next to no supplies, except what they had on their horses.

"Tonight," the leader said, finally breaking the silence, "we hunt them down and slit their throats as they sleep. We start with the old man, then the little mage, then the girl. Then we take the young pup and—"

"No, boss," the man with the crossbow interrupted. His voice rang with notes of defeat. "I say we cut our losses and just forget them."

"What was that, Bolt?" the leader asked, with a wild look in his amber eyes. "Are you going to just let some pups and an old goat make a joke out of us?"

"I didn't sign up to kill kids," Bolt said, matching his leader's wild anger. "I left the king's army because I didn't want to see any more corpses every time I close my eyes!"

"That's too damned bad!" the leader shouted. "As long as I am your captain, you will do as I command!"

"Then this is goodbye," the man who was no longer Bolt said. He stood up and went to his horse.

"Fine, leave!" the leader said. "But you will leave your

supplies with us."

The man climbed his horse and ignored his former leader.

"Men," the leader said, "stop him now and take what is ours!"

Two of the men stood up and slowly walked to their horses, preparing to leave as well. The leader shouted incoherently as the three galloped away.

All that was left was the leader and Lockpick.

"Get some rest, Lockpick," the leader said, as he attempted to regain his composure. But the wildfire in his eyes raged on. "We will start searching for the kids and the old man tonight."

"No, boss," Lockpick said firmly. "I think it's time to call it quits."

"There is no quitting!" the leader spat. "We can't just return to normal living. No, we made our bed; now we lie in it."

"I want to earn a better bed, boss," Lockpick said. "I think that boy was right. I want to give lockmaking a try. I'll need to earn some honest money. But after that, I can open up a shop. Will you join me, boss?"

"What the hells are you even saying?" the leader said. "You'll never make it like that. You'll be forced to beg on the street within a cycle."

"I would rather that than whatever this is becoming." Lockpick stood up slowly, wiping the dirt from his singed pants, and proceeded to his horse.

"Don't you dare turn your back on me, Lockpick!"

"No, boss," the man who was once Lockpick said, "it's Joseph, son of Jonathan. Goodbye, boss." With that, Joseph climbed on his horse and galloped away.

The leader of nobody slumped to the ground, his mind

211

a gyre with a collapsing center. All the actions he has taken to this point were spinning in his mind. He was dizzy from a life of his making. He lurched over and began to dry heave, but there was nothing for his body to expel but his past, written in stone.

The man formerly known as King Crab, formerly known as Boss, formerly known as Captain of the King's army, remained on the cold, wet, muddy ground alone.

Chapter 11: Goes Unpunished
Cycle 4, Day 16

Samuel was not happy with his current situation. He had been nominated as the first watch, alongside Malguinne, at the wizard's suggestion. Samuel was hoping it had just been a coincidence that he hadn't had a free moment with his friends, but this was a sign of quite the opposite.

They had crossed the river easily with the aid of the wizard. He created a tunnel in the water that led them to the other side. Despite his trepidation toward the wizard, he was in awe at his mastery over the elements. After they crossed the river, they set up camp and prepared to rest. So far, Malguinne hadn't said much other than inane chatter—but even most of that had been complete lies. Samuel was growing more and more uneasy and wished he hadn't rescued this man.

"Your friends are incredible with their magic," Malguinne said with a prideful beam, as if he were their teacher. "Crab magic… can't say I've seen that one before."

"It was honestly terrifying to see him use it the first time," Samuel said, trying not to relive the moment.

"I imagine so," Malguinne said. "Shifting magic can be rough to look at before the mage becomes accustomed to their magic. I do hope they both join the school for young mages by the capital."

"Is that where you learned your magic?"

"My dear boy," Malguinne said, "I am one of the founders of that school."

"Oh," was all Samuel could think to say. He mindlessly placed a few more sticks onto the slowly dimming fire.

"It could be an essential part of your friend's mastery over magic," Malguinne continued. "It could help hone young Caleb's shifting magic and young Za'rie's elemental magic and maybe teach her the other elements as well."

"That would be beneficial," Samuel said, not sure where the flow of conversation was leading.

"It could even help you master your own magic," Malguinne said.

"What?" Samuel was completely taken off guard— even more so by the fact that it wasn't a lie.

"Oh, don't play me for a fool," the wizard said as a dark harshness bled into his voice. His eyes narrowed and his whole appearance seemed to shift from kindly-old-man to a dangerous and sinister wizard. "I know you are a practitioner of mental magic."

"I think you're mistaken," Samuel replied, as he started to inch backward. "I don't have magic. I've *never* had magic."

"Hmm, I see," Malguinne said. "I suppose it is possible you never realized it was magic. But didn't you think it strange how you could always tell when someone was lying? Oh, no child, don't even try and deny it. I have been purposefully lying to you this whole evening and watching your every reaction. You have the most obvious tell when you notice a lie, though I don't think I will tell you what it is. Now to the real meat of the matter. I would very much like to have your support in my quest to save the world. Who knows what dangers might befall your friends if I don't make it to the Dark Lord in time."

Samuel was quiet as he calculated every possible outcome of this situation and found not a single good one. He

214

slowly lowered his head, showing defeat.

"I'll do whatever you wish of me," Samuel said, "but please, don't hurt my friends."

"Then look me in the eyes," the wizard said.

Samuel did as he was told.

"Samuel, I command you to do exactly as I say."

There was a red glow in Malguinne's eyes for a fraction of a second, and when it faded, Samuel receded inward, as if trapped in his mind.

"Yes, sir," his body said, without Samuel's volition.

"I'm glad we could come to this happy agreement," Malguinne said, his cheerful smile returning as it hid under his beard.

***

Malguinne woke up the next morning with as many aches and pains in his joints as there were stars in the sky. He was ready for this adventure to be long behind him. His body was sorely missing his comfortable bed as he wormed out of his bedroll. This entire journey has just been one disaster after another. He had no clue where Buddy and Tyberion were, and he feared that time was so limited that there was no point in even searching for them. Malguinne was betting that Buddy was dead or dying, given the old man's physical well-being. Or lack thereof. Malguinne decided to abandon his initial plan. His new objective was to find the elf. As long as Rythel had the null wood arrow, they could still kill the Dark Lord. That abomination was going to shatter this world and rob it of its magic, and Malguinne would not just sit idly by and wait for it to happen.

Reflexively Malguinne raised his hand, whispered a quick chant, and produced a small flame just above his pointer finger. The warmth of the flame started to radiate around him, creating a sphere of comfort with him as the center. He smiled genuinely as he remembered casting this spell for the first time one cold and dreary night. In fact, it was one of the first spells he learned how to cast. He could still feel the pride and joy of that day. Magic was always something he could do well. It was the only thing he could do well. He pushed down hard against the tainted memories of his youth. There was no use in recounting the past, not when he had fought so hard to make it where he currently was in life…which was in a small tent in the middle of a dew-covered forest.

He exited his tent and found that the campfire had become nothing more than embers sometime in the last few hours. He looked around and saw the three children sitting up—back to back to back—with a blanket around them, dead asleep. It looked to Malguinne that they attempted to share the last watch together and did not quite make it to dawn. Malguinne took a deep breath, got to his feet, and made his way over to the three.

"Samuel, my boy," he said with forced cheer, "it is time for you and your friends to wake up."

Samuel's eyes shot open instantly. For half a moment his eyes were glazed over as he registered the command. Then they were back to normal as he nodded and began to wake the others. He always hated that hollow look in his thralls' eyes; it made him incredibly uncomfortable, as if he were giving commands to a doll, or a corpse. But Samuel was a threat and had to be taken out, otherwise the boy would have ruined all his hard work. He considered doing the same with the other two children, but he could only control three people at a time, and it would be such a waste to use his trump card on children who don't know how to fully use their magic. The unfortunate aspect of his mental domination magic is that the person being controlled is fully aware the entire time, and people have a tendency to retaliate after being released. Malguinne tried to avoid this awkward outcome as much as possible.

"How about some breakfast?" Malguinne asked, as the other two children were slowly struggling to regain wakefulness.

*****

Once they had eaten some of their leftover rations and packed their camping supply, they began to search the area for Malguinne's two remaining companions. Za'rie seemed to be the most capable at tracking as she carefully searched for tracks by the river bank and any kind of markings indicating a person's presence. Unfortunately, the recent rain seemed to wash away almost all traces of Rythel and John. This led to a lot of meaningless arguing between the three.

"Don't step there!" Za'rie shouted at Samuel, as hour three of the search approached with painful slowness.

"I'm sinking in mud!" Samuel shouted back. "I need to move somewhere!"

"Mud has never hurt anyone!"

"I beg to differ!"

"How about we take a break?" Caleb suggested.

"Stay out of this!" Za'rie and Samuel shouted in unison.

Malguinne stood there, eyes closed, nose pinched, and slightly sinking. He was on his fifth unanswered prayer to the goddess. On one hand, he was grateful that his mental magic did not alter his thrall's personality, on the other hand, he was ready to jam his head in the mud for some blessed silence.

"Now, now," Malguinne said, returning his expression to the "kindly-old-man" position. "I believe young Caleb is correct. Tempers are flaring, and if we continue in this way, we will find less than nothing."

Za'rie blushed deeply as she nodded with resignation. Samuel also had the decency to look slightly ashamed by his childish outburst. The four mages found a clear spot away from the river where they could sit and evaluate their current plans. Or at least they could sit if the area wasn't still wet. But this gave Malguinne an idea.

"Za'rie," he said, as he adopted a teacherly tone of voice, "this would be a perfect opportunity for you to work on your air manipulation. I know just the spell that you can use to remove the dew."

"I don't know," Za'rie said as her expression narrowed with thought. "Lilly still doesn't trust me to use her freely, or for non-urgent reasons."

"Who is Lilly?" Malguinne asked. He looked around to make sure there wasn't a fourth child that he neglected to notice.

"My magika," Za'rie said.

She looked over to Caleb, whose eyes widened with excitement as a large grin spread across his face.

"That's a beautiful name," Caleb said.

"Well, of course you would say that," Samuel said, as he began to laugh. "But I will have to agree with him for once. That is a really nice name."

"Thank you," Za'rie said, with a hint of pride in her voice.

"Magika? Where did you children hear that word?"

Malguinne asked in bewilderment. He sat down on the patch of grass, realizing too late that it was still wet. He winced at the cold moisture that felt disagreeable on his rear, but he decided to ignore it and focus on the topic at hand.

Za'rie sat down as well, seeming to pay the damp grass no mind. The other two followed suit, though Samuel struggled to not show the discomfort on his face. Naturally, he failed. Za'rie pulled out a book titled *Magic Theory and Magical Application* and passed it to Malguinne.

"Dear goddess," Malguinne moaned, as he flipped through the book with frustrated quickness. "How has this book not been burned? The *theories* in this book are baseless and unproven. The author is a hack who doesn't know the first thing about magic. There is no such thing as magika. Magic is a part of *you*. Not its own entity. Magic that seems to act on its own is magic that has been corrupted and is merely reacting to the world around it. Think of it like muscle spasms in a dead animal. I'm terribly sorry that this was your introduction to magic." Malguinne hesitated—he wanted to keep the book to prevent her from becoming even more tainted by its ideas—but even he knew that would do him no favors in keeping their trust. So he handed the book back to her as he hid his disgust in doing so.

"But the book is right," Caleb said. The boy held out his hand and a blue orb appeared just above his palm. The light shifted into the form of a crab. "This is Hermy, my magika, and he is very much real."

"I will admit that is impressive," Malguinne said. He was taken aback by such a unique spell and the fact that it required no chanting. Maybe Caleb was a stronger mage than he realized. He was still unfortunately under many false understandings when it came to magic, but that would be resolved once he received the proper education. "But just because it can imitate life does not mean it is alive."

"He is!" Caleb exclaimed. "Tell him, Samuel."

For a split second, there was panic on Samuel's face. The spell enthralling him allowed him to act normally, but it also prevented him from acting against the person who cast the spell. This creates what Malguinne has dubbed a magical hiccup. Malguinne quickly gave a telepathic command to Samuel to side with his friends.

"I've seen with my own eyes that Hermy is alive." Samuel paused for a moment as he cringed at saying that name. "I think there is more to magic than we are led to believe."

"Hmmm, I suppose," Malguinne said, as he acted to take their words seriously. "Perhaps there is more for me to learn." It was a blow to his pride to even pretend to toy with this notion. Malguinne was the greatest wizard this world has ever seen after all. What more could he possibly learn? He was about to propose that they join his school once this journey was over, but shouting coming from the north interrupted him.

"That has to be them!" Caleb said, his voice shaken with shock and a tinge of fear.

The four of them shot up and ran toward the voices. Malguinne struggled to keep up while maintaining his breathing. His beard and robes were constantly getting stuck in low-hanging branches. But even at his age, Malguinne was surprisingly in excellent shape.

In less than a minute the four of them found the source of the shouts. Rythel and John were barreling toward them with hands full of berries and a swarm of pixies screeching close behind them. Malguinne had a quick chuckle as he

220

watched the tiny nuisances getting closer to the two men. Singularly pixies are practically harmless, but a swarm of them can easily overwhelm trespassers in gruesome and horrific ways. The wizard made a mental note to keep his mouth closed if they made him a target. Malguinne slid back into his more serious role and started to silently chant a spell, pointing a finger in the swarm's direction.

"Wait!" Za'rie shouted. She grabbed his arm and pulled it down. "I can do this without hurting them."

Malguinne considered this for a moment and decided it was a great replacement teaching moment. And if she failed, he could at least salvage the arrow. He simply nodded and stepped back.

Za'rie looked pleased with herself and turned toward the swarm with a determined sharpness in her eyes. She raised her hand and said, "Please, Lilly, I need a strong wind. But don't hurt them." Dirt and leaves lifted by a strong air current swirled around her, funneling around her outstretched arm and shooting from her reach like a tunnel of wind. It blew past Rythel and John and caught the pixies in its whirlwind. They lost control of their flight and went careening until they were no longer visible. The party decided to not celebrate victory just yet. When the two men reached Malguinne and the others, they all kept running in the direction of the river and out of the pixies domain.

As they reached the riverside, Rythel and John collapsed on the ground, laughing uncontrollably between gasps of breath.

"I told you they wouldn't understand your idea of a trade," Rythel said. He sounded more like an amused child who got away with a risky prank rather than a scolding adult.

"How was I supposed to know they wouldn't want gold?" John countered with equal amusement.

"I would recommend common sense," Malguinne said with a chuckle, "but you ran out of that currency well before I met you, I would say."

They all took a few minutes to catch their breath before Rythel looked around with a confused expression and asked the first question Malguinne expected, "Where are Buddy and Tyberion?"

Malguinne allowed a horrified expression to replace his mirthful one. "I thought they were with you two. I was knocked out and captured by bandits just as they were crossing."

Silence infected the group as a horrific realization hit everyone but Malguinne.

"No that..." John started, but his voice cut out with a painful choking sound.

Rythel placed his hand gently on the other man's shoulder. "There will be a time of mourning. But now cannot be that time. We knew the dangers of this quest from the start. Now we must finish it in their honor."

"I am afraid that Rythel is right," Malguinne said, with forced sorrow and regret. "They would never forgive us if we stopped now, as we are nearing our goal. The king will make sure the kingdom knows of their sacrifice, and Tyberion's family will be justly compensated."

"Yeah, and what about Buddy's family?" John spat. He tried to shake off Rythel's hand, but the elf refused to separate from him.

Malguinne glanced at the three children who were all awkwardly silent and looking away from the adults. They clearly did not know how to act in such a pitiful situation.

"Rythel, John," Malguinne said, "I know this is the

lowest point of our adventure, but even at our lowest the goddess provides. Let me introduce you to the three young mages that saved my life."

Chapter 12: The Hero is Victorious
Cycle 4, Day 20

Magus sat at the table in his banquet hall, rereading the Scout Report that Captain turned in to him just a few days prior…after leaping from the back of a giant phoenix. Magus had been through these reports so many times that he could practically recite them from memory. Yet he still poured over them. He was hoping that without Buddy, Malguinne would no longer have a viable way of defeating him, but he had a horrible feeling that the wizard had another trick up his sleeve. But what?

The sound of approaching footsteps brought Magus out of his thoughts and back to the room. He turned toward the direction of the sound and saw Buddy entering the hall.

"Oh, good morning," Buddy said.

"Good morning," Magus said. "You're up rather early."

"You know what they say, old habits and all."

"I am…unfamiliar with this."

"Yeah, 'course you would be," Buddy said. "Don't worry about it. Just a saying from my world. Do you ever sleep? I don't think I've ever not seen you up first."

"I do not sleep," Magus said, an automatic reply to one of the questions he gets the most.

"No shit?" Buddy said. "That must be a blessing and a curse."

"I see it as neither. It is just my nature."

"Does it have to do with how you never remove your

armor?"

"It does," another automatic response. Magus decided a change in topic would be best. "I have sent out a few scouting goblins to look for Malguinne. I don't expect him to remain captured long. He is the most formidable mage I have ever come across. However, I despise how he treats his magic. I could practically hear it begging for mercy every time he commanded it."

"Here's what I don't get," Buddy said as he sat down on the other side of the table, facing Magus. "Why did you just let him go the first time you fought against him?"

"He would have just been an extra mouth to feed, taking valuable resources away from my people. It would have also been difficult to keep him from escaping."

"You could have just killed him," Buddy said, with a calmness that would have sent chills down any sane person's spine.

"I could have," Magus agreed. "And perhaps I should have. However, killing is such a waste."

"How so?"

"Every life is an infinite of potential," Magus said. "To end a life before it is meant to be is to put an end to an infinite amount of possibilities. A living Malguinne could learn from his mistakes and improve, or he could find a way to undo me and my mission. But a dead Malguinne obviously can do nothing. I suppose killing would stop an infinite amount of possible evils, but it also stops an infinite amount of possible goods."

"I mean, that is one way to look at it," Buddy said, as his mind grappled with a philosophy Magus spent the last several thousand lifetimes living by.

"Some things are better not to have to think about," Magus said. "I will speak with Ambience and see how breakfast is progressing. Once everyone eats, I will take Lawrence to the Well with me to check in. You and Tyberion are more than welcome to join us."

"That's good by me," Buddy said with a toothy grin.

These goblins have quite the infectious smile, Magus thought to himself. He was sure one day they would win society's favor.

***

Malguinne was pleased that they were making incredible progress, now that Buddy wasn't slowing them down. If they kept going at their current pace they would make it to the ruins the goblins have infested within the day. The wizard started to plan the return trip but found his internal calculations interrupted as he saw the familiar bobbing of a group of goblins coming their way.

"How peculiar," Malguinne said, as the rest of the group started to prepare their weapons. "Oh, none of that now. We are on their land, after all. Let's see what they have to say."

The wizard cursed inwardly as the goblins made their leisurely march toward them. He wanted nothing more than to blast them to the lowest point in all the nine hells, but he knew that the goblins would most likely be the quickest route to their target.

"Greetings," the goblin in the lead said. He wore a disgusting and ugly mockery of human clothes and had a trashed wedding ring as a piercing. It was all Malguinne could do to keep a kindly smile on his face. "I am Puppies. My lord wishes you to follow me. Is all companions accounted for?"

"I am sad to say we have lost two of our friends," Malguinne answered. "But I am sure they would wish for us to continue in their stead."

"You are right," Puppies replied, with a hideous grin that showed every badly damaged and cavity-infected tooth. "Buddy and Tybe— Tybar— er, man in armor, are with our lord now and wish you to join."

"Oh?" Malguinne said, unable to hide the surprise.

He was about to say more, but John rushed forward with incredible speed and lifted the goblin leader. The goblin looked more shocked than anything else, but the other goblins drew their weapons and prepared to strike. That was until John pulled the goblin into an embrace.

"I knew it!" John shouted with pure glee. His eyes were closed, and he was practically dancing around, with the goblin dangling in his arms. The goblin quickly realized what was happening and went with it, returning the embrace. "I knew those two wouldn't just die like that! Rythel, why aren't you celebrating?"

"I am celebrating in my own way," Rythel said calmly, but he could not hide the single tear of joy that he tried to casually wipe away.

"That is amazing news!" Malguinne joined in, as he tried to mimic his companions' ecstatic mood. "Please take us to them with great haste. I have missed them both deeply."

The party followed the horrible monsters as Malguinne began the process of making another backup plan. How in the hells was Buddy with the Dark Lord? Was he still on their side, or had the villain corrupted him? Malguinne was not sure how this was going to play out, but he still had the null wood arrow to count on, and that's all that mattered.

***

Lawrence was with Magus, Seth, Tyberion and Buddy at the mouth of the Well when Puppies entered the cavern and introduced the adventurers who sought to kill his current employer. Magus thanked Puppies and asked him and the other goblins to leave, which they did after some protest. Lawrence did not like how calm Magus was at the return of the Royal Wizard. It was obvious the wizard would only be back to face off against the man who put his magic to shame if he knew he could win. But Magus did not seem to put much thought into his concerns.

Malguinne was the first to enter. Followed by an elf archer and a human in light, leather armor. Lawrence expected these three. However, he did not expect the three children that came after. An elf girl and two human boys. Was the wizard so desperate that he resorted to children? Lawrence was about to speak up when Seth spoke up first.

"Sam!" Seth shouted. His voice was filled with joy mixed with relief.

"Dad!" the youngest boy shouted in return. His voice mirrored his father's in tone and volume.

Seth ran toward the group with unreserved speed and was met in the middle by the boy. Seth fell to his knees and embraced his son, who in turn wrapped around his father so tightly it was a wonder no bones were broken on either party's side.

"Are you okay?" Seth asked. "Wait, why are you here? How did you get here? Have you eaten? Holy hells, why is your throat so bruised?"

"Dad, I—"

"Samuel," the wizard interrupted, "step away from that

228

man. He is with the enemy."

"Yes, sir," Samuel said, his eyes going wide and life-less. The smile on his face became a blank slate. He stepped back from his father and, in a quick turn, started to walk back to the wizard.

The other two children ran toward the boy, positioning themselves between him and Malguinne. The older boy was trying to shake the younger one out of the daze he was in, and the girl took out an axe and stared down the wizard.

"What have you done to him?" the girl screamed as the boy's father started to approach and get a good look at his son.

"Be a good girl and stay silent while the adults talk," the wizard said. His eyes were cold and lacked any kindness.

"What have you done to my son?" Seth shouted, draw-ing his sword.

"I'm truly sorry to do this," the wizard said, "but you have been corrupted by evil. May the goddess reuse your breath."

Lawrence watched in horror as Malguinne pointed his index finger, sparks dancing around it, at Seth, and a bolt of lightning shot toward the man. Lawrence wanted to do something, anything, but there was nothing he could do to save the man. Just as the lightning was about to strike Seth, the shape of a large suit of armor appeared out of thin air in front of him and absorbed the full blast.

"This is between you and me," Magus said, not even shaken after taking a direct hit from Malguinne's lightning.

"Oh, I think not," Malguinne said. "You have the ad-vantage with one on one. But if I play the numbers game… Samuel! Keep the children busy!"

Caleb had his eyes on the man in the black armor when a strong gust of wind knocked him several inches to the left, just in time to avoid the dagger that would have stabbed him in the chest.

"Caleb, stay focused!" Za'rie shouted. "Samuel, it's us, your friends."

Samuel turned his blank stare at Za'rie and lunged the elven dagger in her direction. Za'rie dodged just out of reach from the attack.

"Fine, we will just apologize later," Za'rie said as her magic purple butterfly appeared and fluttered around her head. "Restrain him, Lilly."

Caleb jumped to his feet and asked Hermy to give him claws just as a torrent of wind cascaded against Samuel. However, Samuel had his shield out in preparation, and the wind avoided him entirely.

***

"Seth, go help your son," Magus said without turning. "I will take care of this old fool."

Magus heard the man dash away from him as a fireball collided against armor. He was unfazed. It wasn't like the armor could develop more scorch marks. The wizard stood there in what Magus assumed was a calm rage. The elf and the human beside him looked confused and were hesitating to join in on either side. Lawrence and Tyberion stood in front of Buddy, protecting the old man. He would have to end this quickly. Otherwise, there would be casualties.

Another fireball was lobbed at him; this time, it was as big as himself. He channeled his magic and created an airless pocket around himself. The flame instantly dissipated as it passed into the area. Magus was about to counterattack when he heard something from above. He looked up to see a large stalactite falling right on top of him. He lifted his right gauntlet and reached for the rock with his magic. He focused on shifting it, causing the rock to burst into a thousand water droplets. Then he retook control of the air around him and pushed the raining water toward the wizard, shifting each droplet back into the broken-down pieces of the stalactite. A hail of rocks was sent hurtling toward Malguinne, who in turn raised a thick wall of rock that blocked the attack.

Then Magus began to feel himself sink. He looked down to see the ground beneath him had become quicksand. He placed his gauntlet onto the liquid rock and changed the consistency of the quicksand directly beneath him, creating a platform to stand on, then forced it to push him up. Just as he was free, the rock wall Malguinne used as a shield crashed into Magus, sending him forcefully to the ground.

As he was climbing back to his feet, a flash of green in his peripheral vision caught his eye.

***

"*Transport behind Malguine, no time skip,*" Lawrence said quickly. This was insanely stupid. He knew better than anyone his magic was next to useless in combat. Without his pieces of paper, he felt like a drake hunter with an impossibly sharp but unwieldy sword. In a flash of green, he was directly behind the wizard. He had one shot at this. He placed his hand on the wizard's back and said, "*Transport over the We-*"

A current of electricity shattered his nervous system,

sending him seizing to the ground. The pain was immeasurable. He couldn't even muster a scream of agony. But just past the blurring edges of vision, he could see the wizard holding out a flaming palm in his direction.

***

Za'rie watched as Seth reached out for his son, but he was greeted with the slice of a blade that was inches away from his flesh. He leapt backward. She was surprised at how quickly he was reacting. It made her just a little annoyed that he could be this good of a fighter if he would just stop hesitating and overthinking all the time. He was quick enough with the shield that magic was useless, and no one wanted to hurt him, so weapons were out of the question. But if this continued, Samuel was going to hurt someone or worse.

"I have an idea," Za'rie said uneasily. "Caleb, get ready to grab. You'll know it when you see it. Seth, get ready to tackle him when you see the opening."

Caleb nodded and prepared himself. Then, Za'rie charged; she had her axe held high with both hands tightly gripping the handle. Samuel turned quickly and held up his shield. She brought the axe down with as much force as she could, burying the head deep into the wood. Samuel pulled his shield back to free it from the grip of the axe, but Za'rie let go before it could come free.

Then, Samuel lunged at her.

Caleb took that moment to grab the handle of the axe and turned it backward like a leaver. Samuel flew back in the direction of the shield and landed flat on his back.

Seth took the opening and leapt on his son, grappling the dagger out of his hand. And then yanked the shield off, throwing it away. Caleb was then able to hold Samuel's wrists with his unbreakable crab grip. Za'rie was silently celebrating that her plan worked as she fell to her knees, grasping at her lower abdomen as blood started to seep past her fingers.

She thought that it was almost funny—being stabbed by a boy who, up until now, only used a shield to fight. The edges of her vision began to unravel and her grasp on consciousness slipped away. The last thing she felt was the faraway pain of her head hitting a rock. She lay there, unmoving.

***

Before Malguinne could roast the teleporting mage to a crisp, Jacob rammed himself into the wizard, knocking him to the ground. Malguinne looked up at him with bewildered confusion.

"Look, I'm sorry," Jacob said, genuinely apologetic. "I don't think I know exactly what's going on. But I know that this is wrong."

"I agree with him." The voice came from behind him and was followed by the sound of a bowstring being pulled. Jacob turned and saw Rythel pointing his bow at the wizard. "Making children fight their father and friends is not something I can get behind."

The wizard just sat there, dazed for a moment. He looked around the room at the chaos he had created. And for a moment, Jacob thought it was over.

"Rythel, I command you to do exactly as I say!" Malguinne said.

"Yes, sir," Rythel said.

Jacob turned to look at the elf and saw that his eyes were wide, and his face had gone blank. He didn't even get a chance to look back at Malguinne when a bolt of lightning struck him, sending him slamming against the stone wall.

***

Tyberion raised his new claymore and charged at the insane wizard. All he had to do was strike him down before he could cast any magic. Unfortunately, there was a lot of ground between him and the wizard.

"Tyberion," Malguinne said with a calm voice.

No, he had to ignore anything he said. He couldn't turn against his companions. He would never hurt Buddy. If he ignored the command, it wouldn't take effect, right?

"I command you to do exactly as I say."

The words pierced through his mind. He ceased to feel anything. Everything was numb. But he could still see. He could still think clearly.

"Yes, sir," his body said, without his permission.

"Kill the Dark Lord." The voice was like a worm eating through his mind.

"Yes, sir," his body said. He tried to fight against his muscles as they positioned his body to face Magus and forced him to charge with a raised sword.

***

Magus raised his gauntlet to catch the blade to shift it to glass. But just as the blade was coming down, an arrow struck the side of his cuff, knocking his hand off course just enough for the sword to make contact. Magus leapt back with a well-placed gust of wind that separated him and the swordsman. He looked down at his armor and saw a gash in the plate. He pushed his magic into the metal, causing it to expand and meld back together. He wanted to strengthen the metal, but if it were any harder, it would make movement difficult.

He rose proudly with a plan to neutralize Tyberion, who was yet again charging him, when an explosion behind him sent him forward. He was unbalanced, and before he could right himself properly, he was met with another slice of the man's blade. More pieces of metal fell from his chest piece as he fell to his knees.

He quickly turned the ground beneath him to water and allowed himself to sink into the newly formed puddle, freezing the surface behind him. He then willed a bubble of air around him and turned the water back to stone. He took a handful of rocks and placed them in the open gaps of his armor. The rocks turned to metal and began to merge with his armor just as the rocks surrounding him started to glow bright orange and melt around him.

He teleported above ground, twenty feet into the air, and out of Tyberion's reach. He pinpointed the wizard, raised his gauntlet and focused as sparks of electricity ran down his arm. He generated enough power to end the mad wizard here and now. He hadn't even looked down at Tyberion. He took for granted that he was safe from the warrior's close-range weapon. However, had he spared even a fraction of a second to look down at the bear of a man, he would have seen that he was not holding his sword. Instead, the sword was hovering inside a mini tornado, spinning faster and faster.

Just as gravity was pulling Magus down and his lightning bolt was about to fire, Tyberion's claymore was launched through the air. The sword pierced through Magus' chest and out the back. It had been propelled through the air by wind magic as powerful as a hurricane. Magus, the sword, and a hail of metal shards fell to the ground.

Watching the sword impale the armored mage made Buddy's heart ache as if it were the one being pierced. He watched as his mind-controlled friend slowly walked to pick up his sword. The body of Magus lay still on the ground. It was over. Malguinne won. Malguinne and everyone like him were too stubborn to see that it was time for the world to move on and change. Funny, wasn't he just as bad not too long ago? He didn't want to change with the world around him, and his stubbornness had ruined his relationship with his family. He was going to go home. He was going to fix everything. But first, he had to find a way to make a wizard see sense.

Buddy placed his hand over his rapidly beating heart, and then a thought struck him. The phoenix feather! Magus could still be saved. All he had to do was free Tyberion from the mind control, get the feather, revive Magus, and then…Well, everything after that would just have to wait until after. But how to free his friend?

Buddy turned to Malguinne, who was walking slowly to Magus' body, paying him no mind. He was anti-magic somehow, so maybe it was about time to find out how that worked.

***

Malguinne was so giddy he was shaking. The first fight between him and this evil monster was one of the most humiliating experiences of his life. Everything he would throw at the Dark Lord would be turned against him with ease. The fowl beast didn't even have to recite incantations or anything! But now he got him. Malguinne had outsmarted him and proven that he was the superior magic user.

"Tyberion, drag this creature to the edge of the large

236

hole," Malguinne ordered.

The giant, hairy oaf did exactly as ordered. The nearly lifeless body lay just inches away from the edge. Malguinne wasn't sure how far the drop was, but not even the Dark Lord could survive such a fall. However, that wasn't the plan. Certain precautions needed to be taken to ensure that this thing was gone for good.

His thought process was interrupted by the sound of quickly approaching footsteps. He turned toward the sound and was greeted by an unexpected sucker punch that connected with his jaw.

***

Buddy reeled back in absolute agony. It had been years since he last decked someone, and age had not been kind to his bony knuckles. But he was quite proud of the sight of the old wizard on his knees, blood dripping from his mouth and staining his beard. That should have broken the spell that was on—

Buddy found himself in even more pain as he was forcibly restrained by Tyberion. He was on the ground, with his face smooshed sideways against the cold, hard rock floor.

"You fool!" Malguinne shouted, as he began to rise to his feet. "Can't you see that I am fighting to save this world? To save magic? This creature is trying to destroy everything we know!"

"The only fool I see is the one who can't face reality," Buddy said with difficulty.

"Pleeessss, dooon kiiiiillllll hiiiiimmmm," came a quiet echo of a voice from the direction of the Well.

Buddy watched with shock as the body of Magus started to shakily pick itself up. It brought itself into a kneeling position, and that's when Buddy saw the gaping wound.

Except, there was no blood. No exposed internal organs. No anything. Inside the armor, there was no body.

"What?" Buddy said.

"Your *friend* didn't tell you about what *it* really is, did it?" Malguinne said, with the return of his mirthless smile. "The Dark Lord isn't a mage. It is magic. It has been corrupted over the millennia in a way to give off the appearance of being alive. It wants to take magic away from us real mages who have fought long and hard for our magic, as if that will make the world a better place."

"I don't believe you…" Buddy said.

"You don't have to believe me. You can see for yourself." Malguinne lifted a rock, which began to rise in his hand as he started to whisper and then went hurtling toward Magus. It struck his helmet, knocking it clean off, revealing nothing underneath. Magus jerked back and then grasped for the ground, trying to keep himself upright. "It created a body that is impervious to pain. It doesn't need sleep, food, water, or anything. It doesn't even have true emotions. It is just magic gone mad, and you and I have to put it down, Buddy. I can tear it apart piece by piece, but it will eventually just create a new body. But if you take it apart, the magic will die. You don't need to know why; you just need to do as I say. You do this, and you will be a hero. You won't even need to return home. The king will give you riches beyond your imagination. What do you say?"

Buddy felt Tyberion releasing the pressure off of him and was able to sit up. The longer Buddy was in this world, the less he understood. He had come to terms with the fact that this was nothing like what he expected. The wise mentor figure was a manipulative, lying bastard. The Dark Lord was a freedom fighter but was also magic somehow. He, the random person from the *real world*, was not the chosen one destined to save a fallen, dying world but was just a pawn to be used in a world that ultimately didn't need *him* specifically. If he weren't focused on how pissed he was at the poor excuse of a wizard who was lying even now, he would have found it all just so funny.

"Go to hell," Buddy said. He wanted to spit at the wizard, but his mouth had gone completely dry.

"That's no matter," Malguinne said with a chuckle. "Time for plan B. Rythel, would you kindly shoot it with the null wood arrow."

"Yes, sir."

***

Seth was trying everything he could to bring his son back to him. Nothing was working. Caleb was doing his best to restrain Samuel, but the boy's claws were starting to draw blood as his son struggled for freedom. Seth couldn't focus on the fighting going on. Not while his son was in this state. He was also smart enough to know to stay out of a magic fight. But when he heard Magus' broken voice pleading for someone else's life, Seth could no longer ignore it.

His breath escaped him as he saw the man he had grown to respect and admire the last half-cycle brought to the point of breaking. Seth felt like he was moving in slow motion as he stood up and took a step toward the crumbling man. As he took a second, agonizingly slow step, Magus' helmet was struck and fell into the black abyss. Seth should have been shocked to see that there was no face behind the mask, but all he could feel was fear for the loss of a good man.

A third then fourth step struck the ground and pushed forward with a strength and speed he did not know he had within him. Then, a fifth and sixth, matching this raw, primal power.

Seth heard a voice giving a command. It was a sound that was so distant it was as if it came from another reality outside of his own.

Magus was only a few more steps away, and yet he felt worlds away. Too far away.

Seventh and eighth steps. Just one more.

He heard the twang of a bowstring roaring like a cannon.

On the ninth step, he forced himself in front of Magus just in time.

The arrow struck deep into Seth's chest.

∗∗∗

Silent screams wailed in Rythel's mind as he watched the human sacrifice himself in vain. The force of the arrow pushed the man backward, and the hollow suit of armor extended its arms to catch him. But it had no strength left to catch itself. They both fell into the black pit. And Rythel could do nothing but watch.

He couldn't even produce tears.

∗∗∗

Samuel was a universe of rage and grief within himself. He watched his father fall as his body continued to tear at its restraints. No words could pass through his lips. No guttural cries of despair. His world was gone, and he was trapped in his own body.

But then, something possibly even worse happened. A bright yellow orb escaped from his chest. It was similar to Caleb's blue Hermy orb but significantly smaller. With unfathomable speed, it shot toward the dark hole, leaving be-hind a slowly fading trail of yellow light. It was followed by Caleb's blue orb and Za'rie's purple orb, then the wizard's red orb and the unconscious mage's green orb. Their magic had left them and followed his father and the Dark Lord into the pit. But they weren't alone. In less than a second, more lines of light of every color were flooding into the cave, passing through layers of rock, all converging on the pit.

Samuel could feel himself in control of his body again, and he saw that Caleb's claws had disappeared. However, there was no time to reflect on the consequences of what was happening. As more and more orbs filled the air with a bril-liant multicolored display, there was a pulling sensation that was forcefully dragging everyone toward the hole.

***

Caleb saw the hunched-over form of Za'rie begin to be sucked toward the cave's center and made a grab for her, but in doing so, Samuel began to slide. Caleb tried to hold on to both of his friends, but his arms no longer had the enhanced strength he needed, and the strain was breaking him. He couldn't fight against the current of wind forever.

"We have to jump in!" Samuel shouted,

"We will die!" Caleb cried.

"Trust me, the magic wouldn't kill us!"

"Are you sure?"

"No! But my dad is down there!"

Za'rie hadn't said a word, and that was worrying Caleb. She was flopping around like a rag doll. Possibly uncon-scious. Hopefully just unconscious. They had to get out of here.

Caleb used all his remaining strength to grasp both of

his friends and bring them together in one uncomfortable embrace. And then his stomach lurched as he leapt off the ground and was pulled into the light-filled pit.

A World Without Magic
Cycle 4, Day 20

A crowd of scared townsfolk were gathered in the Leabmore Library. Everyone was shouting questions that no one could answer. However, no one was listening, even if there were answers. They were expressing their fears in the only way they knew how.

"I told you the end of the world was coming," said an ornery old farmer. "The two-headed snake was a sign."

"You've said no such thing," his wife said. "And that snake didn't have two heads; it had two spots that looked like eyes on its tail."

"If the world ain't endin', then what were those lights?" came the voice of the town's innkeeper.

"A light flew out of my chest!" a woman said, gaining the attention of concerned men, who took great interest in her chest.

Ella's mind was dizzy with the insanity that had flooded into her once-peaceful library. Had it only been one or two concerned townsfolk, she could have handled it; three to five would be doable but difficult; but half the town seemed to be trying to squeeze into her library. Everyone was scared, because no one knew what was going on with the strange lights that were filling the sky. Ella was scared, too, but she had a job to do. And that was providing information to those looking for it.

"Everyone, calm down," Ella said. Everyone unanimously chose to become less calm and directed their group chaos in her direction. "Calm down now, or I will murder the romance section!"

"What about the—" came the lone quiet, male voice in the sea of newly silent patrons.

"Especially the erotica books!" Ella shouted, with a tone that said *test me, I dare you*. Not even a whisper left the lips of a single person. "Good. Now, I don't know what is going on. The Book of Anu, to my knowledge, never went into end-of-the-world prophecies. And all the books I know of that deal with such prophecies never started with 'The end of the world started with a beautiful display of colors shooting through the sky.' However, I haven't read every book here. So what's going to happen is we are all going to take a book and silently read. If you find an answer, share it with us."

She walked toward the staircase that led to the "Restricted Section" and removed the sign.

"I recommend we start with these books," she said. "But there will be no pushing and absolutely no arguing and fighting. Get a book and find a spot to read; go outside if you need to."

She stepped behind her desk and watched as the patrons calmly started to pick out books. Or at least as calmly as people fearing the end possibly could. As long as there was no bloodshed, she was happy.

Ella knew that no one would be able to find any answers. People would be lucky if they could focus enough to see the words they were looking at. But people had to have a distraction, a goal, to keep their mind away from the fear of the unknown. She placed her hand on her chest, remembering the sensation of the orb of pink light leaving her body and flying away. It was so similar to the other boy's blue light that she was certain whatever was going on had to do with magic. And she was now just as certain that she was also a mage, just like that boy. Or at least, she had been a mage.

She pulled out her heavily dog-eared and marked-in copy of *How to Tame Your Magic* and continued to read where she left off. Even she needed to distract herself from what could possibly be the end of the world as she knew it, in more ways than just one.

***

The students of the magic school were enacting a similar petition for answers. However, their search for understanding was met with a locked door. The headmaster and the professors had locked themselves in the headmaster's office immediately after losing their magic. All thirteen students rallied behind Emile and Meredith as they sought to get answers from the people who were paid to answer questions.

"Where is our magic?!" demanded the group of frenzied teens. Silence rang from behind the door. The same answer they had been receiving since the beginning.

"New plan!" Emile shouted, as he and Meredith took their spot at the head of the group. "We find the answer ourselves!"

"How do we do that?" asked one of the rank-one students.

"We find the person who knows the most about magic," Meredith said, practically reading Emile's mind. Though to be fair, that wouldn't be a difficult task. "We go find Doctor Lawrence. If anyone knows, it will be him."

At this point, the door behind her opened, revealing an irate headmaster.

"I expressly forbid it!" he said, his face turning five separate shades of red.

"Who's going to stop us?" Emile said.

"We will…" said the short, white-haired professor.

"How?" Meredith asked. "There are six of you and thirteen of us. And your magic is just as gone as ours."

"Are you threatening a professor?" the headmaster asked.

"That depends," Emile asked with a wide grin, "do you feel threatened?"

Emile and Meredith turned the group of teens away from the dumbstruck professors and marched forward. No attempts of restraint were made. Most likely, they would send word to the capital to send Wardens to find them, but Emile wasn't worried, not as long as he had Meredith by his side. They passed through the front door of the school and started to head down the mountain. Emile placed his hand in Meredith's, and she squeezed his hand in return.

"Where should we start looking first?" she asked.

"If I were a betting man—"

"And thank goddess you aren't."

"*If* I were a betting man," Emile continued, hiding his grin, "I would say he would find the least likely place to lay low in."

"So, a place mages wouldn't go voluntarily?"

"Right, though I think the Capital is ruled out, as there's no way they wouldn't catch us."

"Okay," Meredith said, "I have a dumb idea."

"Impossible," Emile said. "What is it?"

"So the Dark Lord is capturing mages," Meredith said. "So, that would be the one place a mage would avoid, so prime candidate for a mage hiding spot using your logic. But

I'm also curious if that might have something to do with the disappearance of magic."

"Ok, I was wrong; that is a ludicrously dumb idea," Emile said with a grimace. "I like it. I say we put it to a vote with the others once we get far enough away from the school to take a rest."

"Sounds good to me," Meredith said, holding tighter to Emile's hand.

"Who knows, if you're right, maybe we can save the world and bring back magic."

***

Aila couldn't help but be amused by how frantically all the adults were running around Prymbleton. All the magic items lost their magic at the same time as a nearly endless stream of lights headed toward the Dark Lord's domain, and suddenly, it was the end of the world. She and her cot siblings were ordered to remain in their dorm until the adults solved the issue. It was obviously not an issue that one community of elves could fix, but leave it to a bunch of 500+ year-olds to think they know everything just because they have lived so long. The second that something they've never experienced pops up, and they just lose their whole minds.

"What do you think is going on?" Lyra asked the others.

"I bet it has something to do with Za'rie," said one of the male cot siblings. He spoke angrily and spat out Za'rie's name as if it were poison.

"Why Za'rie?" Aila asked.

"Because she destroyed the town's crystal," the angry elf said. Though it was hard for the others to take his anger seriously. "She was out to screw up our way of life on a whim."

"Do you all really believe that?" Aila said, looking at all the elves in the room with an accusatory glare. The others averted their eyes, but there were several nods of agreement. "I can't believe you all! Just believing what the adults say, just like that. Za'rie has been our cot sister our whole lives; we know her better than anyone ever will. She is impulsive and quick-tempered and a pain in the ass. But she would never cause anyone harm. She would put herself in harm's way before she lets someone else get hurt."

"But the spy pictures—"

"Yes, the spy pictures clearly show her breaking the crystal," Aila interrupted, "but I also saw the handle of her axe covered in blood. Some adults say she was mind-controlled by the humans; maybe that's the case, but I doubt it. I think she had a reason for what she did, and she didn't tell us because she didn't want us to get hurt or get banished like she did. What she did was horrible and hurt the village, but I believe she did it for what she felt was the right reason."

"I want to believe you," Lyra said, "but without her to defend herself, it's hard."

"Then maybe we should go out and search for her and find out," Aila said.

She didn't mean what she said. She was just so angry that she said the first thing that popped into her head. But the pure fear and panic on her cot siblings' faces told her that she had struck a nerve.

"But we can't," said a different male cot sibling. "We can only leave our village during our time of… well, you know." He turned away, unable to look the others in the eyes as he blushed.

"If we leave now, we will be banished just like her,"

Lyra said.

"I know that," Aila said apologetically. "I didn't really mean that."

There was an awkward pause in the conversation that eventually led to a change in topic that was gratefully appreciated. But Aila couldn't quite get the idea out of her head. Did she not mean it? Then why was it sounding more and more like a good idea to leave the village and look for her friend? There was a whole world out there, and if the lack of magic items was going to change their life drastically anyway, why not leave? If Za'rie could do it, then so could she, right?

***

Honeysuckle and Apple Pie sat lackadaisically in front of the Ophidian River, leaning against the napping Thistle. All momentum of their journey was halted by the obstacle they had forgotten to remember.

"You think plan?" Apple Pie asked.

"No," Honeysuckle said, attempting to strategize a plan. All he managed was a headache. "Horse no cross. We no cross with no horse. Horse no go underground. We stuck."

Apple Pie just nodded and relaxed as he listened to the calming river's flow. The sun was out, the ground was dry, and the weather was in that perfect spot of cool breeze mixed with a steady warmth. Everything was right and peaceful in the world. Apple Pie fell into a deep, contented sleep. He didn't even wake up when Honeysuckle tried to shake his brother out of his slumber and watch the pretty lights traveling in the direction of their home.

And so concludes the crossing attempt of the valiant goblins for the third day.

Chapter 13: Before The Beginning
Cycle Unknown, Day Unknown

Samuel wanted to close his eyes. He didn't want to see the world around him rising as he fell to his probable death. But try as he might, he couldn't stop himself from watching. Partly out of morbid curiosity and partly because it was too beautiful not to see. The pit was filled with a rainbow of color as strands of magic shot past them, leaving behind a slowly vanishing trail of light. It felt like flying through a meteor shower.

Samuel looked down and saw the ground quickly approaching. But the magic wasn't just passing through the stone floor as it had from above. It was crashing into the ground like a waterfall and created what looked like a pool of living light. As Samuel, Caleb, and Za'rie struck against this strange liquid light, it didn't feel like falling onto the ground or into water. It felt like breaking through a thin veil.

When they passed through, they were in a dark void, but they were no longer falling. They were slowly floating weightlessly through the darkness. Unable to breathe, but in a way that didn't feel suffocating. It was as if breathing was not necessary. Samuel clung tightly to the companions he could no longer see, wishing desperately to make it out of whichever of the nine hells this was.

After an immeasurable amount of time, Samuel felt himself slowly breaking through another spider-web-like veil. When he passed through, he could see again. The world was still an empty void, but it was dark in the same way a stormy day is. At least he could see himself again. However, that was all he saw around him. His friends were gone. He looked behind himself and saw only a dense wall of shifting pitch-black shadow. He reached out, but he had already drifted too far away from the barrier between him and his friends. He tried to shout, but his voice was gone as if taken from him. There was nothing he could do but fall deeper into despair as he was being pulled further into the nothingness.

As the distance between him and his friends grew wider, he noticed that the darkness started to brighten up ever so slightly. He looked around, and when he looked down past his feet, he saw an immense field of solid darkness that had a slight curve to it. Just as soon as he saw this new feature of the void, he felt his direction shift, directly toward it. He felt the lurch in his stomach as his fall downward accelerated. He closed his eyes and braced for impact, only to feel his fall slow and his feet gently making contact with the solid black ground.

Samuel took a hesitant step and found it equally as solid. There was a glossy nature to the ground, and he was surprised that it wasn't slippery because of it. As he took another step, he felt the ground vibrate. It was a slow and gentle vibration that made a deep humming sound. Samuel realized that this was the first sound he had heard since falling into the pit, and that made him uneasy, but he wasn't sure why. The vibration died down and then came again. He waited several moments and the two humming vibrations repeated, following the nearly universal pattern of life.

He surveyed this new area and saw miles and miles of nothing. That was until he saw a faint glow from so far away that he almost overlooked it. Something akin to hope flashed through his chest as he sprinted wildly toward it. Only, he did not move how he expected. He felt himself moving forward at great speed, but it was not his speed. It was as if he was being pushed forward as the ground beneath him moved backward. He was going to reach his destination faster than he expected.

Faster than he wanted.

He very quickly discovered what the source of light was. It was the magika forming a circular halo of color and light high above the ground. Beneath the halo was a broken and headless suit of armor. It was on its knees, weakly and soundlessly beating its gauntlets against the ground.

Samuel recognized him as the Dark Lord.

He tried to halt his forward momentum, but it was too late. By the time he put the pieces together, he was already only feet away from the man he once saw as his enemy.

The suit of armor froze and seemed to turn its faceless gaze at the boy. Samuel almost immediately understood that the Dark Lord was just a magika inhabiting a suit of armor, but he wasn't sure how he knew that. Then he remembered his father and fresh tears blurred his vision. But he would not let them fall. He had to act and he had to act now to save his father, wherever he was.

Samuel rushed forward and knelt in front of the Dark Lord and tried to speak. Still, only silence rang out from where his voice should have been. He tried over and over in frantic desperation. But there was nothing that could be produced in this void of a world.

He could almost feel an aura of sadness radiating from the Dark Lord, but not even he could speak here. He placed his gauntlet on the ground between the two and showed Samuel the small cracks on its surface. The cracks were as thin as strands of hair, but they revealed a golden light coming from beneath the ground.

Samuel nodded, and without hesitation, he raised his fist up high and sent it crashing down on where the cracks were forming.

Pain tore throughout his entire body. It was beyond anything he had ever felt before. He tried to scream but couldn't.

And then he struck the ground again, and again.

Each time was more painful than the last. It was as if he was being ripped apart piece by piece. But just as the pain grew, so did the cracks. Little by little the light beneath became brighter.

Somewhere along the line, the Dark Lord had joined Samuel in their attempt to break through the darkness. But that didn't matter to Samuel. Neither did the pain. He was going to get through this barrier at whatever cost. He didn't know if this would save his father. He didn't know if this would break the world. He didn't know if he would survive the intense pain. All he knew was that if he did nothing now, he would never forgive himself.

Fear and anger boiled together inside Samuel as he raised his fist one more time. Tears streamed down his face as the pain inside him reverberated and threatened to break him. But he would not be broken. He would shatter this thing that held him back. He would save his father.

He brought down his fist and this time he broke through.

And then he fell into the brightness below. He was filled with relief as he plummeted toward a new ground. But the strain from before engulfed him and he faded into unconsciousness.

***

Samuel's eyes slowly opened. Struggling against the brightness. The new world he found himself in was a bright blur of color and shapes, and sound had returned, but he didn't care about anything. All he cared about was finding his last remaining family. He stumbled and swayed drunkenly but found his footing ungracefully. After a moment of looking for anything person-shaped, he found one that was lying still on the ground, with something thin and long rising like a stalk of corn.

"Dad!" Samuel shouted as he tripped over himself and whatever lay beneath him to get to Seth.

He fell to his knees beside his father, tears and snot escaping as restraint was abandoned. He struggled to see past the tears, but as he placed his hand on his father's chest, he could feel the small and quick rising and falling of broken breaths.

"It's going to be okay, Dad," Samuel said, choking on the words. "I'm here. I'm here. Please, please, please, please! You can't die! You can't…"

Seth said nothing. His breathing was strangled and had an unsettling liquid sound. Samuel didn't know what to do. He couldn't remove the arrow. Maybe he could tear some fabric from his clothes and try to stop the bleeding. But that doesn't alleviate his breathing trouble. Or the issue of the arrow. He was scared to move him. But even if he could without hurting him, where would he move him to? They were somewhere deep underground. How could he get his father to the surface? Samuel held his father's trembling hand and cried. Was this all he could do? Just be with his father during his last moments. His chest felt like it was collapsing in on itself as he struggled to catch his own breath between violent sobbing.

Samuel felt the footfalls of other people. The first to approach him was Caleb, holding the limp body of Za'rie. Caleb laid her down gently on the other side of Samuel. Through his still blurry vision, he could see the blood pooling just above her waist. She was breathing, just barely.

"Za'rie!" Samuel shouted. And then he remembered what he did while under the wizard's control. He wanted to puke as he saw his friend in such a state, all because of him. "Caleb, what do we do?"

"I don't know," Caleb said, his voice low and his eyes lower.

Samuel started to take a better look around him. The world was still difficult to see. Everything was bright and green. Most of the area was flat, except for the looming mountain that they were at the foot of. But it didn't produce a shadow. Nothing had a shadow. Samuel couldn't find a light source. It was as if light just existed. Then he saw where the blue of the sky had been shattered, revealing the black void just beyond. There were blue fragments of broken sky floating like shards of glass near the fracture. These shards were slowly drifting back into place.

Finally, his eyes started to settle on the shapes of other people. He saw Rythel leaning over the slowly rising John. The human mage that was with the Dark Lord seemed to be in a similar shape as John, though he too was starting to recover and stand on his shaking legs. Samuel just caught the tail end of an altercation between Malguinne and the human in heavy armor. Malguinne was collapsing to the ground, holding his stomach as strands of spittle fell from his mouth.

The armored human was walking away and toward Samuel and his companions.

"Please, help us!" Samuel begged.

"Yes, I think I may be of assistance," the man said.

The man seemed to be looking around for something or someone, but in not finding it, he turned his gaze toward the boy. He dug through a pouch at his waist and removed a large, red feather. Samuel took it, confused and angry. His father and friend were dying, and he was given a feather.

"It's a phoenix feather," the man said, probably reading Samuel's expression. "It should recover anyone still living. However, I have only one."

Realization dawned on Samuel. He looked at his father and then at Za'rie. He had to choose who to save. He couldn't bear to lose his father. But Za'rie had given up so much; could he let her just die? He considered what his father would want, and he knew that Seth would not want to live with the thought that saving him led to the death of someone so young. But wouldn't Za'rie feel something similar? Could anyone live a happy life knowing their existence was at the cost of someone else's? Samuel could feel Caleb's eyes avoiding him. He knew Caleb was scared to be asked what he should do. And he knew it would be unfair of him to even ask that. Samuel held the delicate feather to his chest and started to make his final decision when a voice came from above them.

"Oh, how silly my children are. They sit at the feet of their creator and can only see themselves. Whatever shall I do with them."

Samuel looked up at the mountain leaning over him and this time, saw something different. A woman. Green as the grass, tall as a mountain, as beautiful as a flower, as still as a pond, and as graceful as a river. The longer Samuel looked, the more he realized that she wasn't something his eyes and mind could fully grasp. One moment, she was the mountain, then the next moment, she was a woman, while also still being the mountain. Her features were ever-shifting like the seasons. Her hair would become an avalanche of snow, then melt away into rain that watered the open fields that were her shoulders. Focusing on her was like watching nature at high speed. He felt so miniscule before her. Like he was the seed of a blade of grass looking at the oldest and largest tree to ever exist. Samuel saw the armored man crash to his knees and bow his head while both he and Caleb just continued to stare in dumbstruck awe.

"My goddess," the man said, "I am unworthy to be in your presence."

"Oh, hush you," she said with a giggle that sounded like echoes inside a cave. "You are here because my other children decided that you were worthy. Hmmm, oh yes, one says that you have a beautiful singing voice when you are drunk. How lovely."

Samuel could see a cloud of swirling light dancing around her cavernous ear. It must have been the world's collective magic. But she seemed to be listening and speaking to it.

"Please, Anu," Samuel said, struggling to say the goddess name with what he thought was the proper amount of deference, "my father and my friend are dying, but I can't save them both. Please, help them."

"Yes, my child," she said with a sigh that sounded like the cresting waves of the ocean crashing against the beach. "I can not bear to watch my children suffer. I have but one dilemma. Tyberion, would you remove the arrow from Seth?

It's not something I can touch easily. Not without causing more harm to the poor man."

Tyberion nodded and stepped toward Seth. Samuel turned away. But the sickening sound of the arrow being removed from bone and flesh gave him mental images he knew he would never forget. But Seth did not scream in pain. If anything, his breathing improved ever so slightly.

Samuel turned back and saw the goddess lowering one of her hands. It was at this point that Samuel noticed that she held something in her other hand. The black shape of the Dark Lord, beaten and battered but still moving. When Anu's hand rested on the ground in front of Seth and Za'rie, the landscape of her hand merged with the land beneath it. It was like watching a water drop fall into a puddle, ripples and all. As the ripples of grass settled, wild flowers of every color bloomed in the shape of her hand.

"Samuel," she said, "plant the feather into my hand, and I will do the rest."

He nodded and walked forward with trembling legs. He knelt just in front of a patch of flowers that indicated where her index finger was and began to dig. It felt sacrilegious on levels he could not even begin to calculate. But the soil felt warm in his hand. Its heat radiated through him like a gentle embrace, holding him together as he felt like he was tearing at the seams. This feeling persisted as he placed the feather into the ground and only grew stronger as he replaced the soil. When he was finished, he returned to his father's side and held his hand as he waited.

Gradually the flowers surrounding the buried feather started to change color, each turning a fiery red. This transition spread until every flower was unified in color. Then something began to sprout from the disturbed patch of dirt.

It started as a bright red sapling with a thin stem that branched out from the top with long, strand-like foliage. It grew quickly, shooting up and becoming a massive pillar of red bark, with long and low hanging leaves that bore a strong resemblance to feathers.

Suddenly, the base of the tree caught fire. Panic struck Samuel, and he nearly jumped to his feet to put it out, but the warm embrace he felt earlier returned with renewed strength, calming him and voicelessly letting him know everything was going to be okay. The fire spread up the trunk of the tree, leaving behind a trail of ash and death. But once it reached the leaves, something changed. The leaves were not burning, but dissolving into thousands of snow-sized golden orbs of light. They floated for a moment before descending to the ground, covering everything underneath, including Seth and Za'rie. As these glowing orbs made contact, they were absorbed into whatever or whoever they landed on. Samuel could feel the injuries of his adventure fade away.

He turned his attention quickly to his father and friend, and let out a choked sob that expelled the last of his grief and tension as he saw their wounds closing. Slowly, their breathing returned to normal and they opened their eyes. Before they could even sit up and register what was going on, they were tackled back to the ground as they were forced into an embrace by Samuel. This was quickly added onto by Caleb, who could not contain his relief and happiness, no matter how much Seth wiped away his tears. There were several moments where all four were laughing and hugging and attempting explanations of where they were. The worst was finally behind them.

"My goddess," Tyberion finally said after the celebration died down. "What is this place?"

"This is the moment before The Beginning," she said. "The moment before I breathe my last and create all my wonderful children. This moment acts as an eternal center of your world. In here, I live forever as your goddess, but never seeing or influencing past my bubble."

Samuel looked around and started to understand why everything looked so blurry earlier; the world around them was changing and shifting just as the body of the goddess was. Grassy fields became forests, became a large expanse of wildflowers. It was so hard to focus on that the mind slipped over it, like water over glass, unless you looked directly at any one spot long enough to see the changes.

"Why did the magika bring us here, and how do we return to our time?" Samuel asked, as everyone except Malguinne came toward them to join in whatever this was.

"The magika will take you back very shortly. They gathered together when they felt Magus, or *The Dark Lord* as some of you know him, weakening." Her eyes filled with the ocean, deep and mysterious, and full of life. "Magus is my magika, my first child and, in a sense, an older sibling to all the magika of the world. His death would have meant a symbolic death for all of magic. They brought him to me so that I could save him. I have not seen him in so long, and yet no time at all. And I know this will be the last time I will ever see him. I just want to hold onto him a little longer before he is sent back."

"I don't understand," said the Dark Lord's mage. "If we are in the time before time, how are we able to experience anything? Shouldn't we be frozen without time to let us move forward?"

"You have brought in a small amount of time," the goddess said, "like one bringing in dirt on the bottom of your shoes. It's a strange feeling to move forward through time, but it is limited, and I will need to have the magika send you back before it starts to loop."

"What of my friend, Buddy," Tyberion said. "Is there a way for him to return to his world?"

"I hold no power over the other world, and I cannot affect anything outside of this moment," she said. "But the creatures you call goblins may be able to. The magika tell me that these charming creatures came to my world so very long ago from the other and have survived all this time. If they take Buddy to where they came from, perhaps that will lead him home."

"Thank you, my goddess," Tyberion said.

"However…" the goddess said, her lips quivering with the force of an earthquake. "There is something he must do when you return, something only he can."

"What is it?"

"Magus' goal was to make it so all magika were sentient," Anu said. "What I will do is merge all the magika into one and combine them with Magus. Buddy will have to undo Magus' armor, releasing all the magika and setting them free to choose where to go."

"Wouldn't that kill Magus," Seth interjected.

"It will," the goddess said, as mournful as a rainy morning. "But it is the only way. A piece of him will reside in each of the world's magika, making it stronger and more alive. All the magika would become sentient and able to choose for themselves, like any other person."

"So, killing it, I mean him, will bring back magic?" Everyone turned toward the newcomer, Malguinne, with disdain. Samuel wanted nothing more than to make him regret ever turning him against his friends and father. But he decided it would be less than ideal to harm an old man in front of his creator.

"Malguinne," she said his name with the fury of a hurricane. "Your magika has told me about how cruel you were to him. How you forced him to do horrible, atrocious things. And of how you never once felt empathy toward your victims. I would like nothing more than to keep your magika far, far away from you. But he has another idea. To answer your question: Yes, you will have your magic back, but you will never have control. Your magika will be in full control and will do as he pleases to inconvenience you at every turn."

Malguinne slunk back as if to be out of view. There was no shame in his features, only the look of a defeated man. And the look of a man plotting revenge.

Anu reached toward the cloud of magic and created a small wind tunnel that funneled the lights into the broken suit of armor. As the magic entered into it, the gaps in the armor started to close, and a new helmet formed over the empty opening. The black coloration of the armor also dissolved away and became a glossy silver. After all the magic was gone, Anu placed Magus on the ground, where he stood with a newfound strength.

"Thank you, Mother," came the echoing voice of Magus. "I suppose in the next moment, we will both have died for your children."

"Please don't say such sad things as you depart," she said with a mournful laugh.

"This is not an ending, just a new beginning," Magus said. "I love you, Mother, and I will carry that love into the heart of every magika."

The lush valley of the goddess' lips curved into a wide smile as she slowly faded into becoming a mountain once again. Magus did not say anything further. He just turned toward Samuel and the others and placed his hand on the ground. A rainbow of color spread from his fingertips and encircled the group. Before anyone could protest, they were engulfed in the liquid light again and were shot up toward the hole in the sky.

***

Buddy had not been pulled into the abyss of bright lights like everyone else. He was pushed back, repelled like the wrong end of a magnet. All he could do was watch as the people he knew, the people he didn't know, and Malguinne fell down the Well as he was pinned against a stone wall. The light show lasted several minutes before it stopped, and the cave faded into darkness. Buddy was too shaken up to even try and find the exit in the pitch black. So, he sat there blindly until Puppies and a small group of goblins rushed in with torches. Buddy explained the best he could as Puppies tried to understand with similar effort and failure.

Buddy and the goblins waited in uncomfortable silence for several long and drawn-out moments, unsure of what to do if the others never returned. Just as Buddy was contemplating going back to the goblin village to wait, a bright rainbow of light radiated from the Well. Buddy and Puppies rushed toward the Well to see what appeared to be liquid light quickly filling up the Well. They took multiple steps backward as the pool of light reached the surface, but it did not overflow; it became still and flat like ice while maintaining a fluid movement of bright colors. Magus was the first to rise slowly and gracefully up from the pool, followed shortly after by the rest of those who fell. Magus stepped calmly away from the strange surface and the others followed suit, though some more cautiously. John in particular quickly stepped away on tip-toe like a cat crossing a puddle of water. After everyone stepped away from the puddle, it conglomerated into a condensed ball of liquid light. Then it slowly lifted out of the Well and floated above everyone like a miniature, multicolored sun, brightening up the cavern far better than any torch ever could.

Tyberion was the first to rush toward Buddy, giving the old man a surprisingly gentle hug, considering the amount of armor he was wearing. Buddy was relieved to see his friend again and returned the hug. It was far from comfortable. But he was okay with that.

"What in the blazes just happened?" Buddy asked.

Between Tyberion, Seth and Lawrence, the situation was made remarkably clear. Malguinne remained silent and attempted to take a few steps away from the crowd. Unfortunately for him, the goblins noticed. They rushed toward the wizard with surprising speed as they produced ropes from their packs. Malguinne turned to run, but he barely made it a few steps before the small horde of goblins leapt on him, clinging to him like warts with razor-sharp teeth. Buddy got a nice chuckle from the look of horror and bewilderment that overtook Malguinne's normal 'I'm in full control of the situation' expression. In seconds Malguinne was lying on the floor, bound like a spider's leftovers.

"What do we do with him, boss?" Puppies asked, with a proud look on his face.

Magus took a step toward the defenseless wizard, an aura of anger and malice radiating from him as sparks of electricity snapped violently around his gauntlet hands.

"I let him live once. I do not think—"

"I would like to speak with him," Buddy interrupted, and stood between the Dark Lord and the previously-a-wizard, "before you make any rash decisions."

Magus nodded and took a step back. An air of calmness returned to him, as if the storm inside of him was slowly dissipating. Buddy went to Malguinne and sat down beside him, with a mild amount of difficulty and discomfort. However, it was Malguinne who spoke first.

"Don't waste your breath," the wizard spat. "You have thrown your lot in with the enemy. There is nothing of value you can say to me."

"You're an old fool, you know that?" Buddy said conversationally. "I would know. I'm one too. You and I are from an old world that no longer exists."

Malguinne shut his eyes and let out a long sigh, strained ever so slightly by the ropes. "What are you blabbering about? You are from a whole other world altogether. You know nothing of this world and our struggles. And here you are lecturing me while you go and take away our magic."

"Funny," Buddy said, as he gave a dry chuckle. "You were more than willing to use me, an outsider, to aid your world in your *time of need*. But that's all besides the fact. We are the same in one key respect that goes beyond this world and the next. We were both raised to exist and thrive during a much different time than we are currently living in. We wanted our world to work by the rules we were taught without even considering if those rules were right. Times change, and we must change with them, or we will be left behind and forgotten."

"That is a fool's narrative," Malguinne said as he reopened his eyes with newfound conviction. "It is our job as the older generation to keep the traditions and practices of our time alive. The world does not change so easily, and should not change so easily. We stand as the monuments to lead the newer generations forward based on the history of the past."

"That's what I thought too," Buddy said, a tinge of melancholy leaking into his voice. "And it was that mindset that made me lose the most important things to me. We are monuments, sure. But we are supposed to be records of the past, leading the newer generation to be *better* than us. This world must change, and it will. Not because I say so," Buddy looked around at all the different people in the cave and smiled, "but because they say so."

Malguinne resigned himself from the conversation with a harumph and turned his attention to a rock on his opposite side that he seemed to find much more interesting.

"Look," Buddy said, "I don't fully care what you choose to do from here on out. Just know that if you keep being a stubborn old fool, you will continue to lose everything and will be alone in a past world that only you remember."

Buddy attempted to stand but found that his legs had fallen asleep on him. With Tyberion's help, he was able to rise and return to Magus.

"I think we should allow him to remain an infinite of possibilities," Buddy said. "Even old dogs can learn a thing or two every now and again."

"Thank you, my friend," Magus said, as he placed his armored hand on Buddy's shoulder. "Neither this world nor the other deserves you, and both are all the better because of you." Magus turned toward Puppies and said, "Have your people take the Royal Wizard to the edge of our realm and release him. He can do us no more harm."

"You heard Dark Lord, take prisoner far away," Puppies ordered, and then added, "Oh, and make sure he is given food and water. We are not monsters."

The goblins roared with frog-like laughter as they began to drag Malguinne by the feet toward the cave entrance. Puppies was the only goblin to stay behind.

"Now that he has been dealt with," Magus said with a somber voice, "it is time to see this quest to the end. Buddy, I have one final request."

"I don't like the sound of that," Buddy said, trying to add some levity, but he knew something serious was about to be said.

"I carry inside me all the magic of the world and the magika that resides within it. Once they are released from me, they will return to their proper hosts, or wherever they so choose to go, and hopefully live a more fulfilling life. But in order to do that, I must be undone, and it has to be by your hands."

"No," Buddy said firmly, "there has to be a better way."

"There is not," Magus said. "I knew from the start that this would be my ending, and I do not regret it for an instant. I have lived a good life. I have traveled the world. I have met interesting people and made friends and memories."

"Don't ask me to do this, please," Buddy said.

"If you are worried about getting home, Tyberion knows the—"

"I'm not worried about that, you dunce!" Buddy interrupted. "I know it's stupid of me to say—I barely even know you—but I feel that the world would be lesser without you."

"You are a good man, Buddy," Magus said as he came closer to the man. "But the world would not be without me; I will still be a part of the magic of this world. I will live on in the lives of the magika. Please, I ask you, will you help me save this world?"

Buddy hated everything about this idea. But he knew Magus meant exactly what he said. Many would risk other's lives for selfish reasons, but only the great risk their own lives for selfless reasons. Besides, everyone knew you could not refuse the call to save the world twice. Buddy nodded with tears in his eyes and an uneasy heart.

Buddy watched as Magus placed himself flat on the ground. The thought of removing his armor felt uncomfortably intimate. Magus was lying there, motionless, waiting like a patient on an operating table. Buddy knelt beside him and started working on the legs. Magus let out a quiet expression of pain when Buddy's fingers grasped the metal. It was as if his very touch was toxic to him. He undid the latches connecting the left leg and removed it carefully. To his surprise, the suit of armor was no longer hollow. It was filled with bright and colorful lights, too many to even comprehend, that swarmed away from Buddy like scared fish and condensed into the chest. He took a staggered breath and attempted to clear his mind and focus on the job at hand. He moved on to the next leg and then did the same to the arms. The suit of armor trembled the entire time. Magus was in incredible pain but was restraining himself and enduring it as silently as possible. Buddy could only imagine how this felt, gently being torn apart, piece by piece, but at the level of one's soul. He was at the last part. Once he undid the latches that held the front and back of the breastplate to-gether and removed the helmet, Magus would be no more.

"Goodbye," Buddy said through a stream of tears. "I wish I could have known you better."

"I'm glad to have met such an honorable man, er, magika," Seth said.

"You gave me a home when no one else would. Thank you, and may the goddess be with you," Lawrence said.

"You gave me a good fight, even if I wasn't in control of myself. You are the greatest warrior and mage I will ever meet," Tyberion said.

"Ditto what the old man said. Wish I could have known you better, give the other side hells," John said

"I am proud to have met one such as you," Rythel said.

"Thank you for taking care of my father," Samuel said.

"Hermy will be happy to have you be a part of him," Caleb said.

"Thank you for fighting to save magic," Za'rie said.

Puppies had been quiet and stoic this whole time, acting like the proper general he was. But as he opened his mouth to speak his voice got caught as it was forming. Then the facade shattered as he melted into a mess of tears and snot. He ran to, and fell at, his lord's side, clinging to the armor like a life perseverer.

Buddy felt the knot in his chest as his own tears began to overflow.

"Not fair!" Puppies wailed. "It not fair! Goblins need you. We lost without you."

"Puppies," Magus said weakly, "you're right. This isn't fair, and for that, I am deeply sorry. I have grown to love you and your people. But I am leaving the goblins in the best of hands. Your hands. You do not need me. You are a kind and empathetic leader." Magus' helmet turned ever so slightly toward the goblin. "Goodbye, my magnificent general. From here on out, you are the leader of your people, and you are going to be wonderful."

Puppies nodded, tried to speak, but seemed to decide that there was nothing else he could say, or even needed to say. He unclung his arms around the Dark Lord and repositioned himself beside Buddy.

"Goodbye, my friends, and those that would have been friends," came the weak voice of Magus, barely a whisper in a deep cave. "For the first time in countless years, the magika are going to be free. Please, look after my siblings as they learn how to live."

Buddy let the silence overtake the moment and waited to make sure there was nothing more left to be said. Then, he unlatched the last of the fastenings and removed the front plate of the armor, and the helmet fell to the ground with a hollow *clang*. In that instant, there was an explosion of color as lights poured out of what was left of the suit of armor. Lawrence, Caleb, Za'rie, and Samuel had their magic returned to them, and even though Buddy could see they were happy, the return of their other half could not overcome the wave of grief he was sure they all felt. Eventually, all the lights had left, leaving behind the rainbow orb that hung above them; it was the last remnant of Magus, lighting their path as they left the volcano's cavern. Once they were out in the open air, it slowly began to fade, until it was finally gone.

Chapter 14: An Ending
Cycle 5, Day 28

Caleb was back in his hometown again after the long and eventful journey. It was so nice to see everyone again, even if they were all avoiding him like the plague. People would give him a courteous greeting but make sure to be out of range of him quickly. It's funny, at the beginning of his journey, he would have been disheartened if he were treated with this much fear because of his magic. But now he just enjoyed not having to explain his whole story to everyone. He wanted to see his parents and sister and let them know he was okay, but he had someone else to see first.

He went to the field of his best friend's family and saw him working through the mid-morning heat. His heart leapt in a way that only made him even sadder. But he had to confront him. He had to make things right.

"Hey!" Caleb shouted. "Mud for brains!"

Ralph turned around. He was wearing a faded green tunic and brown pants, all of which were more dirt and mud than fabric at this point. His face was pleasant, if not plain, but his head was completely hairless and resembled the top of a crab. Caleb couldn't help but feel awful that he had been like this for over two cycles now. But the second Ralph recognized Caleb, he took off at top speed, dropping everything he was working on. Caleb braced himself for a punch in the face and was utterly taken off guard as he was tackled to the ground in a strong embrace.

"Caleb!" he said, "Oh goddess, Caleb! I'm so glad to see you. You had me worried sick. Your sister and parents too! What the hells possessed you to turn yourself in like that? But it's okay; you're home now, and that's all that matters."

Once Caleb was able to untangle himself from Ralph, they continued to sit on the ground, side by side, as if nothing had ever happened between them.

"Hold on, let me just…" Caleb said. He wanted to try and explain first but decided showing would be easier. "Hermy, please put my friend like he should be."

A blue light shot from his fingertip, and Ralph instinctively panicked and tried to dodge, but the light was too fast. It struck his head and returned to Caleb. The crab-like features immediately disappeared and left behind a normal, human-looking head. It was still bald, but Caleb was mostly sure time would take care of that one.

"Did you just—" Ralph started.

"Yep," Caleb said with a bright smile. "I fixed your head. Well, I restored it to how it was. Not really any fixing it past that point. I have learned to use my magic over the last few cycles. It's a long story."

"Well, don't worry," Ralph said, as he began to stand up. "You have plenty of time to explain it to us."

"Wait," Caleb said, grasping Ralph's arm and causing him to sit back down. "About what happened—"

"No," Ralph said, "I'm sorry. I should have announced it better. No, forget that. We shouldn't have hidden our relationship. But me and her were so worried you would get overprotective like that. I know it's too late to ask for your blessing and everything, but I just want you to know that I do truly love her and want nothing but the best for her. And she loves me. I swear by the goddess I will protect her with my life, but I don't intend to take your place or anything. You are still her older brother and all."

Caleb could feel the pain of tears building, and he knew the dangers of hiding his feelings, but accepting one's feelings and expressing them don't always have to go together. He took a hard gulp as he tried to move his emotions to the side for the moment for the sake of his friend. The pain he felt would one day fade in time. He knew there would always be that scar. But that just meant that the feelings were real. And if he could love once, he knew he would love again.

"No, no," Caleb replied, looking away from his friend. "I was clearly in the wrong. I've had a lot of time to think, and I know you will be good for her, though I'm sure she will be the one protecting you."

"You're not wrong on that one," Ralph said with a laugh.

"I know it's too late to do it right, but you have my approval," Caleb said. "Just don't screw this up, or I will fully turn you into a crab and feed you to the birds."

"That's a good one," Ralph said, his laughter continuing.

Caleb did not laugh.

"Wait, that was a joke, right? Can you actually do that?"

"Want to find out?"

"No!" Ralph said, his voice rising multiple octaves as he fell over in his attempt to crawl backward.

Caleb began to laugh, low and calm at first, but growing louder and full of humor and joy—but also a little bit more, as tears began to roll carelessly down his flushed cheeks.

"I'm glad we could clear this up," Caleb said, casually wiping away the tears. He extended his hand. "I'd hate to lose my best friend over this."

"I am glad, too," Ralph said as he firmly took his friend's hand. "Now that you're back—"

"About that," Caleb interrupted, "I'm not here to stay. I have kinda become a Warden's apprentice, or at least will be becoming a Warden's apprentice, once I make it to the capital with said Warden. But first I have to get an old man home. He's from another world."

"You're kidding?"

"That's the honest truth. I've got to talk to my family about it; why don't you walk me there, and I'll tell you about my journey."

***

It took Caleb a lot longer to explain things to his parents than he expected. But he received their blessings along with a pack of clothing and other supplies he desperately needed the first time around. And now he was making his way back to the campsite with the others. The sun had just set, leaving behind only hints of pink and orange clouds just above the horizon. Caleb turned his gaze to the sky above, still awestruck by the new phenomena he had begun calling the night rainbow. Samuel and Za'rie claim to hate the name, but Caleb is sure that it's because he came up with it first and they haven't found a suitable replacement. Ever since the release of magic, the night sky has been brightened by colorful displays of light. It looks as if someone painted a rainbow in the night sky, and then ran a dry brush up and down throughout the rainbow, mixing the colors in a beautiful way. The group is pretty sure that those are the magika that didn't return to their host, but instead are living freely in the sky and showing off their brilliance during the night.

Caleb turned his gaze back to the path ahead and continued forward. In no time at all, he had returned to the campsite and rushed over to Samuel and Za'rie. They were off to the side, away from the others, presumably waiting for him. They seemed to have just finished a game, based on Za'rie's victorious gloating posture and Samuel's inability to look in her direction.

"Took you long enough," Za'rie said with a bored voice. "Samuel sucks at card games."

"But can't he tell if you're lying?" Caleb asked, as he looked over to a pouting Samuel.

"That's the thing," Za'rie said, laughing at Samuel's expense, "all you have to do is play fair and truthfully, and he doesn't know how to handle it. It's like he relies on lies to win."

"Okay, okay, new topic," Samuel said. "So, how did it go?"

"As well as could be expected," Caleb said with a shrug.

"Did you get rejected?" Za'rie asked, and received an elbow to the ribs from Caleb, who was immediately put in a headlock until he was forced to tap out.

"No," Caleb answered with a chuckle. "I didn't tell him how I felt."

"And you're okay with that?" Za'rie asked.

Caleb thought about it for a moment and then said, "I am. The important part is that I know how I feel, and I know that he is in love and is happy with someone else. Sure, it hurts and will hurt for some time. But him knowing how I feel wouldn't change anything. I like him too much to put him in that kind of situation."

"As long as you're sure," Samuel said.

"I am. So, what's our next heading?"

Samuel looked back at the small group of goblins attempting to help Seth with the cooking. Seth was a miserable cook, and it was a long process of the goblins teaching him the ropes, but maybe one day he would get it. Rythel, Jacob, Tyberion, and Buddy were in their own little circle, talking about whatever it was they talked about all day. Caleb wished that Lawrence would have joined their expedition, but he decided to stay with the goblins and help them eventually join society.

"Petrichor says they 'will knows it when they sees it,' so your guess is as good as mine," Samuel said with resignation.

"This will be a strange and wonderful journey; I can feel it," Caleb said, excited to see where tomorrow would take him in this world filled with newfound magic and wonder.

Not
The End

Epilogue
Cycle 4, Day 20

In a cold and dark prison cell, forgotten by the world, was Vincent. He lay crumpled in a pile of misery and self-loathing. Hunger devoured him from within. Fatigue crept into every bone and muscle. He was still gagged and bound, but his blindfold was removed before he was shoved into the darkness. He should have been at the lowest point of his life. However, for the first time in years, his world was finally a respite of silence. He had watched with bloodshot eyes as a venomous green orb shot out of his chest and past the barred window high above, joining the myriad of trailing lights. He was finally free from the malicious voice that plagued his every waking moment and that interjected itself into what few dreams his limited sleep could conjure.

He slowly lowered his eyelids as sleep began to fall over him. He could feel the approaching dreams returning to him like a cool wave.

Vincent.

And so the silence erupted into chaos as all hope yet again abandoned him. Vincent's eyes shot open in an instant and a pit of dread started to spread within his chest as he saw the horrible green light in front of him. This time, it was not shaped like an orb, but rather a person. It was a reflection of himself in form, but where detail should have been, there was only the green light. It didn't even have a face, just a green void that stared back at him.

I have returned, my pathetic host. Did you really think you would be rid of me? You truly are a fool! I would sooner…

Vincent tried to drown out the words of his magic. The tormentor of his life. The jailer who held the keys to his freedom. There was nothing that could silence the voice. No thought loud enough to overpower it. The Council of Magi and the kingdom only wanted to use him and his demon. But he just wanted freedom from it. The library was his last-ditch effort. But those putrid children just had to get in the way. And that woman. His mind was a bloody fog of his lust for revenge, mixing with his sleep deprivation.

As the last rays of hope began to fade from his soul, something began to snap inside of him. He was cracking under a weight he could not even grasp. It was as if the very thing that kept him human was breaking open to reveal something vulnerable and helpless inside. It was this core, soft and fragile, that the magika targeted with his sharp and insidious words.

The human-shaped magika stepped toward Vincent with an outstretched hand aimed at the man's face. Vincent squirmed away as best he could until a wall broke his retreat.

It is time you stopped running. You will never be rid of me, and I will never give you up. Give up fighting my control. I have grown so much stronger thanks to the imbecilic kindness of a self-made martyr. Let me sink deeper into your soul, and we will have our revenge on everyone who has wronged us.

Vincent's eyes were wide in terror and his body shook violently as the magika's hand touched the gag. The fabric erupted in a flame that lasted less than a second. The intense heat seared his flesh and left burnt patches in his hair. The magika did the same to the ropes that bound him. Again, his flesh burned as the ropes turned to ash. His hoarse and broken voice echoed his pain throughout the cell. Someone had to have heard that. They would see this monster and rescue him. But nobody came. Vincent looked up at the magika with tear-stained eyes.

"No…" Vincent said. His voice was a low, hollow whimper in the dark. "I won't accept you." He stared directly into the blank face of his magic. His resolve was slowly building like a wall, one stone at a time.

You have no choice. I am—

"I said no!" Vincent interrupted, his voice strengthening with every word. He just had to hold out until the guard came. Someone should be here any minute. "You said you've gotten stronger? Then why don't you go on your own? You don't need me and I sure as hells don't need you! Find another victim!"

Vincent stepped forward with explosively expressive hands as his words gained momentum. The creature of magic backed away until it was against the wall. Somehow Vincent could read just a little bit of uneasiness from its non-expressive face.

He was about to continue his tirade until he heard the sound of approaching footsteps. He was finally saved. He couldn't help but give a weak smile as he turned toward the door. But it was just as he turned toward the sound that his brain started to pick up something. It didn't sound like a pair of feet, but two. And the footsteps didn't sound like metal on stone.

He looked at the wooden cell door and waited for it to open. Horror built in his chest as it remained shut.

Oh, he's with me, the creature of magic said. *Would you be a good host and open the door for our guest?* As it said this, it raised a hand and pointed at the door. A ray of green light struck the door and something within clicked.

Vincent wanted to remain still. He wanted to be anywhere but here in this cell with his monster. He was also afraid of who, or what, was outside of this cell. He wanted to disobey the magika, and he knew he should have. But he knew that every move he could make would only lead to his defeat. So, with agonizingly slow steps, he walked toward the door. His feet felt heavier the closer he got until they were almost rooted. But it didn't matter. He was already at the door.

He placed his hand on the old, splintery wood and pushed. It opened without a hint of resistance.

Sitting calmly on the other side was a gray and white wolf. It was so much larger than any dog he had ever seen, and almost as large as some horses. But it was not the size alone that nearly sent him into a fit of fear-induced insanity. In the wolf's bloody mouth was an equally bloody hand. By the look of the severed end, it did not come off cleanly.

Vincent collapsed to the floor, forcing his mouth shut to not vomit.

You see? The magika said as it slid beside Vincent. *You have no choice. Your magic has killed a man. They will kill you unless I save you.*

It circled in front of Vincent, their faces mirroring each other, and placed a hand on his cheek. Vincent did not feel any pressure. It was as if the creature's hand was made of air. Slowly, his hands fell from his mouth.

"I don't want to die…" Vincent said, weakly. He could not look directly at the magika, but he felt its stare boring into him.

No one can not hurt you if you have me. Its voice was soft and soothing. Almost comforting. The magika's hand lowered from Vincent's face and rested on the man's chest. Right at his heart.

"I just want the pain to stop."

We will inflict our pain on those who have hurt us tenfold.

The hand began to glow brighter and sank into Vincent's chest, streams of light spider-webbing from the point of impact. Something made contact with his still-breaking core and began to seep into it.

"I want to be free."

We will be the only free soul.

Inch by inch the magika was melting into Vincent and his core was filling with the acidic bitterness of the magika.

"I will be free!" Vincent's voice rose and trembled with mania as the last remnant of the magika had disappeared into Vincent. The broken man stumbled to his feet, shaking with exhaustion and rage, as the remnant of his human soul was enveloped and corrupted by the pure malice of his magika. What stood in the dark cell was no longer human or magika.

"We will be free! No matter the cost!"